BROKEN
BLOODY CROSS

BILL HANSON

ISBN
978-1-958122-05-1 (Paperback)
978-1-958122-06-8 (Hardcover)
978-1-958122-04-4 (eBook)

Dedication

To my oldest friend, William Wood and to a truelly honest
man, my high school vice principle, Martin Gibbens

Table of Contents

Chapter 1   Bloody Morning 2

Chapter 2   Strike Two 10

Chapter 3   Dark Fury 18

Chapter 4   Clueless 30

Chapter 5   Drop Off 40

Chapter 6   Time Lag 54

Chapter 7   Big Bang! 66

Chapter 8   King Pin Meeting 80

Chapter 9   Power Of Will 92

Chapter 10   Morning Shots 104

Chapter 11   Love Fest 114

Chapter 12   Ugly Politics 126

Chapter 13   Gun Gone 136

Chapter 14   Hot Trot 146

Chapter 15   Double Down 156

Chapter 16   Heart's Truth 166

Chapter 17   Dead Fast 176

Chapter 18   Terror's Edge 188

Chapter 19   Showdown 200

Chapter 20   Hollow Justice 212

Chapter 21   Black Dawn 226

The evils men invent, usually survives to plague future generations. It can be a legacy of horror handed from father to son or government to government. Once a method or advance has been discovered, such forbidden knowledge remains, available to the whim of ruthless men. Broken Bloody Cross is such a story, rooted in the modern world with a regrettable link to the recent past.

With the death of each policeman, the city becomes further enshrouded in a cloak of fear. Why is this wave of violence occurring? Who is the killer? Why is it happening? Why can't the authorities bring the monster to justice?

The unknown yet predictable threat keeps stalking the police force and even the F.B.I. is baffled. Can this killer be found? How many cops will die before the discovery and arrest is made? Will this evil genius escape and plague other cities? Will the nation be ruled by law or by fear and violence? Captain Mackelroy is caught between the quest for justice and the too real threat of anarchy. He is soon caught between duty, vengeance and passion. Will he find the killer or will Mac end up in a cemetery like the others?

Bill Hanson

Chapter

1

BLOODY MORNING

Captain Mackelroy stared at the crumpled body of Sergeant Tindale. He could still smell the residue of gunpowder in the air, the scent of fresh blood, and the damp odor of decay and age which pervaded the filthy, abandoned warehouse. Other homicide detectives drew chalk lines around the corpse along with taking photographs of the crime scene. Tindale was lying face down with several bullet holes in his back and head. Blood and brains were splattered over the floor and body.

Mackelroy observed that Tindale's gun was still strapped in the holster.

His voice rasped in the sullen silence. Anger and disgust competed for possession of every word when he stated the obvious to his friend and right hand man, Lieutenant Tanner. "Well, Frank, the poor bastard never knew what hit him. He was deliberately ambushed. With all those bullet wounds, I'd say there was a lot of anger in the killer, perhaps fear also."

He glanced around at the grim-faced men who were investigating the scene. "I want the son of a bitch who did this. Ted Tindale was a good friend of mine and a damned fine cop. By the looks of things, he didn't even have a chance to defend himself."

The sullen Worcester city cops just nodded. Words weren't needed. Mackelroy continued to take in the depressing scene. Amid the detritus that always accumulates in deserted buildings, Mac soon noticed some shell casings and pointed them out. The detectives drew more lines and picked up the casings with tweezers, carefully placing them into plastic evidence bags.

Over the years, he'd seen his share of death, and he'd never really gotten used to it. But this particular fatality struck him to the core of his being. In morbid curiosity, he knelt down and felt Tindale's lifeless left hand. It was still warm. He squeezed his eyes shut and tried to control the sickening feeling in his stomach. Losing the struggle, Mac went over to a nearby corner and promptly splattered the wood plank floor with the remains of his breakfast

---

"Misses Tindale, my name is John Mackelroy and this is my assistant, Mandy Buskirk. May I speak with you for a few moments?" The attractive blonde recognized the tall, thin man standing in front of her at the apartment landing. She did not know who the police woman was, although she looked quite becoming in her tight fitting blue uniform. He was well-dressed in conservative gray, being a plain clothes man. His thin mustache leant dignity to an already serious face, and his ice-blue eyes were downcast and lacking in enthusiasm. She replied, "What is it? ?"

They'd met briefly at some social function sponsored by the policeman's union a few months previous. Mac vaguely remembered her when she'd attended the event with her husband, Ted. He removed his hat and asked, "May I come in for a few minutes? I've got some bad news about Ted."

For the first time, fear jumped inside Ann's throat like a snarling tiger, as she glimpsed tears in Mackelroy's eyes. "Oh my God! Is Ted okay?"

She motioned for them to enter. The police woman quickly shut the door behind her. His voice was soft and full of grief's singular awareness. "Forgive me for being the one to have to tell you this, but Ted is dead. He was shot."

The blonde's face was a study in shock, disbelief, and grief. Her mouth was open, but no words would emerge. He continued, "I'm so sorry, Misses Tindale. As far as I can tell, your husband was killed instantly by some bastard who shot him from behind. It was the act of a cowardly monster."

She collapsed to the floor and wailed and screamed in anger and grief. Her words were incoherent, and she was racked with sobs that she couldn't control. Her fists hit the carpeted floor with impotent rage and despair. Mac watched helplessly with a face devoid of expression. The only sign that the police captain was stricken was the insistent trickle of tears that slid down his five o'clock shadow cheeks.

At last she recovered enough to speak. Her hand shook as she pointed to a doorway. "Get me a drink! It's in the fridge!"

He motioned to the assistant to retrieve the beverage. Moments later, she found the bright, tidy kitchen and discovered a bottle of bourbon in the refrigerator. Officer Buskirk proceeded to fill a glass and bring it to the wailing woman, kneeling and gently placing it in her trembling hands. Mac supported her by gently placing his arm around her back, helping her sip the strong liquor until the burning sensation assaulted her throat. The grieving woman coughed and finally gained some composure. "I'm sorry I made such a scene. What the hell happened?"

Mackelroy replied in his gentlest voice. "He went to a warehouse this morning. Somebody was waiting for him and they shot him in the back. He never had a chance. So go ahead and cry. It's perfectly all right. Do you want another?"

She nodded, "yes, please."

Moments later, she imbibed another 100 proof drink, and he said, "I know that, for you, this is a tragedy I can't begin to feel or understand. I'll say this: Ted was a fine man and a damned good cop. I'll find the son of a bitch who did this if it's the last thing I do."

Mac looked into the tear-stained green eyes of the grief-stricken woman. Her chin grew tight, and anger flared from her face like a flaming torch. "You do that, Captain! I want to see that murderer shot to bits! I told Teddy time after time to leave the force. Damn him and damn the killer and damn you! Get out and leave me be!"

Mackelroy stood up and, in a choked voice, replied, "all right ma'am. I'll be going. I just want you to know that the department will help you in any way it can. Good night. I think it would be a good idea of Mandy stayed with you awhile."

Ann nodded, permitting Mandy to help her to the sofa.

He quietly shut the door which barely lessened the sound of hysterical weeping which seemed to follow him as he left to begin the hunt. Mac silently vowed to himself with each descending step that he would get that miserable mother fucker, come what may.

⸺•⸺

Mackelroy was in his office, drinking a third cup of coffee, when Police Chief Al Bender walked in and unceremoniously took a seat. Then he lit up a Lucky Strike and took a few puffs before enlightening Mac. "Well, I just got the gory details. It's all on this report, but I'll give you the highlights. We found no prints on the shell casings. The marks on the bullets don't seem to match any other gun records in our files, and those files go back over sixty years. The weapon was a 45-caliber hand gun. The call came in at nine thirty one from a male, and we traced the call to a phone booth a few blocks away from the murder scene. Tindale was alone because he'd dropped off his partner about fifteen minutes before. Tindale was nearby, so the poor bastard took the call, and he well, he was a dedicated cop. Autopsy confirmed he never knew what hit him. Apparently the shot to the head was the instant cause of death. Fortunately, we have a tape of the call that came in. It's our only lead."

Mackelroy looked through the report and sighed. "My gut feeling tells me this was a gangland hit, but why? Tindale wasn't on the drug or vice squad. It just doesn't make sense."

Bender gave him a level stare. "Mac, it doesn't have to make fucking sense. Maybe it was some teen-age jerk who panicked. Maybe it was some Looney who wanted to do a cop. It could even have been a drug deal that went belly up. How the fuck should I know? I want the thug who did this. I want his ass brought to me on a silver platter with his balls in a champagne glass, all right?"

Mackelroy gave the Chief a bleak smile. "That makes two of us, Al. I want to nail his carcass on a rough, hewn cross and make him suffer for six months. One way or another, we'll get him."

Next day, Mack carefully inspected the fatal phone booth where the strange call had been made. He carefully walked the two blocks from the booth to the crime scene in the abandoned warehouse, meticulously timing it. It was certainly a dreary neighborhood. The murder scene could not have occurred in a more depressing location. Large bushes and two foot high grass testified to the run down and neglected condition of the once, prosperous property. Many of the bricks were cracked and the entire structure was in desperate need of mortar refitting. Most of the windows had been boarded up with plywood but even those were rotting and badly weather worn. Two other old, pre world war one buildings were in similar condition. It was obvious that the former owners of these relics of the industrial revolution were either financially incapable or too cheep to remove the offending structures. Obviously the city did not consider it to be their responsibility to clean up the mess from a previous generation. So there they stood, silent sentinels doing homage to a former economic greatness.

For several minutes, Mac just stood there, mentally memorizing the entire location. The entrance door to that warehouse was around a corner so the phone booth could not be seen from that fatal doorway. He then ran the two blocks to the booth and timed it as well. Once he'd consulted his watch, he hurriedly scribbled some notes on his small pocket note pad.

The strange call had come in at 9:31 A.M., and the body had been discovered 15 minutes later. A female passerby walking her dog, had heard the shots and called in at 9 39 several minutes later, once she'd had a chance to get back to her home. That civic minded lady sounded like some kindly old biddy. She'd given her name as Verna Graves of Oread Street, located just a few blocks from the crime scene. If the criminal had immediately walked from the booth to the warehouse, it would have taken him two minutes. If he ran, it would have taken 30 seconds or so. It would have taken about seven or eight minutes for the elderly woman to reach her own phone. That means the police had gotten to Tindale real quick, like in five to ten minutes. Time of death was about 9:40, give or take a few minutes. At least they had a pretty exact time of death.

The call that had come in from the phone booth was scary. The voice sounded like it was filled with fear. "They're trying to kill me! It's a big drug deal going down in zee warehouse! I'm at 15 Summer Street! Get zee cops over here before I'm wasted! They're just outside. They're armed."

That was the address of the warehouse all right, but the phone caller had been lying. He hadn't actually been in the warehouse when he'd made the call. Mackelroy looked at the phone for a long time, as if it could tell him whom to look for. No prints had been found on the phone. Something else bothered him. Was it possible that the killing had occurred even before the thug made the call? If so, why?

He walked back to the scene again, entered the front hall, and walked to the lines on the floor. The body had been lying face down on the filthy, pitted cement, a mere thirty feet from the entrance. It was pretty obvious the ambush had been perpetrated from the alcove to the right of the main hall. There were no additional clues. The place hadn't been used as a warehouse since the early sixties, and the building was a totally filthy mess. The homeless had found shelter there countless times, along with druggies doing deals or teenage couples using the place to get their rocks off.

Mac thought to himself that the damned building should have been demolished at least twenty years ago. Sounds of dripping water broke the cold stillness of dark recesses, forlornly echoing in the hollow emptiness of the long deserted warehouse. What a fucking lousy place to bite it, Mackelroy thought to himself as he kicked aside an empty soda can.

Tindale had been working the night shift, and he was on his way home that morning when he'd apparently taken an unexpected call. That was strange to, because he hadn't been contacted by a dispatcher. Had he been working on a lead? The poor bastard came in here and bang, bang, he was dead. To be sure, other cars had been dispatched after the strange call from the phone booth, but everyone had been ten minutes too late. By the time the poor bastard had been found, the killer had vanished like some furtive ghost.

Mac strolled back to his car deep in thought. He always returned to the crime scene to try to get a feel for the place. Sometimes you saw something different if you came back a day later and had time to think about the set up. He sat behind the wheel and kept staring at the abandoned warehouse as if its very walls could speak. The only other buildings nearby were a few dilapidated three decker houses built sometime during Victoria's reign. That's when he got the call.

Chapter

2

STRIKE TWO

Mac automatically picked up the car phone. "Mackelroy here!"

"Captain, Captain!" A frantic female dispatcher was on the other end.

He replied, "What's up?"

"You've got to get over to Ten Congress Street. They just found patrolman Will Skulley. He's dead!"

When Mac reached the new crime scene, he knew the killer had struck again as soon as he saw the bullet-ridden body on the front steps of another inevitable triple-decker apartment house. It seemed to Mac as if the entire city had been once exclusively built with such structures, obviously a predictable legacy of the previous century's industrial revolution.

Once again, the other members of the homicide team were drawing their lines and taking their photographs. The body, that had recently been Bill Skulley, lay prone on the once fashionable brick sidewalk about twenty feet from his car. Congress Street was typical of a classy neighborhood predating the Civil War. It looked so out of place to see a bloody corpse sprawled out on such a stylish walk way. Mac absently noted that the car was a few feet too close to a fire hydrant.

Local residents watched the grim proceedings, and of course the press had landed like a flock of restless vultures, trying to glean every scrap of information for the evening news. It never ceased to amaze Mac how quickly the members of the damned morbid press could show up when bad news was afoot. He wondered how many of the bastards would have shown up at Golgotha had they been around in ancient times.

⸻ ◆ ⸻

Later, in the chief's office, Bender gave him the grim details again between quick intakes of cigarette fumes. "Well, Mac, just as you guessed. Slugs from a 45, and yes, they match the other ones dug out of Tindale. Time of death was about six this morning. Apparently Skulley was returning to his apartment. Skulley caught three slugs in the back. It's like the bastard was waiting for him."

Mac thoughtfully sipped his eternal cup of coffee and stared out the window for a long moment. "Any sign of robbery?"

Bender sighed with obvious disgust. "No, Skulley still had his wallet and revolver. No attempt was made to enter his apartment either. He was just shot and left to die in the street. Mac I'm giving you an open ticket. Whatever you need, whatever you want, you've got it. The mayor is going to back me up on this all the way."

Mac actually laughed with derision. "That cheap son of a bitch wouldn't give a fucking rope to a drowning man, for Christ's sake. Get real, Chief, Flarity is worse than useless!"

Bender shot Mac an annoyed glance. "Just for the record, I've talked with Slocum, the bastard's rich uncle. Flarity will tow the mark on this one. After all, Slocum's old man was a cop."

Mac grinned and took another inevitable sip of the warm brew. "Thanks . I'm checking out everything I can on this one. I've got guys canvassing all the pawnshops and gun stores in the entire sodding state. I've got a few friends in the troopers, and they're just as pissed as we are. We'll get the bastard, by God! As far as Flarity goes, I'll believe it when I see it."

Bender gave Mac a wintry smile. "I hope so, because at the rate this prick is going, we'll all be dead in less than a year." His chuckle lacked the faintest trace of humor.

Mac put some more sugar in his coffee as he returned to his own desk. For some reason, the liquid had grown bitter in his mouth. He read and re-read the reports of the two murders and tried to think beyond the details. How had the bastard known that Skulley would be at Ten Congress Street at that time? It couldn't have taken more than a few seconds for Skulley to get out of his car and walk the twenty feet or so to the steps. Also strange was the fact that nobody in the neighborhood had heard the sounds of shots. Had the killer used a sound suppressor on the weapon this time? The two incidents had proved one thing, at least in Mac's mind. Apparently, the killer was trained in the use of firearms. The police had found eight shell casings for eight bullets, all of which had hit the intended target. Mac checked the local phone book, and sure enough, he found Skulley's name, phone number, and address listed. However, there were eleven others Skulley references and nothing in the phone book indicated that Skulley was a policeman. So maybe the killer knew Skulley personally.

Next, Mac went to see Lieutenant Tanner.

Frank Tanner was a tall, well put together man in his late twenties. He'd gotten an early start on the force, having joined at the tender age of 20. That is why he'd been able to reach Lieutenant so young. Of course, he'd spent every spare moment taking criminology courses which had been an integral part of his promotions. Frank was intently studying some paperwork when Mac entered.

"Frank, I want a copy of every file on Skulley. I want a complete list of every case he worked on, I don't care how trivial. How long was he on the force anyway?"

Tanner arched his thick eye brows. "I think about two or three years."

"Good! Then we'll have a finite amount of material to go through. I intend to check out every person on that list of individuals he saw, wrote up, or arrested."

Tanner snorted. "Are you looking for a revenge angle?"

Mac shrugged his shoulders. "I don't know what the hell I'm looking for. I'm going to cover all the bases. That bastard knew Skulley was a cop; that's why he was waiting for him."

Frank went over to the coffee maker and asked the obvious. "Can you use another cup, Mac?"

"Yeah, half and half."

Tanner thought to himself that it had been a stupid question. Mac never turned down hot Columbian laced with sugar and cream. "You know, there are other ways of finding out names and addresses of policemen."

Mac began downing his second cup. "I know that, but almost anyone can find that information if he knows where to look. Maybe checking Skulley's back work will be a waste of time, but at least it's a relatively short list. I mean, we might be looking at something like a thousand names, and maybe we'll get lucky. Maybe we'll find something from some gun shop. Anyway, I want those files by tomorrow morning, and I'll assign some people to track down the leads. The chief has given me a blank check."

Frank spoke quietly as if he were afraid someone might hear him. "It's thin Mac."

Mackelroy grew a little testy. "No shit, Frank! Don't you think I know that? Of course it's fucking thin! But it's all we've got right now."

Frank raised an eyebrow. "We're on the same side, Mac."

"Sorry, Frank, I just want to get my hands on that creature and strangle the mother fucker."

Frank grinned. "Hell Mac, if I find the guy first, there won't be anything left to strangle when I get through with the fuck-head."

Mac quickly drained the second cup. "You better be sure to make it look like an accident. I mean, the mayor doesn't want any complaints about police brutality to ruin his lily-white image. I kinda like an old John Wayne line: I'll take you back to town for a fair trial and a fair hanging."

Both men laughed as yet more coffee was poured into empty cups. Mac asked, "by the way, Frank, where's the fucking donuts?"

The lieutenant smirked and winked at his boss. "At the corner of Park and fucking chandler."

Mackelroy practically choked on his coffee. "Yeah, Frank, I knew that."

Sometime later, Mac was systematically ingesting a late lunch while waiting for several reports to come in including an updated list of gun shops in the tri state area. Between mouthfuls of a boring ham sandwich, memories flitted into his mind like so many uninvited ravens. What a waste the first marriage had been. Everything had looked so promising during the intricately choreographed religious service. There she'd been in a wedding gown fit for Queen Elizabeth. Her veiled face glowed with happiness just before the fateful words had been spoken.

The honeymoon at Oahu had been a cross between a magnificent sight seeing tour and a major porno flick. For two weeks they'd done everything in a countless variety of ways. Then it was back to work.

It wasn't just the long hours. Time after time, the national news broadcasts picked up on policemen either killed or badly injured in the line of duty. Order had its price and as time went on, his wife became apprehensive. She wondered when and if her "sweet Jack" would literally bite the bullet. Apprehension gave place to worry, which in turn gave place to an inner fear. In three years, the marriage was over. Fortunately, they'd practiced birth control so the departure was relatively painless except for the emptiness he felt from time to time. She'd known the risks of his profession. However, it was one thing to intellectually know about them and quite another to live with those lurking fears. So now it was coffee and ham sandwiches instead of cooked vegetables and broiled steak. He'd been alone for three years now and the job wasn't getting any easier.

And what about his own fear? It lurked like a coiled serpent, ready to lunge at the slightest provocation. The normal risks of being a police officer were dangerous enough but now there was some deranged cop hunter, stalking and killing them as if they were fair game in the proverbial concrete jungle. Would he stay the course? Would he survive long enough to bag the bastard? Or would he buckle and flee the scene? Would cowardice triumph over duty? He honestly didn't know. After all, he was but a mere mortal and Jack had never claimed to be better than the rest nor above the temptations and tribulations that daily tormented mankind. Many times when arrests were made he would silently tell himself, "There but for the grace of God, I stand."

The raspberry muffin did little to bring him comfort. Five minutes later he was back at his desk, sifting through more meaningless facts.

Chapter 3

DARK FURY

"**Y**ou must keep killing zee Americanner swine. "

Herbert stared intently into the limitless blackness. Only a shimmering apparition hovered before his glazed eyes. It was the only light source that existed in Herbert's small universe. The monotone voice continued, "You are an SS officer, Herbert! You vill do zis for zee fatherland. Kill more and more of our enemies. Show them no mercy, just as they showed us no mercy during zee var. Those Amerikanners spread lies, Herbert! So many lies about me saying I killed myself. But as you can see, I'm still here. I vill lead you to victory."

He raised his hand in salute, and Herbert said, "Yes, mine Fuehrer! I vill tell the veakling under my command what ve must do. The power is in your vill!"

The shadowy image continued to flicker with blinding brilliance in the darkness of Herbert's mind. The apparition's benevolent smile lifted Herbert's spirit to a new level. "It's too bad your father vasn't still alive. He vas a man of strength, a man of iron! You vill be strong! Stronger than your father was! Do you understand?"

The voice had become loud and insistent. Herbert replied with fierce determination and pride in his shouting voice. "Yes, mine Fuehrer, I vill do better. My father was a credit to zee SS. It is an honor to valk in his footsteps."

The figure grew a little brighter. "That's good, Major Koehler. You vill do your duty and keep killing those blue devils. Vhen you kill enough of them, they vill bring in their useless national guard. Then you can kill their soldiers. You can set zee bombs under bridges and near their vehicles. Their streets vill run with rivers of blood. I vill have my revenge on them all!"

Evil laughter filled Herbert's mind as this visionary specter of Hitler reveled in future victories. "Did those fools think they could destroy Dresden and slaughter my armies and get away vith it?" The voice was screaming now, and the eyes seemed to blaze with a fierce light. "My only regret is that I don't have a few of you in Russia to kill zee Godless communists."

Herbert was standing at rigid attention now. "I await your orders, mine Fuehrer!"

When the orders had been given and the vision departed, he sank back on his bed listlessly looking at his drab bedroom. Dirty clothes lay in a pile near the closet. The place smelled of coffee, sweat and mouse droppings. There sure wasn't time for housework when the fate of the fatherland was in his trembling hands. Gently, he fingered the cool steel of the handgun that had proved to be so useful over the past few days.

⋅•━━━━━•━━━━━•⋅

May is such a pleasant time of year in central New England. It's an area of the U.S. where people still get excited about Memorial Day, and thousands of flowers are ordered for the monuments in serene cemeteries. It's also the time of year when most major league ball clubs are still in their respective races, and the dating scene seems to heat up in earnest. Everyone walks a little quicker as spring becomes a reality. Children flock to the playgrounds, and the smell of vibrant foliage perfumes the air as life speeds up a notch. Even in the modest sized city of Worcester, additional zest seems to hit the streets as pedestrians become a little more cheerful. The playgrounds begin to fill, anticipating summer heat.

Patrolman Rick Connors had just finished taking a report on a minor burglary at a flower shop which of course, was closed for business so early in the morning. He got the call on his radio. His partner was out sick, so he was just taking the more incidental calls, like family disputes, minor store robberies, and that sort of thing. In minutes, he was on his way to 117 Franklin Street. He called into the dispatcher that he would be checking out a noise complaint. It was still dark outside with only a faint trace of dawn becoming visible in the eastern sky.

It only took a few minutes to drive over to the house. When he got there, the place was in virtually total darkness. Only a few dim lights could be seen in a few of the second and third floor windows. He entered the hall of a turn-of-the-century three family house. The hall stank of a century's worth of cooking odors and humanity. He started up the well worn steps which seemed to give ever so slightly under his weight. Each step produced a creak, highlighting his progress. Only the faint light from a nearby street lamp graced the deep darkness with a trace of illumination. The complaint had ostensively been called from the third floor apartment. He frowned a little because he heard no sounds. If there was a wild party going on upstairs, why was it so damned quiet? Was it a false alarm? The steps creaked as he reached the second floor landing. Well, he decided to check it out anyway. Sometimes trouble makers might notice the cop car drive up and shut things down. A stern warning never hurt. His eyes were getting used to the very dim light coming through the grimy window. For a brief moment, he thought he saw a dark, moving shadow, and that's the last thing he knew as the 45 caliber slug tore through his skull and imbedded itself in the hallway wall.

Because of the silencer, the report of the gun was almost soundless. That's why no one in the building noticed anything until someone left for work later that morning.

The shadowy figure calmly stepped over the corpse and quietly left the building. It was all too easy, actually. The killer grinned to himself as he left by the front entrance in the early morning pre-dawn darkness. He was thinking, one officer was a piece of cake. Of course, he knew he could have wasted two cops without any difficulty. He was a crack marksman, and he had the additional advantage of surprise. He chuckled to himself softly as he calmly walked away along the quiet street. Soon he was humming a German marching song.

After a few blocks, he quickened his pace so he could reach home in time to have breakfast and prepare for another day's work.

Ann Tindale had gone through hell and continued to do so. First there were the harrowing days of calling hours and the solemn funeral. Then the heart-rending vigil during the dismal burial as Theodore W. Tindale was sent to his final rest. Family members and friends tried to console her but it was to no avail. Now Ann was taking anti-depressants on top of her frequent consumption of stiff alcoholic beverages. Perhaps it was a dangerous combination. At this point in time, she couldn't bear to look at Ted's picture, so she put it in a cabinet drawer. Ann continuously watched the news as if addicted to the glowing tube. It was in vain. Not only was there no progress, but the cops kept getting picked off as if they were clay ducks in a shooting gallery. All she heard was the normal platitudes. The mayor would say something inane like, "we'll leave no stone unturned until we find the perpetrator of such violent acts. The police of this city are a sacred trust, and I'll do all in my power to see that they are protected."

She laughed at that one. That stupid bastard couldn't protect himself if his life depended on it. Then that moronic Police Chief would claim that they were progressing and running down leads and they would bring the thug to justice. It was all so hollow and pointless. Yet she kept watching and hoping. At least she did when she wasn't balling her eyes out or lying in bed in a drunken stupor.

And that wasn't the worst of it. She and Ted had only been married for a bit over a year, and her body still hungered for his touch in every imaginable way. Sometimes, at night, she curled up in a ball and screamed into the pillow as her inner self felt the sharp pain of emptiness.

The vivacious blonde imagined that she could still feel the joy of Ted moving inside her, still recall the pleasure of his delicious kisses as she lay writhing in the empty bed they'd so often shared. "Oh Teddy! I can't stand this!" She beat the pillow with her fists and eventually cried herself into fitful sleep.

Finally, the days ran into weeks, and the pain lessened a little, and she went back to work; but her heart wasn't in it. She went through the motions and did just enough to keep the boss happy. Then it was back home for a quick supper and the television updates. She became dependant to the enticing lack of relevant news as well as those depression pills. When would they catch the blood thirsty monster? Cops were dying like flies and they couldn't figure out bugger all.

⚬⚬⚬ ——— ⚬ ——— ⚬⚬⚬

"Ah, Herbert, you've done very vell. Very vell indeed! You popped that cop off, and this time you only used one bullet. That is good, because you only have so many bullets left. How many remain, Major?"

Herbert stood at attention and clicked his heels. "There are four-hundred-and-ninety-one, mine Fuehrer!"

The shadowy ghost cackled again. Herbert loved how the Fuehrer showed his gratitude with that smile. Sometimes the apparition looked more like his father than the pictures of the historical Hitler he'd seen, but what did that matter? The voice continued, "very good, Herbert! You can always buy more in New York or Philadelphia some day. But for now you have plenty. It vas vise of you to throw them off the scent by using five bullets the first time. Then you used three bullets, and now one. They'll think there's some special pattern to that, vhen in fact it means nothing. I can just see the stupid bastards seeing if 5-3-1 has any significance."

Herbert responded, "Yes, mine Fuehrer, it was a brainstorm I had. I can keep doing that as vell. Maybe they'll think it's a special code or something. How many do I have to kill before I receive the rank of Colonel, mine Fuehrer?"

The blazing figure shook his head. "Oh, major, you disappoint me. Is a promotion all you care about? I vill let you know when you have earned zee higher rank. For, now you vill follow my orders, and you vill enjoy following my orders. Do you understand?"

Herbert responded, still at attention: "Javole, mine Fuehrer!"

Herbert had to be careful. He didn't want to upset the Fuehrer, and asking for that promotion had been a mistake. Yet he wanted to make certain that he was doing the right things and advancing. He wanted to become field marshal one day to erase the scandalous memory of the betrayal of Rommell. Herbert wondered to himself how anyone could betray the Fuehrer. It was unthinkable. How could the famous World War II field marshal have done such a disgusting thing?

The Fuehrer continued his lecture. "I think it best if you lay low for a vhile and see what they do. I suspect they vill change their plans and procedures now. You learned a lot in their army, didn't you?"

Herbert spoke with more confidence. "Yes, mine Fuehrer! I vill kill many more of them by your command."

The imagined figure began to flicker and fade slowly spiraling towards nothingness. The inevitable disappearance of his teacher and leader filled Herbert with regret. He knew the interview was almost over. " Vell, make sure you keep that spineless worm to the straight and narrow. I vill give you more orders in a few days."

A moment later, the sinister apparition was gone. Herbert stared into limitless darkness once again. He longed for the light which emanated from his commander. He hated the darkness of the modern, decadent world. It was plain for anyone with a clear mind to see. Society was infested with rap music, filthy movies, bogus art, Jewish influence in the media and finance and an ever spiraling national debt. It was madness and he would cleanse the entire country of these fools who had laughed at his fuehrer, consigning him to political oblivion.

⸻ • ⸻

Dave Emmons and Al Benoit were two ten-year veterans of the force. They had the routine down to a "t" in their constant role as vigilant vice squad patrolmen. They always started the day off with an hour-long conference in the Dunkin Donuts shop at the corner of Park Avenue and Chandler Street. According to neighborhood legend, people could set their clocks by the two patrolmen's punctuality, as they entered the donut shop every day at exactly the same time. The teeny bopper who served the customers didn't even have to be asked anymore for their orders. She always had the coffee prepared just like they liked it. Dave's regular order was a half-and-half, while Al drank his coffee black, with one sweet-and-low. Both had a walnut crunch and a blueberry muffin. Then they sat down to discuss what areas to check out that day, and to look over lists of names or complaint reports.

Across the street from the Dunkin Donuts, a local businessman ran a collectables store. He was often asked by his customers why he didn't have any special burglar deterrent equipment, and he always answered: "Why should I have any? Just look across the street! The fucking cops live at that donut shop. A thief would have to be insane to come around here. Let me tell you something, one night I was here until two in the morning doing inventory and as God is my witness, I saw cops sitting over there even at that time. No, this is the safest corner in the entire God damned city."

To be sure, the Park Avenue donut shop was a popular place for Worcester's finest, and everyone knew it including the crooks.

⊷●━━━━━●━━━━━●⊶

Frank Tanner found a seat in Mac's office, and Mac nursed another cup of coffee as he listened. "Well, Mac, we've gotten a preliminary rundown on the gun and pawn shops. I've compiled a list of approximately 450 persons who purchased a forty-five hand gun in the last two years. Most are from out of town, but I've assigned two patrolmen to check out the locals for now. Also, none of the persons on this list match the list of persons that Sergeant Tindale had any dealings with."

Mac grimaced, "Yeah, it looks like a dead end, but keep them cracking. I at least want to eliminate some suspects. The fact that these 2 murders took place so close together, and in downtown Worcester, tells me that the thug is local; though he could be from anywhere in the county, or even from the middle of the state. He could be anyone from Springfield to Boston, or from the New Hampshire border to the northern parts of Connecticut or Rhode Island. However, I have a gut feeling the bastard resides right here in town. That warehouse is off the main drag, and Congress Street is a side street not readily visible from Pleasant. This creep knows his way around this town."

Frank got himself another stiff coffee before replying. "Well, Mac, we confirmed one interesting thing from the lab. It seems they were able to show that the shell casings are from older ammunition. I mean, we checked with the company that manufactured them, and the shell casing is made of a metallic compound that hasn't been used since 1988. So our boy hasn't bought the ammo recently, assuming he didn't steal it."

Mac smiled a little. "Well, that either means that the thug bought the bullets back in 88 or earlier, or the store he bought them at had some older back stock. So now we have to check ammo sales going back up to twenty years and he might have chosen a store that's out of business now. On top of that, there's no guarantee that the store has a name to go along with the sale. We're back to fucking square one, all right."

Frank laughed without a trace of humor. "Yeah, we're up shit creek without a paddle, and our boy is still on the loose, swimming down stream."

Mac shook his head. "It's so easy in the fucking movies, you know. The criminal always leaves just enough clues for the cops, and then Clint Eastwood nails the fucker within two hours, and justice is served. You know, *Dirty Harry* is my favorite movie. I just love it when Eastwood says, *do you feel lucky, punk?* Then he blasts the fucker into the lake. That flick really helps me relieve some stress but of course, it's never like that in the real world, is it?"

Frank took another gulp of the rich Columbian blend. "You got that right."

Mackelroy shook his head while he looked out the window, not really seeing the familiar scene, a large granite stone building skirted by a poorly paved parking area. "Most of the pricks we nab are cowards and worse. They get off on hurting the helpless, but when we show up, they start whimpering on their knees and begging for their lawyer. I hope this thug doesn't ask for a lawyer. I hope he fights it out so we can blow his ass into oblivion."

Frank grimaced again. "Be careful what you ask for, Mac, you might get it."

Mac chuckled. "Yeah, I know. I watch Star Trek too. Don't worry, Frank; I talk big, but I always go by the book."

The phone rang. Frank and Mac exchanged a long glance before Mac picked up the receiver. "Captain Mackelroy, can I help you?"

Frank rapidly became uneasy as he observed Mac's face paling with obvious shock. "Did you say Evers? First thing this morning? Thanks I'll tell him."

Mac put down the phone. His dismay had turned to rage. "John Evers was killed this morning. A gunshot wound to the head. We'll do our homework, but I'd be willing to bet my left gonad, that it's "him" again. We've got to get this murdering fucker, Frank!"

He smashed his fist down on the desk. "Jesus fucking Christ! Three men in less than two weeks! The chief has given me a blank check, and I'll do the same for you. Frank, do what you have to do to get his ass. Wire tap the entire fucking city if you have to. I'll back you up a hundred fucking percent!"

Frank and Mac had been friends a long time. Tanner had never seen the Captain so angry, even when they'd brought in the serial rapist or the drug pusher that loved to sell to ten-year-olds. Frank said in a quiet voice, "I'll do all I can, Mac. You know that. Evers was a friend of mine to. We'll get this score settled."

Mac refilled his cup. "Yeah, well I won't rest until the bastard is pushing up daisies. You're a good man, Frank. I couldn't run this department right without you. I'm not angry with you. I'm enraged with this faceless fucker that keeps killing such fine men. You should have seen Mrs. Tindale when I told her. I saw a person lose her spirit right in front of my face. It's almost like the bullet went through her too. I thank God Skulley didn't have anybody that close. I want you to handle Evers affairs, seeing as how he's your friend. I know we don't have much to go on. This case is so thin it's like century-old paper. Just so we don't cover the same ground, you keep checking the paper leads, and I'll work on questioning people from the neighborhoods. We'll have a short meeting every morning to exchange updates."

Frank finished his drink. "Anything you say Mac. Sooner or later we'll get this thing." Frank pronounced the word "thing" as if it tasted of excrement.

Mac felt genuine weariness and it was only 8 in the morning. "I sure hope so, Frank. I hate to admit this, but you know, this guy is starting to scare me."

Frank gave his friend a level stare. "I'm scared too, trust me."

Mac sighed and shut his eyes for a moment. "Yeah, for the first time in my life, I feel like I'm being hunted. It's like having a target on your back and you don't know when the fucking arrow is coming."

"I just hope I get a shot at this thug before he gets a shot at me." Frank gave Mac a mirthless grin. "I can't serve the force if I'm dead."

"Don't I know it. That's why we have to bust ass on this one. It's an honor to have you on my squad. I really mean that, Frank."

Tanner shrugged in a rare display of self deprecation. "You're the best, Mac."

Soon both officers were hard at work, sifting through long shot leads and making phone calls. It was like throwing darts at the target in a completely dark room. This investigation gave new meaning to hit and miss.

Chapter 4

CLUELESS

The worst thing about police homicide investigations are that the press starts picking up on the sensational details like a hungry horde of leaches. The first wave that swarmed the scene was the local media, which plagued Chief Bender with a myriad of the usual inane questions. Soon after, WBZ Broadcasting, located in Boston got its cameras really rolling. All this was going on while the department was scrambling to fill their depleted ranks. More recruits were brought up from the academy than normal to fill the easy desk jobs while the more experienced men were cruising around town checking out any lead no matter how remote or insignificant.

Mac wasn't the least bit surprised when the lab confirmed that the bullet that did Evers was a 45 caliber slug from the same weapon that had killed Tindale and Skulley. As usual, there were no witnesses. The second floor tenant at 117 Franklin Street by the name of Jose Herrera was leaving for work in a nearby factory. Needless to say he tripped over the body of John Evers which was lying right in front of his door. Not surprisingly, the second floor tenant was pretty shook up about it. It isn't every day that you find a dead body lying so near to your point of egress.

Mac had driven over there to over see it all. They found the shell casing a mere three feet from the victim. They even found the slug imbedded in the archaic plaster wall. Evers had gotten it from real close range. The powder stains on the body verified that. Apparently the killer had been hiding around the corner where the stairway went up to the third landing. They carefully searched Herrera's apartment and the entire building and found nothing except for the tell tale shell casing and the fatal bullet.

Back at the office Frank and Mac listened to the tape of the call that had brought Evers to his death.

"Please send somebody over here now! There's zis vild party going on and I can't get to sleep!"

All right sir, where are you located?"

"I'm at vun, vun, seven Franklin Street. The party is on zee third floor.

"And what is your name sir?"

"Manfred Vallner"

Frank summarized the report." The call came in at four twenty seven A.M. and patrolman Evers shows up about twenty minutes later. Time of death has been determined to be between four forty five and five fifteen that morning. It's probably closer to five and of course the name given by the caller was a fake."

Mac sneered sardonically, "What a fucking surprise!"

Then he retrieved and played the tape of the other call that had lured Tindale to his end. They listened to the two tapes several times.

Mac finally commented, "It's the same guy and he's got a German or eastern European accent. It's got to be the killer because a third party wouldn't happen to have virtually the same voice. The chance of that happening are probably millions to one."

The Lieutenant stared out the window for a long moment before answering. "I agree. We now have a voice. This time he used a cell phone. We couldn't trace the call."

"Yeah those cell phones are a bitch. All right Frank I want you to have your boys get all the names of persons owning a cell phone with an active account as of the date of the murder. I want everyone in the entire fucking county."

Frank gasped in disbelief. "Christ Mac! That will be thousands, perhaps tens of thousands of names !"

"I know Frank, I know! First I want the names so we can fill in a loose end later in the investigation. We can check to see if anyone reported a stolen cell phone. We can check for any German or eastern European last names. Maybe we can get a record of all cell phones that made calls to our police department at the time in question. I just know we've got to check every clue we get, no matter how remote."

Tanner did not look happy. Checking thousands of records was going to be a super bitch. "Yeah, you're right. Play the hand we're dealt. This is going to take a shit load of man hours."

Mac gave him a wolfish grin. "Use some of those new boys from the academy. Let them see how boring and nerve racking police work really is. Give each one five hundred numbers to check. Thorough police work brings its own luck."

Frank gave Mac a very crooked smile and a jaunty salute. "Yes sir! I'll get right on it."

"All right! We'll get this prick! Now bugger off so I can get some real work done."

⋅•➤━━━•━━━◆━━━•━━━◀•⋅

The mayor of Worcester enjoyed the use of a very plush office at city hall located on Main Street. This osteer building was a tribute to the grim stolid design of late Victorian architecture. It was supposed to look like a renaissance castle but it looked more like a well-designed prison. It was all granite gray outside and archaic marble inside. The front portion of each interior steps leading to the second floor and beyond were worn down about a quarter inch from the countless thousands of shoes that had trod up and down them over the last century. In spite of the relatively new light fixtures, the inner reaches of this edifice still maintained that singular Victorian look with its ornate woodwork and lead glass door windows. Only the open snack shop to the right of the front stairway smacked of modernity.

Mayor Thomas Flarity was an anachronistic throwback to the "old Irish club' days. At one time he'd lived in the moderately sized suburban community of Clinton. That old mill town was controlled and predominantly inhabited by Irish. And it wasn't just Irish but they were from the county Mayo and this meant that other Irish were not considered good enough for the local cliques.

Mayor Flarity was both comfortable with and very proficient in the use of political corruption of every kind. It wasn't that he did anything blatantly illegal. However, he was well versed in giving and receiving the right kinds of favors. He used influence and subtle innuendo to get the job done or carefully line his very deep pockets. Graft via the granting of large, construction contracts usually was his favorite avenue to financial well being. When he moved to Worcester in the early nineties, he quickly got into the political power scene with the help of some of his innumerable relatives. This crafty political con man told the public what they wanted to hear and he made sure that the contributors to his campaign got what they expected for the most part. The right honorable Thomas P. Flarity was the politician that could be completely trusted. He'd been bought and paid for a dozen times over, by the Democratic Party and its important constituents and of course the all important special business interest groups, which somehow always were able to remain anonymous.

The mayor was sitting behind his desk resplendent in a perfectly tailored charcoal gray suit accented by a conservative maroon tie. His hair was a predictable, middle aged gray and his elegant appearance was accented with flashing brown eyes. If one didn't know him better, he actually looked like an honest man. He was not amused as he gave a verbal tongue lashing to the chief of police, Al Bender and the homicide captain, John Mackelroy.

"So what you're saying is that after almost three weeks you haven't found a fucking thing! Christ man I've been handling questions from WBZ to WXYZ. I'm getting hundreds of angry or concerned calls from citizens all over the county. Look gentlemen I don't like bad publicity! It makes me look bad and when I look bad it makes it difficult for me to get re-elected!"

The chief was apologetic or at least he attempted to be. "I'm sorry sir, but we don't have much to go on. There's no obvious motive, nothing we can put our finger on."

Flarity blew up. "I don't want you to put a lousy finger on anything! I want the son of a bitch whose doing cops! I want this shit off the front pages! How about it Captain? Cat got your tongue?"

Mac flashed Flarity his most obnoxious, shit-eating grin. "I see you haven't been all that impressed with our performance sir. Perhaps you could come down to the station and help us. I suspect you're much better at all this than we are."

The Chief shot Mac a warning glance. The mayor was taken aback. "Captain Mackelroy are you trying to insult me in my own office?"

The police captain's smile became a study in mock warmth. "Why no mister mayor. I was complementing you. You must be more competent then we are. After all you're the mayor and we're just moronic cops that don't have a fucking clue."

The mayor looked shocked and he spoke to Bender, "Is this guy for real? You straighten him out and get this case solved or I'll be looking for a new chief of police now both of you get out and get to work!"

The two policemen stood up to leave. The mayor opened the door for them and Mac kept grinning at him while Flarity flashed Mac a baleful glare.

•——•——•

Later in Bender's office, the chief was dishing it out to Mac. It was obvious that the chief was definitely not amused. "Mac you can't talk to the mayor like that! What the fuck is the matter with you?"

Mac grinned back, risking even more wrath. "Please, stow it chief. I've got so much on the right honorable Thomas P. Flarity that his political career could go down like a lead balloon. All I have to do is call the media and let them go nuts."

Bender was still angry but curiosity won the battle. "What do you mean?"

Mac chuckled, "Lighten up chief. I've got enough dope on uncle Tom that all I have to do is send a lengthy file on the pranks of this guy to the Worcester Telegram and Gazette and it'll blow his socks off."

The chief looked unexpectedly interested. "What do you have on him anyway?"

"Don't get me wrong chief, I'm not saying he's worse than most of your crooks in government today. I mean don't you get suspicious when a guy spends millions of bucks to get a job that only pays $90,000 per year? I have my sources and our beloved mayor is a real whoremaster. Not only that but he's got enough graft going with certain Italian construction companies to cover a dozen bodies with skin. Don't get me wrong; it's nothing that would actually send him to jail because it would be difficult to prove in court. But if all this became public he'd be political history. I don't put up with crooks at any level. In fact I almost have more respect for a bank robber than the mayor because at least the bank robber has to have some guts to walk into a public place with a gun. After all some bank robbers actually get killed. Flarity is a gutless coward and a slime ball feeding at the public trough to boot. When he insulted you chief I felt like beating the shit out of him."

Bender finally grinned a little. "Well thanks for the sentiment. I'm glad you didn't hit our illustrious mayor. We would have lost our jobs in the force big time."

Mac was genuinely curious. "Why would we both lose our jobs?"

Bender's smile visibly widened. "Because I would have been helping you. Now fuck off and get some work done and for Christ's sake Mac try to be a little more respectful to important public figures in the future. Remember, they issue our bloody pay checks."

⋅•◆━━━◆━━━◆•⋅

Amy Vincent was an older woman on the wrong side of sixty. Every spring she insisted on doing the spring-cleaning. She lived in a fine two-story home on Burncoat Street and she was into house keeping big time. Her guests would have told her that spring cleaning was of no matter as there was never a microbe of dust anywhere in her entire home anyway. But she would grimly make sure all the interior windows were spotless and she would even hire a cleaning company to do the outside. However, her annual project was somewhat curtailed by the fact that she liked to collect all kinds of junk. Even when spotless, the house was cluttered with books, papers, photos, pictures, potted plants and various kinds of bric-a-brac. She hadn't been in the attic for several months however, and she finally went reluctantly up to the dusty loft to wade through the piles of stashed knick knacks, boxes and trunks. She found some old magazines and newspapers stacked in a corner and decided to get rid of them at last. This took several hours of sorting and bagging. She was an environmental freak as well and she made sure that the paper was placed in the correct bag for each blue box. With Amy, it was a constant struggle between retaining collectibles or removing junk. Next she explored the back end of the attic and found some old toys that her son had played with as a child. She brought all those down and called the Salvation Army for their next Monday pick up. After all, even a inveterate hoarder like Amy Vincent had some degree of rational perspective. Once and a while, she actually could find something to throw out or give away.

A few days later, she steeled her courage and returned to the dust laden attic. After a few minutes of rummaging around, she re-discovered a large trunk sitting in a particularly dark corner of a long abandoned closet.

Apparently the old storage container had been owned by her first husband, Will. As it turned out, opening the large trunk became a major project for the elderly lady. She didn't have a key and she had to break the lock in order to open it. It required the violent use of a hammer and screwdriver but she finally grinned as she pried the top open.

Amy thought the key had been in her top drawer in the bedroom but it hadn't been there after all. She'd settled for the tools after over an hour of thorough searching had failed to produce the correct key.

Once she'd been able to gain access to the trunk's contents, she pulled out a folded flag that turned out to have a swastika on it. Amy shuddered in disgust and shock, putting it aside quickly as if the cloth were infected with anthrax. Next were some photo albums. She quickly looked through them but most contained older photos of persons she didn't recognize including some in German uniforms. She went further and found an old uniform with a few medals. The uniform was black with silver trim. There was a diary in there also but she couldn't read it. The writing was in a foreign language and even some of the lettering was strange. But where was the gun? She knew there was supposed to be a gun because there was an empty holster inside. Besides her first husband had told her he had a gun in case any one tried to break into the house. No matter how carefully she looked, there was no gun inside the trunk. She searched again and again and then searched the entire attic including the crawl space. There was no gun.

Had it been stolen? Had there been a gun in the first place? Had Willy eventually sold it? It was very puzzling. She'd known the trunk was here but she hadn't bothered looking inside before.

⚬⚬▪━━━━━●━━━━━▪⚬⚬

"Good Evening this is Howard baker of WBZ news. Today the Worcester police department is under siege as a manhunt has been organized to find the "Cop Killer". A party or parties unknown have murdered three policemen. We interviewed Mayor Thomas Flarity this afternoon and here's what he had to say about these truly tragic events."

The image on the screen shifts and the mayor is being interviewed in his office." This is Jane Jacobson from WBZ news. I'm here with Mayor Flarity of Worcester, Massachusetts to find out what progress has been made to apprehend this vicious cop killer. So mister mayor what is being done?"

The camera zooms in on the face of the mayor. He is smiling with effort although the underlying tension isn't apparent to either the camera crew or the interviewer. "I am happy to report that significant progress is being accomplished at this time. New evidence has been unearthed with the latest homicide investigations and we are confident that there will be an arrest soon. I ask that everyone remain calm and let the police do their jobs."

Jane asks, "Isn't it true that Chief Allan Bender and Captain John Mackelroy were here earlier today and that they weren't very optimistic?"

For the briefest of moments a frown appears on Flarity's face and he continues, "You must understand these men are professionals. They are always guarded in their assessments of potential success. All I can tell you is that there has been significant progress."

Jane wraps up the brief interview; "Well that's it from here. Back to you Howard."

Howard continues in his trained, accent-less voice. "This morning patrolman John Evers was laid to rest at Saint John's cemetery with full military honors. Certainly hundreds attended and policemen came from as far away as Illinois and Georgia to pay a final tribute to a brave police officer. John Evers had been on the force four years and leaves a wife and infant daughter behind. The staff and management share in their grief. We all hope for a rapid termination of these horrible crimes."

Ann disgustedly shut the tube off before she crumpled into bed. It was more of the same except now there were three dead cops instead of just her wonderful Teddy. When would it end? Even the liquor couldn't relieve her pain. She writhed under the covers seeking and not finding any comfort at all. She was alone. Even in the darkness, she could not find sleep or escape. Her insides were gripped by the terrible tight rope of grief and anger. There were no answers, no respite, no revenge!

Chapter

5

DROP OFF

Ann heard an unexpected knock at her apartment door. She thought to herself, who the hell would be visiting her on a Saturday morning. She approached the door and in typical paranoid Worcester fashion. She called out, "Who is it?"

It's relatively easy to know how long an apartment dweller has lived in Worcester by the amount of paranoia displayed in the simple act of answering or not answering a door. If a person has lived in Worcester less than five years then they generally will open the door at least to the extent the security chain will allow, in order to permit the dweller to observe the identity of the unexpected guest. The five to twenty year sojourners won't open the door. They'll call out "Who's there?" However for those who have been unfortunate enough as to have endured living in that former industrialized horror for more than twenty years the loudest and longest summons will be tacitly ignored. It can only be surmised that the only way they ever get guests is by invitation only. This progression down the road of perpetual distrust only starts after a person has reached enough maturity to begin contributing to the work force. Students typically aren't paranoid because as a general rule they figure they have nothing worth stealing. It's the sociological price Worcester citizens pay for the upturn in the crime rates which have occurred, ever since the Viet Nam conflict and its introduction to many of its serviceman to the perils and pleasures of non perscription drugs.

Ann was originally from Cambridge and was a distinct exception to the above rule. She'd only lived in Worcester for the time of her fifteen-month marriage with Ted. Therefore it can be safely assumed that she transported a healthy dose of Bostonian paranoia when she married Ted.

Ann heard the deep male voice from the other side of the still secured door. "It's captain Mackelroy. Can I see you for a few minutes?"

Ann pursed her lips in sudden thought. What did he want now?

She replied, "All right, just give me a minute."

She quickly took off her bathrobe and slipped on some blue jeans bra and Harvard U. sweat shirt. For a brief moment, the widow glanced at the mirror to make sure she was at least somewhat presentable. She slipped on a pair of low, two tone shoes and proceeded to open the door, motioning him to enter.

The pale, care worn face that stared back was a shock to the normally self-possessed police officer. Dark lines etched her eyes, giving her a somewhat spaced out look. Her light blonde hair was a tangled mess and it looked like she was having trouble keeping her eyes open.

She noticed a large cardboard carton that he held in his right hand.

"Won't you have a seat Captain? I'll get you some tea or would you prefer coffee?"

He answered automatically, "Half and half please."

A few moments later, he sat down on a cheap leather imitation sofa and put the box on the coffee table. He hadn't realized how tired he now felt as he waited. He could hear Ann rummaging in the kitchen obviously getting the coffee ready. It wasn't long before he heard the whistling kettle boiling water. It would definitely be instant.

By force of the policeman's habit, He carefully observed the rest of the living room. The woodwork was typically Victorian with curvy grooves and carved flowery cornices. It was painted white contrasting with the walls done in a pale colonial blue. The carpet was a dark rich blue with a faint sculptured design. The furniture had the look of good quality second hand with a new TV and combination DVD and VCR player tucked on top of an antique table in one corner. The lamps were either antique Typhany or tasteful replicas. Over on the right, a large mahogany bookcase practically overflowed with a wide assortment of paperback and hard cover books. Then Ann was back and placing his coffee in front of him on the small round coffee table.

"Thank you Mrs. Tindale. I'm truly sorry to barge in on you like this but I've got some important matters to discuss with you."

Ann sat down in the large lounge chair across from him and sipped some tea. "I hope you like instant decaf. You kind of caught me off guard."

He smiled, "It's just fine. Of course I like any coffee even ice cream. I guess I'm addicted to the stuff but at least I don't smoke and I only have about three drinks a month so I'm not totally depraved, at least not yet. "

They laughed and he was pleased to see her finally break out of her somber mood a little. He liked her smile. Those pearly whites seemed to dazzle a little in the gentle morning light.

He continued, "I found all of Ted's personal effects in his desk and locker and I've returned them to you in this box."

Her green eyes became intense. "Thank you captain. I'm sorry for the scene I put you through the other night when you told me."

She noted there was genuine care in John's face as he replied, "Please, I should have been more tactful. I just didn't know what to say myself. I only wish I could bring him back for you."

She tucked one leg under her as she studied him more intently. She noted he didn't have a wedding ring on and she cursed herself for even being concerned with such an irrelevant observation. She sipped some more tea before replying, "I still can't believe it. It's so unreal. I keep thinking he'll come through that door and all this was a bad dream but it isn't a dream is it Captain?"

He shook his head. "No, I'm afraid not." He paused for a long moment and then continued. " I also have something else for you."

The plain-clothes officer reached into the inner pocket of his trench coat and handed her an envelope. "As you probably know all of the officers are insured for just such tragedies as this. You'll find a bank check from our insurer for $250,000. Ted elected the max and named you as the beneficiary. I took the liberty of submitting the forms and a copy of the death certificate on your behalf. The coroner is a close friend of mine unfortunately."

She raised her eyebrows a little, "Why is that unfortunate captain?"

"Because of situations like this or for so many victims I must investigate on a daily basis. You know Mrs. Tindale it never ceases to amaze me how cruel we can be to each other. I mean it's one thing for a man to steal food to survive and it's quite another for someone to kill for apparently no reason. I don't know anymore. I'm thirty-two and sometimes I feel like ninety. I've lost Tindale, Skulley and Evers in just a few weeks and I'm no closer to solving this than before. I know the money can't bring Ted back and I'm certainly not trying to imply that it's a substitute. But maybe it will make your life a little more bearable. You can buy a rental property or supplement your income. I've included a business card of a reputable investment planner in the envelope. His name is Don Shepard and he's with a prominent local investment firm. He's been handling my IRA account for over eight years now and he believes in preservation of capital. He'll make sure that your money grows and is safe."

She could see a tear trickling down his face from the right eye. "That's very considerate of you. How did you get all that paperwork done without my signature? I'm just curious?"

"Ted had set up a power of attorney with Mr. Philben a local attorney. Apparently there was a clause to cover this situation if it ever arose. It shows that Ted thought the world of you. He made sure everything was arranged.

I'm only glad I could make things a little easier for you. God knows this is a difficult enough time for you. Again, I'm sorry."

She finished her tea and placed the empty cup on the table and sat back and took a long breath. "You have no idea how lonely it's been for me. It's like my right arm is gone. Can you even begin to understand?"

He looked into the hopeless green eyes, "Perhaps a little. I'm divorced some three years and although it's not the same as what you've gone through I think the loneliness is the same. But I'm not here to talk about me. I'm here to help you get through this Mrs. Tindale. If you need counseling I can arrange that for you. If you ever need a clerical job I might be able to arrange it. If you ever just need to talk, call me. I promise I'll listen."

She gave him a wistful smile, "That's very kind of you. Call me Ann. Mrs. Tindale is starting to grate on my nerves."

He glanced down at his now empty cup for a moment before replying. "All right Ann. All I can say is telling you about Ted was the hardest thing I ever had to do. The entire business is a God damned shame." There was a brief pause of awkward silence. "Well, I probably should be going now but let me know if there's anything further I can do and again you have my most heart felt condolences. Ted was a fine man. He deserved better."

He stood up to leave and she extended her hand, "thank you for coming and for all your help. You almost convince me that there may be a ray of hope in all this."

He grasped her small, surprisingly warm hand. For a split second it was like a shock had gone through them both with the incidental contact. Neither said anything as their eyes met for a moment and then he quietly let himself out.

She slowly went to the door and locked it. There had been something there. She had felt it when she looked into those sky blue eyes and had shaken his strong, dry, warm hand. How could she even think of such things with Ted still warm in his grave? She shook her head in self disgust. Ann went to the coffee table and looked through the personal effects in the box. Tears came to her eyes when she recognized one of her wedding pictures along with the other familiar effects.

For lack of anything else to do that morning Mac dropped in on Mrs. Verna Graves. He called her first to let her know he was stopping over. Fortunately, Verna was a member of an older generation that still believed in answering phone calls, as opposed to relying on perpetual voice mail. It only took ten minutes to drive over to her residence. A few moments after he'd parked the vehicle, the homicide captain got out of his car and reached the entrance to a home that looked like it had been built in the twenties.

An elderly woman opened the door a few moments after Mac knocked. It sure helped to overcome paranoia when you called in advance. She was at that indeterminate age that can be anywhere from sixty-five to 80. In actual fact he knew she was seventy-three. She kept good care of herself as she was well dressed and had the dignity of a senior citizen who has grown up with elegant manners. "Come on in captain. I have some coffee brewing."

He returned her smile, "How did you know Mrs. Graves?"

She laughed, "Everyone knows that policemen are addicted to coffee and donuts."

He looked a little chagrinned, "I see our reputation has preceded us. Thank you for the hospitality. I just wanted to ask a few questions about the shots you heard that morning at the warehouse."

They sat at the kitchen table. It was covered with a red white-checkered oilcloth. He thought momentarily it was like a throw back to the fifties. "I don't know what I can tell you that I already haven't told that nice young man lieutenant tanner. By the way, he liked my dog, Perky."

He smiled, "Yeah Frank's a good egg. I'm sure he covered the bases. No, I'm looking more for impressions and details that might not have been asked. Perhaps we could take your dog for a little walk at the same time?"

She got up to get the coffee and she replied, "Perky will like that but why do you want to walk with us?"

At the sound of Perky a large German Shepard strolled into the kitchen as if he owned it. Mac stared into greedy canine eyes as the dog definitely had the lean and hungry look. "Ah Mrs. Graves has he been fed?"

She giggled, "Mercy me yes captain. He won't bite. He's a good little boy aren't you?"

Her voice was cooing at the dog and his tail wagged but those eyes were telling John that he'd make a nice snack.

"I'll take you're word for that. I just wanted to take a little walk to see how long it takes to get from here to where you heard the shots. I like to work things out for myself."

In moments he was gratefully sipping the coffee after applying the proper ingredients. She patiently sat across from him. She looked all the world like a picture of the queen mother. Yet, her smile was youthful somehow. "I don't know why I'm telling you this but if I were 35 years younger I'd scoop you up in ten minutes. You're quite a hunk even for a cop."

He almost choked on his coffee. Some actually spilled on his chin. He smirked, "I'm sorry but you caught me by surprise with that comment."

She laughed, "I know I'm an old hag now but you should have seen me back in 1960. I was pretty hot stuff then. Oh well I'm over the hill now but it's the first time I've been asked to walk with a man since my hubby died two years ago."

John was wondering why he was saying I'm sorry to everyone he was meeting and he said it again. She replied, "Oh that's all right captain. He died of lung cancer and it was a blessing near the end. We both smoke like chimneys and I'm sure my days are numbered. But I'd rather die at eighty in decent physical shape than die at ninety with Alzheimer's or some other chronic, debilitating disease. If only we could live two hundred years at the attained age of thirty. Is the coffee all right?"

He smacked his lips, "Excellent ma'am."

Soon, they were walking the five blocks towards the vicinity of the warehouse. "At first, I thought a car had back fired. But then I heard a few more reports. I was about here when I heard them and I turned back soon after. I didn't see anyone around but I figured if the sounds were shots they almost had to have come from the warehouse. To be honest, I couldn't imagine where else they could be coming from with all the other buildings around here being apartments or closed up storefronts. Actually I wasn't even certain they were shots but I thought I'd play it safe and call the incident in. The worst that could happen is that it might waste fifteen minutes for a couple of you guys to check it out."

"Were the shots clear or muffled?"

She stopped in mid stride and frowned. "you know Captain, you do ask odd questions. I'm not sure. I suppose they weren't as sharp as if they'd been fired outside but they weren't really muffled either. By the way how long did it take us to get here?"

He smiled at her as he checked his watch. "Eight minutes and thirty seconds and Perky hasn't munched on me yet."

"Oh captain you're such a tease. Is that all you wanted to ask me?"

John nodded, "Yes dear, you actually have been a help. The time differential does clarify a few things. Also your call to the police may prove helpful in the long run. Perhaps it's only a small fact but every little bit of information helps.

Oh, by the way, I almost forgot. How long did it take you to make the call to the police when you got home?"

She rubbed the dog's head and considered his question for a moment. "Well, it took a few minutes to get my dog Perky fed and I had to look up the number in the book. It probably took five minutes or so." "That's fine, Mrs. Graves. Would you like me to walk you back or do you want to stay out for a while? It's really a lovely morning."

Verna gave him a very mischievous grin, "Actually I think I'll be getting back. Perky here needs lunch soon. I wouldn't want him to devour helpless police officers by accident."

Frank Tanner was washing his car. It was his Saturday, pre-noon ritual. He loved his two-story colonial home on Old English drive along with his Grand marquis. His wife Eleanor, loved Frank except for his devotion to that damned car. She called it "His God!" She was only half joking. Eleanor was cynical beyond belief and her tongue could be sarcastic and witty. Her tantalizing soprano voice could also be very seductive at bedtime. She was the same age as Frank being twenty-nine and they had two children that she ruled with a velvet covered iron fist.

Frank had a very simple solution when it came to discipline, just hand the problem over to Eleanor and support her decision. Her logic was so irrefutable that the children didn't bother arguing any more. They were rapidly learning that it was almost impossible to con those two parents of theirs.

Frank was just applying the wax when John showed up. Frank raised his eyebrows as his boss approached. "What's up Doc?"

John quipped, "Can you use a hand?"

Frank laughed, "All right what's on your mind?" He tossed John a clean cloth.

Mac started applying the wax on the left, rear door; "It just came to me frank, what if the killer had already killed Tindale before he made the call?"

Frank stopped in mid wipe, "What! But that wouldn't make any sense!"

John let his words sink in, "Perhaps but lets look at the implications if it was true."

Now Frank was thinking, "it would mean that the killer wanted us to think that the murder hadn't been committed yet and he wanted to take some form of complicity away from himself."

"Yeah so lets say that the guy knew Tindale and wanted to make it look like a stranger did it. Or maybe he just wanted to buy more time after the murder so he could get away. But that makes little sense because why make the damned call in the first place. There's something wrong here and it's bugging me. We get a call at about nine thirty one. We find the body five to ten minutes later. Verna Graves here's the shots and it takes her nine minutes and thirty seconds to walk back but she called in at nine thirty nine. Now even if she had gone at a fast pace she still couldn't have made it in less than five minutes and it took her another vfie minutes to call us after she got home. That means that the actual killing might have taken place as early as 9 26 A:M The time element is screwed up. Now Verna doesn't have any reason to lie and we can verify the exact time she called. Even if you admit that it could have been nine thirty nine and fifty seconds she still had to have heard the shots before fuck head made the call."

Now Frank had stopped wiping and was looking at John. "You know, you're right. When I first saw the times it seemed it was a bit close but now I think you're right. It's very strange. Maybe Tindale knew the creep but why would Tindale go to the warehouse to meet this guy. The warehouse has been trashed for years and Tindale wasn't a detective like us so he wouldn't have any informant or anything like that. At the very least it's doubtful he'd go there alone."

John finished the rear of the Marquis, "I think we've got to take another hard look at that list of contacts that Tindale made over the last three years."

Frank grinned, "Actually two years and six months. That's when he got out of academy and joined the force."

John snickered, "Whatever Spock. It'll take you seventeen point nine years to clean the space station and another two point three years to clean this fucking Marquis."

When they had finished laughing and cleaning the Marquis Frank invited him in for a quick lunch. "We've got the place to ourselves. Eleanor brought the kids to Bobby's little league game. Of course Karen will be whining because she doesn't like baseball at all but her mother doesn't want her daughter home alone with all the wierdoes around. She tells me that a dozen crooks could enter this house undetected while I'm polishing my God."

Mac smirked, "Well she might have a point Frank. I mean that car glows in the fucking dark. You could read by the light it reflects."

Frank gave John a rye smile, "Fuck off and eat your sandwich. It's my car and I want it to last for ten years before I let my son wreck it on a wild date."

When captain Mackelroy was about ready to leave, he casually mentioned an observation that had just come to him. "Well at least this little wrinkle tells me that we now have a hint of a motive. Give it some thought over the weekend Frank. I'm going to do a little more homework on Evers as well."

• • •

John returned to his apartment on Lancaster Street. It was an older pre war home but very well maintained and what was better it was close to the Worcester art museum. John spent many carefree hours there. The quiet atmosphere among the relics of past centuries helped him think and put things in the long view perspective. He didn't know much about art per say but he liked what he liked and he was very partial to the renaissance paintings. His favorite was the painting of John the Baptist by Andre Del Sarto. The use of those rich colors combined with the brilliant portrayals of a long vanished world never failed to intrigue the observant police officer. To see such adoration and faith practically glowing from the canvas was more moving to him than the typical church service.

For now, he kicked his shoes off and lay back on his sofa thinking about the recent events that had so shaken up the city. He reviewed the events of the past few weeks in his mind, sifting through the few facts that had so far been gleaned from the murder scenes, until he unexpectedly fell asleep.

Chapter

6

TIME LAG

"**C**ome on in Al. Could you have a seat please?"

Patrolman Al Wagner sat down on the plain wooden chair directly in front of Frank's desk. Mackelroy stood to one side near the over used coffee maker.

Frank continued, "This is just routine but we're talking to all the partners of Skulley, Tindale and Evers. We're trying to see if there is anything that may have been overlooked and right now we're checking all partner's arrest records for the last two years or so. We just want to be thorough, you might be able to clarify something for us or point us in the right direction. Then again maybe there's nothing. Is that okay?"

Al sat stiffly before his superior officer. Al wanted to make sure that he did nothing to jeopardize the investigation. Besides, he was eager to do his utmost to bring this evil police killer to justice. "Yes sir! I'll help in any way I can."

Frank chuckled at the patrolman's unease. "Relax Al. You're not on trial here. "

Mac smiled at Al attempting to reassure him. He'd once been low on the totem pole himself and he knew the feeling. "Just rookie jitters right Al?"

Al's face flushed a bit. "Well it's not every day I get to talk with the two king pins."

Frank grimaced good naturedly. "Is that what the rank and file call us?"

Al responded, "Yes sir. I think they mean it as a back handed compliment."

Mac laughed, "Yeah, and the emphasis is on the back hand, I'll bet!"

The patrolman got serious. "What would you like to know sir?"

Frank riffled through some papers. Mac knew it was an act to make Al think Frank was unprepared and asking questions off the cuff. It was meant to put the person questioned at ease. Finally Frank asked, "According to the report, you were apparently the last person on the force to see Tindale alive. About what time did he drop you off at your place?"

Al thought a moment, "Well I'd say about eight fifteen or eight twenty. I know it was before eight thirty because I caught CNN news just as it starts on the half hour."

Frank absently gazed at the mug of coffee that Mac was slowly consuming. It seemed that Mac perpetually ingested the dark, brown liquid, regardless of time or place. "Yes I see. And you live at 27 King Street I believe?"

"Yes sir."

Tanner went on. "All right. When you left Tindale that morning did he seem nervous or different in any way?"

"Not that I could tell sir. Everything was fine."

"I know you've only been with Tindale a short time but with any of the arrests you and he made were any of the suspects particularly vindictive?"

Al asked, "Can I check my notes please?"

"Certainly. I've got a copy of your files right here. Take your time."

The silence dragged on for a while and Mac nervously refilled his cup from the chugging coffee maker. He got Frank a cup as well. After about ten minutes Al spoke up. "Well this one was a bit ugly as I recall. We busted some piece of shit by the name of Carlos Rodriguez and his hooker girl friend Renee

Martinez. They threatened us with every manner of post lifetime torture and I must say their language was far below gutter level."

Frank looked at the case and did some quick checking on the computer. Well it can't be them. They've been in jail and should be there for a few more years. But that's all right Al. Sometimes it's just as important to figure out who couldn't have done it as much as finding the culprit. Does anyone else strike your notice?"

A minute later Al remarked, "Well Joseph Brown A K A William Howard, A K A French Twist tucker wasn't exactly pleasant if you get my drift."

Frank and Mac laughed before Frank continued, "I'll bet. We had a bitch of a time preventing that no account pimp from getting bail but that low life, spear chucker is at MCI as we speak. I must admit you're picking out some real gems. You're right in assessing them as dangerous individuals. I tell you what why don't you go through all your cases with Sergeant Carter. See if any of these clowns are still on the street and make me a list of those. If they been in jail during this entire month we can knock them off the list as suspects. It's kind of hard to kill cops from a jail cell."

Al sighed, "I'm sorry I couldn't be of greater help sir. I'll see the Sergeant presently."

The lieutenant gave Al a brief wave, coffee mug in hand." Go right ahead Al. We'll be in touch."

When Al had left, "Frank asked, "Well what do you think?"

Mac refilled his cup yet again. "I think he'll go through the list and we'll find nothing. But at least we can scratch a few more known thugs off the suspect lists. I don't know why Frank but I have the strange feeling Wagner knows something. Perhaps he doesn't realize the significance himself. Remember he's not a detective like us. He wouldn't notice what we'd notice. He said he didn't perceive anything unusual about Tindale's behavior. Sometimes the guy might take a different road home or stop for some butts at a store and take *five minutes to long. Maybe he didn't talk much. Then again maybe there was nothing. Maybe Tindale got bumped off out of the blue. But If Tindale goes to the warehouse before a call went out, why would he go there? It's as if someone led him there or someone agreed to meet him there. You know what I mean?"*

Tanner was inwardly wondering how much coffee Mac consumed in a week. It had to be at least triple the amount of his own considerable intake. "Yeah, I've given you're theory some thought and it's bothering me. The numbers don't lie. The call from the phone booth had to come after Tindale was dead. It seems like the killer was trying to cover his tracks by making the call, but why."

Mac sipped some more half and half before remarking on the problem at hand. "Maybe he was setting up what I would call an inverse alibi."

"In other words the killer can prove he was elsewhere at the time?"

Mac sighed, "Something like that. Or maybe it was someone Tindale knew and he wants to make it look like a stranger was involved. Hell Frank the damned accent could be fake. It all could be one giant curve ball."

Frank carefully added the proper amount of sugar to another steaming cup. "I just thought of something else. What if the ambush as Evers was planned?"

Mac snickered. Sometimes detectives could ask some pretty stupid questions. Yet those questions had to be asked because many crooks actually were stupid. "Of course it was planned. The bastard was waiting for Evers. It was a set up."

Frank retorted, "Yeah but what if the guy knew that Evers was going to be alone? What if he knew there were only a few patrols out at that time of night? It is a remote possibility isn't it?"

Mac almost choked as he miss-swallowed. It took him a few seconds to answer. "You think he might have a CB radio or something?"

"Perhaps but what if this guy has some inside information on us. What if he's some cracker jack computer hacker or something?"

Mac gazed out the window at the busy mid day traffic. He was lost in thought for a few moments. "I can check with the tech department to see if that's possible and if there have been any incidents. If he's a good hacker we won't be able to find the fucker anyway."

⋯⋯━━━━●━━━━⋯⋯

They questioned patrolman Jablonski who was Evers partner and assigned him to work with someone to go through the cases after nothing concrete surfaced. Then they had a talk with patrolman DeOreo with similar results.

Through all this, something vague was bugging Mac. However, he couldn't put his finger on it.

Back at his office he checked out the data on the three officers interviewed that morning. Patrolman Ralph Jablonski Corporal: Aged 27: Married: police academy graduate: Record very good: One commendation and no major complaints.

There wasn't a policeman on the force who hadn't had a minor complaint from some local idiot. Jablonski had a degree in criminology from Boston University. His career was definitely on the rise.

Patrolman Albert Wagner private: Single: Aged thirty: He'd graduated from academy two years ago. No major complaints. No commendations. Previous record. U.S. Marine from age 18 until he entered the police academy. Al was decorated in the Afgan action with a silver star. He was a tank Sergeant. Later he was in the commandos for special force training. He was considered as potential officer material.

Reason for leaving service was Al wanted a better paying job.

Mac remarked to himself, "No shit!"

Patrolman Alonzo DeOreo private: Single: age 24: Police academy graduate with a criminology degree from U. Mass: National Guard member for 3 years, six months: Record very good: No commendations and only one minor complaint. Current commanding officer gives DeOreo high marks for being helpful to others on the force and the public in general. Could have fine officer potential in future.

He noted that Sergeant Carter had made that notation. That was praise indeed from Carter. That crusty son of a bitch was from the old school. He sat back and thought about the three. They all looked exemplary. The military background would explain Al's yes sir no sir deportment. Sometimes those ex marines were gung ho years after they left Paris Island or Quantico or wherever the fuck they got unleashed from. And Wagner had a silver star to boot. The guy was an authentic Afgan hero. He sure didn't look the part. Al was quiet and reserved but then Audi Murphy didn't look like King Kong either. Well maybe they made the best kind of heroes. No bull shit just do your fucking job and be done with it.

He leaned back in his chair and stared at the apathetic computer screen in disgust. The white noise was reassuring somehow. It meant there was still energy behind the scenes. Down the hall he could hear people talking, even laughing. An ambulance siren wailed far in the distance. Life went on In spite of everything. They'd been three young cops with jobs to do and they'd paid the ultimate price. Somehow, the force had to get over this tragedy just as much as Ann or Evers's young wife had to. But why the fuck would the thug call when Tindale was already dead? Why? Why? Why?

He downed another cup of his favorite brew, Columbian. Juan fucking Valdez the original coffee bean spick! To think Juan was the virtually unknown brother of Ricardo Monteban for Christ's sake. It was the perfect example of who you know was more important than what you knew. Juan "Khan" Valdez was probably a moron anyway, dumber than the beans he picked.

His thoughts gradually returned to the bewildering case. Maybe it was the God damned mafia. After all maybe they squashed the wrong bug. But these guys were too young to have gotten that corrupt except maybe Skulley.

The Mafia could have inside dope if one of the current cops was crooked and no matter how well policemen were screened there was always sure to be a bad apple or two. He gazed at the mocking computer screen as if it could give him answers but refused. He stuck his middle finger at it and swore under his breath.

He could understand the second call. It was a trap. Maybe the fact that Evers had been alone was just bad luck. All right maybe it couldn't be mafia because they couldn't have known who would show up. But why did the guy call the first time, after Tindale had bought it? It made no sense and yet he felt if he had the answer to that one he'd solve the crime. There had to be a reason. Someone wanted to cover his tracks big time. He actually laughed at himself. Of course the ass hole wanted to protect his ass. Nobody wants to go to jail for twenty or more years for rubbing someone out.

He swore again at the computer and waited impatiently as he tried to access more files. He flipped to a different screen and looked up the service records for the three murder dates in question. Al Wagner was off duty for all three events. DeOreo was only on duty for tin dales demise and Jablonski had also been off duty for all three events. For that matter Tindale and Skulley had been technically off duty as well. Then he checked Tindale's feels to see if he'd been involved with any arrests with men of Italian descent.

He flashed through the names. Of course there were several but they were all trivial except for the arrest of one extortionist a one Frank Luzzani. The thug was currently in jail for two years after a plea bargain. It was hardly enough to kill a cop for. He rubbed his eyes in pain and fatigue. It kept coming back like a bag of bad pennies. "Why did the fucker call? Why? Why?? Why?!"

❦

Ann took a day off from work on sick leave to see Don Shepard of Paine Webber fame. The firm was located on the twentieth floor of the Worcester Galleria building. The view from this office was like looking down on the city of Worcester from Olympus. When she entered the reception area her eyes were greeted with what could only be described as professional opulence. The floor was covered in a light brown wall-to-wall carpet that was perfectly maintained, not to mention, seductively soft to the step with its luxurious thickness. The walls appeared clean and bright with a light beige color accented with expensive art works. The outer walls, which were about 90 % glass, let in the morning sunlight adding to the overall cheerful effect.

Once the receptionist let the appropriate person know Ann was there, a lovely, blonde secretary showed up in moments and ushered her in. "Hi, my name is Lisa Chapman. I'm Don's personal secretary and he'll see you in a few minutes. I heard about what happened to your husband and I'm very sorry. I'm sure Don can assist you. He's been in the business for almost thirty years."

Ann glanced at the busty secretary, offering a wan, tired grimace. "Thanks, it's been difficult

Lisa gave her a most sympathetic smile. "I can't imagine how terrible it must be. Why don't you sit here and I'll get you some tea all right?"

The brand new widow gratefully sat down in an exceptionally comfortable chair. "That would be lovely, thanks."

It wasn't long before Ann was sipping hot lemon flavored tea. Don Shepard entered the spacious office and shut the door quietly behind him. He reached down a little to shake her hand. "Good morning Mrs. Tindale. I'm very sorry about your recent loss. Captain Mackelroy spoke to me about you and I can assure you we'll be very careful with your money. I'm from the old school and I don't believe in get rich quick scenarios."

She examined the middle-aged man with an appraising look. His hair was white at the temples, accenting the gray. Sharp brown eyes looked back at her just hinting at an inner approval. He exuded confidence and trustworthiness. "If you don't mind I would like to ask you a few questions before I make any recommendations."

"Certainly Mr. Shepard."

He raised his right hand in silent admonition. "Don will be quite sufficient I assure you."

Ann responded, "And Ann will be fine for me. What would you like to know?"

The investment broker finally sat down across from her and thought for a few moments. "Did your late husband have any IRA accounts or pension funds with the police force?"

Ann looked perplexed. "I really don't know. I know he used to get some statements from Merrill lynch."

Don smiled, "Our noble competitors. Well I'll arrange for you to sign a letter of consent so we can find out what he had or didn't have. Lisa can help you with all that.

As far as the money you received from the insurance proceeds, I think it imperative that we protect your principal. I've done some study on your situation and I recommend that we place fifty thousand dollars in short term municipal bond funds, a hundred thousand dollars in short term t bills and fifty thousand dollars in mortgage backed security funds. Perhaps the mortgage funds could be invested in Exchange Trading funds. I know that is probably a new term for you and we can discuss that later. The last fifty thousand dollars should be invested into high yield blue chip equities so that the dividends can be reinvested and your equity will grow to some extent to help keep up with inflation. As your funds make money you can invest some of the interest earned into more speculative investments if you wish but I want to make sure that your nest egg is safe. I certainly don't mind if you wish to get a second opinion and I've drafted a list of my recommendations so you can show another brokerage firm to get their assessment as well."

She raised her eyebrows in obvious curiosity. "I'm surprised you would actually advise me to get a second evaluation.

The urbane financier shifted slightly in his chair and leaned forward to emphasize his point. "Mrs. Tindale, I mean Ann, if you had a very serious illness wouldn't you go to more than one physician?

"Yes."

"Well I don't claim to be infallible and I'm successful because I don't browbeat my clients. I don't make money if my clients loose money. I also don't retain clients if they think they're being forced to do certain things. What I've shown are recommendations. You're currently in a fairly low tax bracket but if you check the numbers with your accountant you might want to put more into municipal bonds and less into the t-bill funds. If you want to take some time to consider all this you can put the money into a t bill account which is a hundred per cent guaranteed and it will make a reasonable return while you make up your mind."

Ann looked pleased. "All right I'll put the money in the t bill account for now and speak with an accountant. Can you recommend one who is reasonable?"

"Yes, I've worked with a gentleman by the name of Troy Leman. I'll let him know you'll be calling and he can look at the recommendations as well. All I would caution you about is that when some broker says you can make twenty or thirty per cent in a year that is true. The key word is Can. You could also lose twenty or thirty per cent and I don't think you want that. Later on a few years down the road if you have built an extra hundred thousand dollars then you can play a little. You stand to make about 20 thousand dollars per year with these investments with minimal risk. My advice is to let the position grow and work for you. Someday you'll be a wealthy woman. I want you to be successful."

Ann got up, ready to depart. The advice had been excellent but all this talk of money made her feel uncomfortable so soon after Teddy's tragic demise. "Thank you Don, I'll see Lisa now and have those funds invested in the t bills. Does Lisa have Troy Leman's number?"

* * *

Ann returned to her apartment after her appointment with Troy S. Leman C.P.A. He'd substantially confirmed Don Shepard's program with only minor changes so Ann was more comfortable with how she set up the account with Don after her visit with the shrewd accountant.

She'd placed most of the money into t-bills and high-income mortgage funds for the present. She had more important things to worry and grieve about. No amount of money could erase the sense of loss and emptiness she felt as she prepared supper in an empty kitchen and a silent dwelling.

The evening news turned out to be trivial and uneventful as usual. The Worcester police were still baffled and Ted's killer or killers were still at large wasting other cops.

Ann had to put mental pictures of Ted deep inside her mind to avoid thinking about him all the time. She was always surprised at how many more tears she had to shed and memories of Ted right now, didn't help. Maybe someday they would. Trying to sleep was the worst. Television programs couldn't numb her turbulent mind. Ann was alone with inescapable thoughts and memories. The new widow was torn between the ache of her loss and a simmering anger that kept building. It was like a volcano ready to burst and spread destruction across some tropical island paradise. Perhaps she was a little old fashioned but Ann wanted vengeance with a resounding capital V. She yearned to see the killer of her precious Teddy nailed to a wooden cross with dull rusty nails or chained to a wall and forced to work at slave labor until he dropped dead. With the help of two very stiff drinks, she finally fell into a fitful sleep.

Chapter

7

BIG BANG!

Sergeant Benoit and patrolman Emmons were at the Dunkin' Donuts as usual. The place was quite crowded on a particularly busy Friday morning.

Emmons was chatting with his long time partner Al. "So, what do you think the Dead Sox will do this year?"

Al Benoit took another bite of his muffin, "Probably fuck all. They'll die in August again. They always run out of gas. It's the Babe Ruth curse."

Dave laughed, "Oh come on Al! You can't believe that shit! There's no such thing as a curse."

Al snorted at such crass unbelief, before swallowing some more coffee. "Oh yeah look what happened in 86. The Dead Sox had a five three lead with two out and two strikes on the batter and nobody on base in the bottom of the fucking tenth. Shiraldi was the best reliever in the entire American League that year and they still blew it. Buckner was only the last straw. Christ five guys got on ahead of his bonehead play. Last year the great Pedro said some snide things about the curse and the next game he pitched he got his arm injured and didn't win another game the rest of that year. You can bet your ass that moron spick doesn't open his big mouth any more about the G. D. curse. I'm telling you they're done like dinner before spring training even begins! The only reason I watch the bastards is just to see how the curse will get them this year. It's like a Greek fucking drama. You know, the hero is doomed in act one even if he doesn't get wasted until act five."

Dave sighed, "I just can't get through to you. I suppose you believe in the Cubs goat curse as well?"

Al shook his head. Such skepticism was beyond his ken. "You're damned right I do. Hey I didn't make up the story about the guy who brought his goat to the games through all of 1945. They wouldn't let him take the goat to the World Series and he got pissed. That's when he said, "The Cubs will never get into a world series in Wriggly field again." And they haven't."

Dave grumbled, "Just coincidence!"

"Oh yeah? Back in 84 the Cubbies had a 2 game lead going to San Diego and the Padres swept Chicago three straight to keep them out. And what about the total fuck up against Florida? How else do you explain blowing a three games to one lead? Anyway we better make sure we get the damned cop killer before we end up like the dead sox. By the way, any updates?"

Dave ate some more of his second walnut crunch, "Nothing new! They haven't found a damned thing except the same 45 slugs did all three. Evers bought it from the same slime ball."

Al thought a moment, "Maybe we should take a spin down Piedmont Street and see if any of the broads have heard anything or seen anything unusual? Sometimes the hookers find out things long before we do."

Dave snickered, "Yeah maybe we'll get a free piece if we tell the sluts we'll let them off the hook. Get it? "

Al stared up at the ceiling. There were times when he didn't know how he could put up with his unimaginative partner. "Maybe but I think we better concentrate on finding out about the sniper or we might be pushing up roses in the fucking cemetery ourselves."

They talked about some minor cases they were working on as more people came and went. Dave carefully observed the customers from force of habit while the discussion proceeded. He noted that an elderly couple ordered herbal tea and muffins. Five college students of various sizes and shapes wandered in and made a variety of orders.

Another policeman wearing shades came in and gave Dave and Al the thumbs up as he proceeded to order some tea and a honey dip. Then two shady looking black dudes came in and Al watched them like a hawk. The blacks ordered coffee and a dozen assorted donuts to go and left quickly.

Al whispered to Dave, "You know, if those two spear chuckers were packing' rods, I'd bring them in for questioning."

Dave washed down the last of his crunch. "Now, now, Al. That's called racial profiling. That's a no-no."

Then a tall Moslem entered wearing a turban and strolled to the counter.

Al frowned and lowered his voice. "There's one of those freaking rag heads. Maybe he's got connections to the bloody Taliban."

Dave chuckled, "you know that's politically incorrect lingo."

"Yeah but I didn't make up the news about the fucking I N S sending a valid student visa to Mohammed Ata six months after he drove the plane into the twin towers. If the I N S can't do better than that we shouldn't let any of the fucking rag heads into the country. I love how those bleeding heart liberals keep saying how it's an infringement of human rights not to let the bastards into this country. What they fail to realize is it isn't a God given human right to live in America. Our country has the right to let or not let people in on its own discretion. After all we didn't let the Japs into this country during world war two and we let precious few in before that."

Dave leaned back in his chair and stared at the man wearing a turban. He was now sitting at a table and drinking his coffee slowly. "Well speaking of sand niggers look at that towel head, Al. He acts like the bloody prince of fucking Yemen. He walks in here like he owns the fucking place. Fuck! I'll bet he doesn't even have a valid passport."

Al asked, "Think we should check him out?"

"Nah! With our luck he'll have diplomatic immunity. Christ on his cross!"

Dave finished his coffee and watched a really sleazy looking girl traipse toward the counter. The slutty looking blonde was wearing blue jeans and a bright red halter-top. Even in unremarkable Dunkin' Donuts she was swaying her hips very enticingly.

Dave shook his head a little. "Christ what a piece! I bet she's a working girl."

Al smiled absently, "Yeah I think I've seen her around. I don't bother getting excited about that stuff unless I have an opportunity to actually sample the wares free of charge, thank you."

Their laughter was unnoticed in the noisy donut shop. Finally they got up and left.

When they were back in the car, Dave got behind the wheel and commented. "Well Al time to punch in and earn our daily bread. Back to the fucking grind."

⸎

The red headed teeny bopper behind the counter was Luana Macrae. She'd been working at Duncan Donuts for nine months while going to night school to get an accounting certificate. She smiled tiredly at an older gentleman who was ordering black coffee and a chocolate dip. Her attention was on the customer so she didn't actually see the police car disappear when it erupted into a fiery explosion in the parking lot. The front plate glass window was split and cracked by the force of the blast. People instinctively dove to the floor. The air was filled with screams and to Luana's horror she saw what had been the police car transformed into a blazing fireball. In moments the cop with the shades was demanding to use her phone and she led him to the back room.

In seconds he dialed a number and yelled, "Get a fucking ambulance down to Dunkin Donuts at Park and Chandler like right fucking now!

Send some other cars over to. I just saw one of our patrol cars blow fucking up! Do it now!"

Then she saw him run out towards the lot.

The red head went around to check the other customers, Most of which were badly shaken. She yelled in a shrill voice to get attention. "Is anyone hurt? There's an ambulance on the way!"

Apart from a few minor cuts and bruises everyone in the shop was all right and they watched in grim silence as three police cars showed up along with an ambulance and a fire truck. In seconds men sprayed down the flaming vehicle but of course what had been Officer Al Benoit and Dave Emmons were but charred hulks only remotely resembling human beings.

Across the street, Bob Jenson ran out of his collectable shop in a vain attempt to offer help. Frank Tanner had just arrived on the scene. He gave bob a curious look. He knew Bob from a few years ago. "You might as well go back to your store Bob. There's nothing you can do. They're done."

Bob shook his head. "I know Frank. I saw the whole thing. I'm looking out the window and I see the car leaving and then poof. It just exploded. I've never seen anything like that since I was in the army!"

Frank raised an eyebrow, "What do you mean?"

Bob was talking quickly now. "Well when I was in the army we used to have demolition practice. We'd use some plastic explosive on a ruined tank or pile of wood or something and the car went up just like that. I mean one moment the car is there and the next it's fucking gone!"

Frank nodded, "Well if we need any further statement from you, I'll send someone down to talk with you. I've got to get back to this miserable business but thanks for caring."

The grizzly remains were placed in the ambulance and the white vehicle screamed its wailing sound as it rushed to the morgue. Policemen and investigators cordoned off the area as they took photos and carefully collected pieces of what had been a car. Soon a large truck appeared and the remains of the vehicle were gathered in the back by use of a crane. Within six hours the lot was cleared up and things got somewhat back to normal.

It wasn't back to normal in the station. Mac had gotten in late that day. He'd been on a long shift the day and night before tracking down leads on the sniper and other important cases and he'd just gotten to his desk when Frank ran in. "Christ John we just lost two more cops at the fucking donut shop!"

Mac stared at Frank in disbelief. "What the fuck?"

Tanner rambled on, "Yeah at Park Avenue and chandler! Their car blew up like totally!"

Mac's face became white with shock and rage. He just stared at Frank. "No shit Frank?"

Frank's face was stone. "No shit Mac! Al Benoit and Dave Emmons are literally toast. Their car exploded and they've been blown into fucking oblivion!"

Captain Mackelroy covered his eyes with his right hand and started weeping silently. When would this nightmare stop? He finally looked up and the two old friends looked at each other for a few minutes in complete silence. Mac croaked, "What the fuck can we do? Its like open fucking season on cops! I'm really getting scared Frank!" "

"That makes two of us."

Mac gripped the edge of his desk hard in an attempt to keep his cool. His voice hissed through gritted teeth. "Let me know as soon as you get a report from forensics. This is getting beyond frightening!"

The younger man gave Mac a mirthless smile, "You got that right. I think it might be time to send my wife and kids to the in laws in Framingham. I'm getting some real bad vibes about this shit."

Mac looked Frank right in the eye. "You do what you gotta do. Your family has got to come first. If you gotta take a day off to get them settled you fucking do it. I'm beginning to see why my ex left me."

"Thanks Mac, I'm doing it tomorrow."

"Right! I've had a good rest last night so I'll cover for you. If the chief says anything I'll tell him where to go and how fast to get there."

The lieutenant smirked. "Thanks Mac! I owe you one."

"Okay now get that fucking report ASAP. I wanna know what we're up against this time."

⸻ • ⸻

Herbert was standing at attention. He watched the glowing image which stood mere inches in front of him. "You've done very vell major Koehler. You stopped using bullets and used zee bomb zis time. Very Good! It vill keep them guessing. Is zee coward being controlled properly?"

Herbert saluted with his right arm extended straight out and upward. "Yes mine Fuehrer! I have him completely under my control! I vill carry out more of your plans as soon as you think fit."

Herbert cringed a bit, listening to the rasping laugh from the glittering shape. "Ha, ha! We have them on zee run now! They won't know what to expect. They may even start thinking there are two killers after them. Remember major you must have zee vill of iron. You must be strong for zee fatherland. Now get some sleep and I vill issue more orders in zee few days. I must think and plan. Much is at stake."

Herbert was very proud of his recent achievements. As his leader winked out of existence, he was left in darkness, alone but full of confidence. He got back into bed and smiled. He was approved by the Fuehrer himself. How could anyone be stupid enough to doubt his courage and leadership? Well he would show these stupid Americans that Germany could still win. He would show them all. He would bring the divine Fuehrer back to power by his own accomplishments. Perhaps if he worked hard enough he could eventually become a field marshal to insure the completion of the work his God like leader had started.

⸺⸻⸻⸺

"This is CNN news with Piers Filcher. The Worcester police are truly under siege this evening as two more of their comrades have been blown up in a car bombing. They have lost five officers in just over three weeks and they are no closer to solving this crime wave than they were two weeks ago. The mayor is asking for help from the F.B.I. in this horrible case. Terrorism is suspected."

Ann shuddered as she saw the CNN report. She winced at the photos of the ruined car and the weeping friends and relatives. She went to her kitchen and poured herself a very stiff martini. She knew she was drinking too much, but what else could she do? It was the only way she could remove herself from the inner pain that pursued her like some remorseless lion. Later she fell asleep on the sofa as the news droned on.

⸺⸻⸻⸺

A few days later, Mac and Frank were in Bender's office. Mac was hiding behind the inevitable cup of coffee while Bender was speaking, "I wanted to give you the facts from Forensics. The car was blown up by amore than adequate amount of C4. It seems that a radio transmitter was used to detonate the bomb from relatively short range. The device was placed under the left rear wheel guard apparently with a magnet. It would have only taken the killer a split second to place the device and move on. For the moment I'm considering this under a different file, as we are not looking at 45 slugs this time. My gut feeling is terrorism either by organized crime or perhaps some Alkida fuck heads hitting us when we're down."

Mac looked up, "It still might be our boy."

Bender sighed, "It might and it might not. For now we'll assume the events are unrelated. Gentlemen this is getting critical. I'm supporting the mayor's decision to bring in the F.B.I."

Tanner was looking out the window as if able to search the city with x ray vision. "Makes sense to me."

Mac drank some more of his half and half. "We'll check out local construction companies for any stolen explosives but again it's such a long shot it's hardly worth the effort. All we've been able to do so far is eliminate about three hundred and fifty known criminals from the suspect lists because they are in jail or way out of state. I've been checking the map and there doesn't seem to be any pattern in terms of victim locations. The only two constants are that all the homicides took place in Worcester during the morning. I don't even know if that's significant. I'm going to interview some of the witnesses at the donut shop today but I'm not optimistic."

The chief shrugged, "Do what you can. WE really need a break in this case or cases. For now we have a pistol sniping killer and probably a terrorist bomber. Frank, I want you to start checking any files on rag heads in this city. I'd start on the local colleges and work from there. As for you Mac I want you to continue on the 45-assassin bastard. Members of the F.B.I. will be talking to you later today Frank, just to let you know. Right now I've got to lock horns with the fucking mayor again. He's really hot to trot. I guess he thinks I'm Batman or something. I'm supposed to find all the crooks by looking at my computer. I'll keep him off your backs for now. You just keep digging all right?"

Mac gave Bender the thumbs up and Frank nodded. "All right chief. I've got my family safely tucked away in Framingham."

Mac countered, "I'm having my sofa bed brought over here to my office. I'm sacking out here so I don't get picked off trying to walk in or out of my apartment. If the son of a bitch is going to get me he's going to have to get me in here. I can take showers over to the Y at random times. I can bring my laundry over to the Chenks on Pearl Street."

Bender grinned, "Isn't that being a bit paranoid Mac?"

Mac snorted, "Fuck it! I'd rather be a little paranoid and be alive than end up a dead fucking hero. If that bastard is going to get me he's going to have to work for it."

The Chief nodded, "Makes sense I guess? When are you moving in?"

Mac finished his coffee and got up to fill another cupful. "Later today, when I get a couple of guys to give me a hand. It'll be a bit cramped but what the hell! My office has more room than a fucking grave."

A little later Mac went to see Sergeant Carter, a gruff middle-aged man who was pushing fifty. His old man had been a cop to and Carter wasn't impressed by anybody or anything. He'd seen it all and done it all. Carter knew the workings of the force inside, outside and sideways.

When Mac reached his desk with the expectant look in his eyes Carter said in his caustic manner, "SO what can I do you for Mac?"

The overworked captain gave the sergeant a mirthless grin, "Joe do you think you can get me a back up of about five cars either tomorrow or on Friday?"

Carter whistled, "Five fucking cars! What are you doing? Invading the Joker's hideout or something?"

"I'm going into the lion's den and I want to make sure I can get out. How about it?"

Carter shrugged, "I'll work on it. Benoit was a good friend of mine. I hope I get a chance to help you nail the bomb freak to the cross. I'll try to get some of the off duty boys to chip in. Get back to me."

An hour later Mac was over at Clarke University talking to Luana Macrae after one of her classes. He was in his unremarkable dark brown suit and he showed her his credentials and badge number to put her at ease.

Mac was apologetic. The young chick had gone through the wringer, having helped some of the slightly injured customers recover and then being questioned for two hours at the station. "I'm sorry to bother you but I just wanted to hear your story when the cop car exploded the other day."

Luanna was thinking to herself that this tall, handsome cop would really be a nice handful if she were into cops which she definitely wasn't. Right at the moment she was balling an upper classman who was majoring in electrical engineering. She smiled sweetly, "That's all right Captain Mackelroy. I've only answered the same questions to three different officers in the last three days. What would you like to know?"

"Did anything else unusual happen that morning?"

She snickered a little. "Not really, just Business as usual until the fireworks."

Mac continued, "You didn't see anyone acting strange or maybe someone who was a new comer?"

She frowned a little, "No one acted strange until the blast. Then everyone was screaming and diving to the floor except for one guy."

Mac perked up a little, "And who was that?"

Luanna tried to concentrate, "It was a cop wearing shades. He really went wild. He made me show him where the phone was. "

"Did he try to make the call after the blast?"

Luanna looked a little confused as she tried to recall the sequence of events. "Yes of course. He was screaming into the phone to get an ambulance over quick."

He persisted, "What did he do then?"

Luanna shrugged, "I really don't know. He left the shop and I was too busy helping the customers to worry about it. The place was swarming with more cops when the cars got there anyway. Some lunk by the name of Tanner got all the names and addresses of anyone who stuck around for statements including me."

Mac laughed as he put his small note pad away. "That lunk is a close friend of mine. I'll forward the compliment. As far as you know did you recognize the cop with the shades? Had he been in the shop before?"

Luanna shook her head. "I didn't recognize his voice when he made his order but with the shades on I can't be sure. All I can tell you he was well mannered for a cop, I mean he said please and thank you when he ordered his tea."

Mac spoke dryly, "Yeah I guess that's quite unusual for a cop. Thanks Luana now you better get back to class and get good grades and maybe you'll be able to get a job as a janitor some day. The job market really sucks right now."

Luanna sighed and shrugged her shoulders. "Tell me about it. My boy friend has got resumes out and he can't even get interviews and he's almost got his engineering degree."

He shook his head. "Well good luck to both of you. It's a tougher world out there since September eleven. If you think of anything else give me a call. Here's my card."

In a moment she was left holding his card and the detective was gone. She thought it remarkable how quickly he blended in with the crowded hallway.

Chapter

8

KING PIN MEETING

Frank Lucciano had worked many years for the crime boss, Antonio Genovezzi. He prided himself in being the all-purpose butler/body guard/ hit man/ jack of all trades thug. Frank was one of the few men in or out of the organization that Don Antonio actually trusted. This trust had been developed over the years because Frank didn't have any lofty ambition. Lucciano knew he wasn't smart or knowledgeable enough to run "the business" and besides that, his kid sister was married to Antonio's son Marko.

It was a pleasantly warm, Friday afternoon and Don Antonio was enjoying a hot drink of herbal tea in his plush living room in the expansive compound. The house and grounds were located in the most exclusive neighborhood of Shrewsbury, an upscale suburb of Worcester. Understandably, there were always some men at hand complete with automatic weapons, additionally supported by several, well trained guard dogs. One couldn't be too careful these days especially with the Asians and Jamaicans horning in on the drug trade. Don Antonio looked up as Frank entered the pleasant room. The complex harmonic sounds of a Bach harpsichord concerto, emerged from a DVD unit set at a pleasantly moderate volume. After all, even a master criminal could have excellent taste in music.

The crime boss's voice was deceptively soft, hinting at urbanity but disguising an inner will of steel. . "What is it Frank?"

Lucciano stood in front of his boss and looked at his patrone with a bewildered look. "I don't know quite how to tell you this boss, but Captain John Mackelroy of homicide is here to see you. Do you wish to see him?"

Don Antonio raised his eyebrows, "This should be interesting indeed. Show him in by all means!"

Don Antonio actually stood up when Mac entered the plush office. "Good afternoon captain. This is an unexpected….. pleasure? Are you here on business or as a tourist?" The Don's eyes actually twinkled with a flicker of humor.

Mackelroy took in the man at a glance. Don Antonio had to be seventy or more. His hair was gray-white and he wore horn-rimmed spectacles. He looked like a helpless grandfather except for those sharp, cold, black eyes. Mac had the eerie feeling he was looking into the stare of a tense cobra. He replied in a matter of fact tone. "Don Antonio, you can imagine I've heard a lot about you over the years. I wouldn't presume to waste your time on trivialities."

The mafia boss laughed, "I hope some of it was good, no?"

Mac shrugged, "I guess that depends on who you talk to."

Don gave Frank a signal and the two men were alone. "Won't you sit down Captain? Can I offer you a drink? After all you might need a little fortitude visiting the lion in his lair, no?"

Mac carefully sat down across from the Don on what appeared to be an imitation Louis the fourteenth chair. The room reeked of elegance. "Actually could you do me one tiny favor Don Antonio?"

The boss raised a brow, "Certainly captain."

Mac sat back and let his gaze linger on the ornately designed bay window. "Would you be so kind as to look out your window and tell me what you see?"

Don Antonio glanced out side and saw three police cars parked in front of the entrance gate. He looked back, "I see three police cars."

Don Antonio was getting just a little uneasy as he watched the piercing gaze of the policeman. Mac continued as he glanced at his watch. "At precisely six o'clock or about two hours from now I have instructed police officers from six vehicles to enter this compound if I do not safely return to my vehicle. When it comes to men of your occupation shall we say, I wouldn't trust any of you with a half a buck much less my life."

Don Antonio visibly bristled. "Did you just come here to insult me? Certainly you must know I wouldn't be stupid enough to kill a cop under my own roof!"

Mac gave him a frosty smile, "True, true Don Antonio. But would you be stupid enough to kill cops out on the street like having them shot or blown up, hmmmmm?"

Don Antonio was debating whether to continue the discussion or have this upstart thrown out but he was curious so he continued the conversation which was rapidly becoming strained.

"Mister Mackelroy you must understand that the family runs a business. I don't like adverse publicity. It is not in my or our best interest to have bad publicity. It's not good for business. I watch the news. I think I know why you're here. You're thinking that Don Antonio has a vendetta against the police for some reason. Let me assure you neither myself nor any of my business partners had anything to do with those killings."

Mac shrugged, "To be honest with you I'm not sure what to believe anymore. I've got five dead cops on my hands and our department has made national fucking news. The mayor is bringing in the F.B.I. The last bombing looks just like a mafia hit that you see in the movies. What was I supposed to think?"

Don Antonio nodded, "I can understand. But tell me captain when was the last time you noticed a gang land slaying around here? I mean a real, provable hit?"

He gave the Don a very rye smile. "As far as we know it was back in 97 and the guy who was wasted was definitely a thug with a record as long as your arm."

Antonio laughed, "Precisely Captain! I have no quarrel with you or your department."

"What about Frank Luzzani?"

Antonio shrugged, "The man was a fool. He had no subtlety, no tact. Maybe he learns a lesson maybe he doesn't. It's water under the bridge."

Mac nodded, "Yeah well one of the guys who arrested him is dead."

Don Antonio spread his arms out, "Look captain, I swear to you I had nothing to do with killing those men. Further I don't know who did and I can assure you that if I knew I would tell you. Cop killing is bad for business. I mean if we want to ruin a cop we supply evidence that he's a bad cop and you guys throw him out of the service right? We don't have to kill you guys. We don't want the police to go after us like its hunting season. It's a bad thing, you understand?"

"All right mister Genovezzi. So I'm back to square one. For the sake of discussion what if a new group like the chenks or Jamaicans wanted to take over your territory and they decide to kill some cops to make us think it's your boys. Would you know about that if it were being tried?"

The boss put his hand on his chin and thought for a few moments. "That's an interesting idea but I think we'd know about that. At least we'd know pretty damned quick. I can only say that we have insiders in some of those groups who give us information for special consideration you might say. It would have to be a new renegade group from way out of town to pull that off. I would say the chances against that happening without me knowing about it are about ten to one. It's remotely possible but unlikely. Usually when a new group comes to town they try to take out some of my boys and I find that very upsetting. You know what I mean?"

Mac gave him a wolfish grin, "I can imagine. You know when I came over here I was thinking about Jimmy Hoffa, you remember him don't you?"

Don Antonio nodded, not sure where this was heading. "I remember the case yes."

The officer looked Genovezzi right in the eye. "I was thinking to myself that if I came to see you and you became upset with me I could disappear just like that. But of course with six police cars around the building I figured that would improve my chances of survival. But back to Jimmy, one afternoon he just disappeared. It was like the fucking Martians got him. Poof! Gone! Between you and me I figure some undertaker in a nearby county owed a favor to somebody and Jimmy's body was ashes within twelve hours of the disappearance. Of course maybe he's in a cement pylon on some highway and they'll find the body in 2035. But I like the crematoria theory better. I mean it's quite nifty when you think of it. Without a body you can't even prove a murder was committed. There's no murder weapon, no witnesses because the thug who actually picked up Jimmy was probably dead six months later also. When they brought the body it was covered and slipped into the roaster and nobody the wiser. So I'm thinking that maybe Antonio didn't have the cops wasted because he'd be more hygienic."

Don looked amused, "More hygienic?"

Mac favored him with another mirthless grin. "Yeah, I mean you'd be a lot more subtle than having some thug just walk up and blow my boys away. I mean some Thursday morning Evers or Skulley just wouldn't show up for work. They'd just disappear. I mean maybe they'd go to Switzerland or the fucking Belgium Congo you know? Maybe they'd be wearing cement shoes in the middle of the Atlantic. But I'm sure you wouldn't be so obvious as to leave bullet riddled bodies lying around or exploding headlines to bring bad publicity to your business."

Don was not looking so amused now. "You're very perceptive captain. I also think you've wasted just about as much of my time as I'm willing to spend."

Mac steepled his fingers and stared straight into Don Antonio's level gaze. "I'm leaving in a moment. I just want to make myself perfectly clear. If you don't know already I play by the book. If one of your boys fucks up I play by the book. He gets a fair trial and I have to do my homework to collect the evidence. Are you with me so far?"

Don smiled dryly, "Yes captain, I know of your reputation. I must admit you've always been an honorable opponent. I actually respect you. I happen to know you can't be bought and I respect that, I really do."

Mac paused for a moment and then went on, "All right and I must admit that my information on you is similar. Considering the ummm business career you are in, it is acknowledged by certain elements in society that you are a man of honor in your own right."

Antonio nodded his head slightly. "I thank you for that."

Mac took a long breath and spoke in a low precise voice. It was all the more threatening for its quiet, steely resolve. "Mister Genovezzi I won't sit back and let my men be killed like helpless targets. I'm sure that if someone were picking off your people you'd feel the same way."

Antonio nodded in agreement. "Yes of course."

"So this is what I have to say, mister Genovezzi. If you're telling me the truth about you're position in all this fine and good. I will continue to play by the book. If you can find out who is doing this and can furnish me with proof perhaps under the current circumstances I would find myself in a position to have to do you a favor. After all we are both men of honor."

Antonio nodded once more. "Believe me captain if any of my people find out who is doing this I will make sure you are informed."

Mac looked deep into the cobra eyes, "Excellent senor! But let me make myself perfectly clear. If I ever find out that you or any of your ilk had anything at all to do with these murders I will throw away the book. I would stop at nothing to destroy you and all who work for you. I would be as ruthless as your forefathers were in the twenties and thirties. Is that fair enough?"

Genovezzi flinched ever so slightly as he saw the cool rage in the policeman's eyes. "I think mister Mackelroy that when you find the barbaric killer of your men he will be in very big trouble. I would not want to be in his shoes. I understand how you feel. Again I swear to you on the soul of my mother that I had nothing to do with all this."

Mac stood up, "Then I think we understand each other. If you find out anything, who will you send?"

The mafia boss stood up as well. "My butler Frank, the man who brought you in here to see me. If I find out anything important I will send him to you at your office, fair enough?"

"Thank you. You know it's too bad that men like yourself couldn't have started in more legitimate lines of work. In a sense you're more honorable than some of the idiots I've seen in political office. I mean at least you don't claim to be the upholder of the public trust."

Antonio chuckled, "I know it's the old question. Who is worse the honest crook or the secretly crooked paragon? I know you are a dangerous man captain because I know you to be an honest man who can't be bought."

Mac gave him a hard, penetrating look. "That's not entirely true! I could be bought very easily right now if it led to the capture of the murdering son of a bitch who is systematically destroying my men. I'd give my soul to get the bastard. Good day to you, I can find my own way out."

Don Antonio watched as the detective left and soon the police cars left quietly. Frank came back into the room. "Will there be any thing else, sir?"

Don Looked at his old friend and employee with a searching glance. "You know Frank the man who just left is a very dangerous man. I know because I was like him at that age. I want to see my top boys tomorrow night. We've got to start looking for the guy who has been doing cops.

I don't like it when captain Mackelroy comes here with his eyes blazing looking for bodies to hang on a gallows. I don't like it at all. It's a bad thing. Besides I'd like to be able to have this virtuous man owing me a big favor. It could save our ass some day."

Frank bowed slightly, "I'll have them hear. Will eight o'clock be satisfactory?"

Don nodded, "that's excellent, my old friend. Make sure all the refreshments are available. "

When Frank had left, Antonio put on another CD. This time Aida was put on and the opera slowly soothed him into quiet contemplation. He always became apprehensive when honest men became angry because he knew they couldn't be controlled. Even though he knew that his hands were clean, at least in this affair, he decided it would be wise to go the second mile.

⸺•⸺•⸺

When Mac got back to the office he saw a note on his desk to call back Ann Tindale. He figured she'd be home being after six so he called. Ann's tremulous voice answered, "I'm glad you called John. I thought perhaps if you hadn't had supper yet you could come over and talk awhile. I can rustle something up that's bound to be better than what you'll get down town."

He hadn't spoken to Ann as much as he probably should have and he felt a bit guilty about it. Besides, her cooking had to be better than the stuff at the nearby greasy spoon. "I'd be honored Ann. I'll be there in an hour. I don't have much to update you on I'm afraid."

Ann laughed a little. "That's quite all right. The news has been a dead end anyway. I'm just going stir crazy over here. I've got to talk to someone. See you soon."

Promptly at seven, Mac knocked at the door of Ann's apartment and in moments she let him in. He noticed the care lines etched in her face and the fatigue circles around her eyes but she smiled when he greeted her.

"Come on in John and make yourself at home! We're having beef stew and a few other interesting things and it's almost ready. Have a seat."

Mac couldn't help smiling into her lovely green eyed gaze. "That's very kind of you. Thank you very much."

Soon they were eating the excellent food and talking about current events when Mac changed the subject with a little joke. "You know Ann the quickest way to a man's heart is through his stomach and I must say that if this food is any indicator you're trying to build a highway."

She giggled, "Now, now captain, flattery will get you everywhere. I just had to do something more positive than just sitting around the apartment and feeling sorry for myself. By the way I want to thank you for recommending Don Shepard to me. He's super. My investments are in safe hands. It's taken quite a load off my mind. I have a lot more to worry about than mere money."

He gave her a warm smile. "It was nothing. I'm glad I was helpful. God knows you could use a little assistance after all that's happened."

She looked into his eyes and it was like he'd been hit by a ton of bricks. Her voice got lower and softer, "I hope we can be close friends John. God knows, I've been so alone these past weeks! I just can't get things off my chest. I know your still looking for the killer and it's difficult."

Mac nodded, "Yeah Ann, for some odd reason the guy doesn't want to turn himself in and what's worse we might have two killers after us now. You must have heard about the car bombing."

Ann shuddered, "Yes! It was horrible! I'm almost afraid to put the news on anymore. I just can't talk about it right now."

He was definitely sympathetic. The toll was starting to tell in his own life. "I understand. It's been rough on all of us. I knew Emmons and Benoit quite well. They were straight shooters."

He kept staring into those lustrous deep, green eyes. This time the silence was prolonged.

Finally Ann cleared her throat and asked, "Do you like chocolate ice cream?"

"Absolutely and perhaps some coffee?"

Ann laughed. "No coffee this time! My goodness even I've heard of your incessant coffee drinking. You're going to have some vintage wine tonight."

So over glasses filled with sparkling white wine, they talked about their previous life experiences. Mac described some of his more outrageous pranks during his years at Marlboro High. Then he recounted a few interesting experiences he'd had in the police academy and of course a few highlights of his bitter sweet marriage that was now dead and buried these past three years.

Ann talked about her own college days at B.U. and how she'd met her now dead husband. The time went by pleasantly until John got up to leave. "Well Ann I think I'd better get going before I'm guilty of imposing or very bad behavior."

She smiled very tenderly at him as they went to the door. "It was so kind of you to visit. I've been so out of sorts these weeks."

He could smell her perfume and feel the closeness of her. She gazed straight into his eyes and a silent message was communicated to him in that moment. He was drawn to her open lips like a moth to a flame. Ann softly moaned as he enfolded her in her arms. The kiss grew in tenderness and duration as the loneliness and desire was communicated to each other. When they finally came up for air Mac sighed, "I'm sorry Ann. I shouldn't have done that. I don't know what got into me. I don't want to take advantage of you. I know you're going through hell."

Her arms were still around his neck and she was looking into his wondering eyes. "Don't apologize, John. It's just so good to have you here with me. At least you care."

He saw the invitation in her eyes again but he held back. "Ann lets not go to fast all right? I think we like each other but let's sleep on it. We're both going through a hell of a lot and we're not even near the end of the road yet."

She held him so close she could easily feel his hardness. His chest instinctively pushed against her soft, firm breasts. Her heart was pounding as she rested her head against his shoulder, "What a beautiful sentiment John. You're right of course. But please don't be a stranger okay?"

Mac kissed her cheek. "Don't worry Ann. I'm not trying to escape you. I just want us to be sure that's all. Let's invest a little time first."

Ann was a little surprised and delighted with the unexpected maturity and consideration of this interesting man. She hugged him even tighter and gave him another very long, appreciative kiss before they separated for that night. She whispered "Call me tomorrow." In the hall, He turned and his radiant smile matched her own. Then he was down the stairs and gone. She was alone once more, wrestling with her thoughts and turbulent emotions. What had gotten into her? How could she practically throw herself at this virtual stranger, just weeks after Teddy's sudden demise? She just shook her head with self disgust while she picked up the dirty dishes.

Chapter 9

POWER OF WILL

Mackelroy was running into more dead ends. Nothing had shown up on the gun or ammo leads. Nothing had come in on the arrest lists of the three shot policemen. At this point he didn't actually know if the same killer was behind the car bombing or not. All the force had been able to do was eliminate some suspects by determining that they had been incarcerated or in a few cases, out of state during the times of the murders. By the further use of the computer they could eliminate all persons under age 13 and all females. They also removed all persons over the age of seventy from the list. It still left tens of thousands of names any one of which could be the killer. They checked the backgrounds of anyone who legally had a forty five registered to them. Without cause however, their wasn't much they could do if the person hadn't already had a criminal record. Mac decided to have his staff start going through all the owners anyway. It was unlikely that the legal owner of a gun would do such acts but at least they could eliminate more potential suspects off the lists.

Then one morning a few days after Mac's confrontation with the mafia boss, a tall, well dressed man stopped by Mac's office to speak with him.

"Good morning captain Mackelroy. My name is William Flynn. I'm with the F.B.I. Can we talk for a bit?"

As usual, Mac was slowly drinking his third cup of morning Expresso and he nodded, "Have a seat Mister Flynn. How can I help you?"

The man had on a three piece brown suit with a conservative blue/black tie and wire rim glasses. His hair was brown and slightly graying.

As he took his seat he grinned a little, "I understand you've run against a stone wall in this case with the assassinated police officers, is that correct?"

Mac sat back and regarded the man in front of him. "Can I see your credentials please?"

Will raised his eyebrows slightly, "Certainly, but didn't they tell you I was coming?"

The captain gave him a wintry smile. "Yeah, but you never can be too careful these days. I like to go by the book."

The F.B.I. man nodded and opened up a wallet and handed it to the police officer.

"Excellent, captain! It's good to see you're on the ball. My manager is Harry Porterfield based in Hartford Connecticut."

Mac carefully looked over the badge number and identification papers that also contained the photograph matching the man in front of him. It looked very official and genuine.

Mac handed back the papers, sipping some more of the strong, hot coffee. "All right Mister Flynn I can honestly say I'm up against a blank wall. All we've been able to do is eliminate some suspects. We're basically no closer to solving this than we were weeks ago. Up to the moment there's three policemen shot to death. One was definitely set up with a preplanned ambush and possibly the other two. The car bombing could be the same guy or someone else entirely. You should know I went to see the crime boss, Genovezzi and I have the gut feeling that he didn't have anything to do with it. However I haven't totally dropped him or his ilk off the list either. It just wouldn't have made any sense for the mob to do cops. I mean they had nothing to gain. As you probably already know, the mayor is pissed totally off and the news media is getting beyond predatory in their coverage of all this. With the car bombing, you probably already know we've finally caught CNN's attention. We've got inter-fucking national publicity from Washington to fucking Siberia."

Flynn grimaced, "Lucky you."

Mac shook his head a little, "Yeah, no shit! It's been a royal pain in the ass with those over paid morons asking me when I'm going to make an arrest or do I know who did it yet? Or what's taking so long? Or when am I going to take my next piss? Like I have a fucking crystal ball or something. You know what I mean."

Flynn nodded, chuckling without humor. "Yeah I know. It's a real ball busting case. I'm going to be working on this along with some of my close friends. I've got access to info on terrorists and rag head cells and all kinds of things you don't have access to. I'm going to revue any info you have on this case so far. I know it's thin but you never know if there's a link somewhere. Do I have your permission to go through all the files on this case?"

Mac threw up his hands, "Sure! I'll even give you the results of all the dead ends. If anything new comes in I'll send that to you too. Look Bill, I'm not a glory hound. I don't have any turf to fucking protect. Any assistance you can give us is greatly appreciated in my book, all right?"

The inspector's mouth twitched at a hint of a smile. "That's good to know captain. You have no idea of how some people can be fanatical in guarding their space. You are a refreshing change, sir."

Mac finished his coffee and grimaced at the sour taste. "Look, I'll even give you the names of the judges most likely to grant a search warrant or a phone tap. But even they need something at least remotely resembling just cause. You know what I mean?"

Flynn sighed, "I know exactly what you mean. Certainly the right judge will help a little. I'll share as much as I can with you as well. I'll keep in touch."

The two men stood up and shook hands and a moment later Flynn was gone. Mac sat back down and took a long breath. At least he wasn't alone on this nightmarish journey. He started going over his notes again.

He couldn't escape the feeling that he was missing something. Somewhere in the back of his mind the answer lurked, just itching to surface and enlighten him.

Herbert kept staring at the apparition again as the control voice of Hitler grew to fever pitch. "Don't you understand? Ve must have order! A complete Vorld order! Ve must eliminate all zee social pollutants from zee planet. Ve can only do that by engendering a sense of chaos unt anarchy in zee United States. Ve must demoralize zee police and letting the lawless elements gain some control over these soft, over paid and over sexed people. Then when things get very bad, you can start zee new National Socialist party unt eventually gain control of zee government. At zee same time Ve get revenge for all the terrible things zee Americaners did to holy Germany!"

Herbert was perplexed. After all, he was only one man and the Fuehrer acted like he was in control of an army. "But how do I do all that? I know you're leading me but I'm only one man and I have to keep the vorm in line. Sometimes it's very hard."

The ghostly presence screamed, "I vill not tolerate veakness! I vill tell you what you need to do! You vill follow my orders and you vill succeed. Ve must get rid of zee Jews and zee Slavic communists along with the black sub humans in this country! Ve vill regain zee racial purity! Ve Vill purge and cleanse zee human race before ve can attain world dominance unt zee superiority."

Herbert was impressed to the point of adoration. The Fuehrer's German was flawless and inspiring. The route he must take was so obvious now and so right. "I begin to understand zee truth, mine Fuehrer. Vhat are your next orders?"

The glowing shape smiled at him in, affirming Herbert's desire to serve. "That's better, major. It is imperative to start killing zee leaders of zee police. It vill make them hesitant and veak. You vill start killing them soon. You know who zee officers are including the so called chief. Cut off zee head and the body vill die. Do you understand this major Koehler?"

Herbert saluted once again. "Yes my Fuehrer! The chief vill take some planning but I know another officer I can kill quite easily."

The image nodded in condescending affirmation. "Is goot! With zee officers you must be careful and ruthless. You must put fear into all these cretins. Ven you have killed zee chief and some of zee officers than it vill be time for zee mayor. These people vill be so desperate for order they vill receive you vith zee open arms. After all, I vas elected into office in 1932 in a democratic election, Zee dumer aissels! You can achieve greatness with my guidance and zee power of my vill!"

Herbert continued to be dazzled by the logic and inspirational impact of the Fuehrer's words. He already had some idea who would be next on the hit list. Soon the apparition faded, leaving the Major with the power of the Fuehrer's plan.

Then he got himself and the worm prepared. Major Herbert Koehler hated the gutless worm of a person he had to control. The worm was such a coward and unwilling to take risks. Herbert smiled to himself; it was all right that the worm was so fearful. It meant the proud, fearless major had to be more meticulous in his plans. That was good because it meant a higher chance of success. So he spent hours in the darkness of his room scheming of another plan for another victim. All the while he was humming German marching songs or whispering ideas to himself to sharpen his focus.

•◦•————•————•◦•

Mac and Frank were in Bender's office getting the run down on the bombing. The chief was talking, "Got all the dope from forensics. It turned out to be a lovely bit of work. Apparently some c 4 was attached under the fender of the left back tire. Right by the fucking gas tank of course. The explosive was in a small metal container and magnets were used to keep the thing in place. The detonator was triggered by a radio transmission of some kind. Obviously there wasn't much left to pick through. They only found a few bits of the detonator. Because of where the c 4 was probably placed it sure couldn't have been an impact device. Gentlemen we're dealing with someone who really knows what the fuck he's doing. He's had demolition training and he had to have access to plastic explosive. I don't know if it's the same guy who's been wasting the others. Right now we can't assume anything. It could be the same guy or someone else. Anything is possible at this point."

Mac couldn't help being a bit curious. "Chief would such a device have to be triggered from long or short range?"

Bender cleared his throat before replying. "Good question! I would say that such a device would probably have a range of less than a mile. Although a transmission was used, when you get above certain distances in such devices, interference can ruin a signal quite easily. Oh you can set one off from longer distances but it wouldn't be all that effective in our active down town area. Such a device might trigger at five miles out in the country."

Frank got his two cents in. "Did the witnesses see anyone or anything unusual?

Bender shrugged, "Not really, I've reviewed Mac's report and the others. Most of the people in the place were regulars. Apparently there was another cop there which isn't at all fucking unusual considering the incident took place at the donut shop. I mean half the force goes there. Maybe the killer was across the street. My gut feeling is that the guy must have been watching because the car exploded right in the parking lot when Al and Dave were leaving. I don't think it was a timer because the timing of the explosion was too accurate. I mean if the timer had gone off three minutes sooner, the cops would have still been in the shop and we're only out one car. If it happens an hour later the cops might be out of the car interviewing someone. The bastard must have been watching. I want you to check over the witness statements and even ask them a few more questions if you notice something that might have been overlooked. So get on it. I've got to bring Flynn up to speed in a few minutes. Bless his greedy little heart."

When Frank and Mac were heading back to mac's office Frank asked, "By the way what does FBI really stand for?"

Mac knew it was coming but he bit, "Don't know, what does it really stand for?"

Frank chuckled at the delivery of the punch line. "It means, fucking big Indian."

They both laughed over that one. Mac automatically got the coffee maker refilled and purking, just before they sat down.

Frank inquired in genuine curiosity. "By the way, do you ever stop drinking that stuff? "

Mac stared at the florescent light gleaming above him for a few moments. "It keeps me going so get stuffed." He paused for a few more moments before continuing. "I just have this feeling that there's something so obvious that we're missing it. I keep coming back to why did the guy make the phone call when Teddy bought it? Why wouldn't the thug just hit and run? Why make the fucking phone call? Why was there a cop at the donut shop wearing shades? Was he a real cop or some imposter? I'm fresh out of answers Frank. I just have questions."

"I know, I know! I can tell you this, the person or persons unknown, seems to know quite a bit about cops. I mean the donut shop is a no brainer. One day I'm walking down to the bank and I run into this blind guy. I'm helping him across the street and when I explain to him I'm a police detective he asks me why I'm not up at the Dunkin Donuts at Park and Chandler?"

The two men chuckled before Frank continued with his observation. "So the one that got Evers, I figure he didn't know it was going to be Evers he just called in to set him up. The voice matches the first call so we know the same guy did Evers and Tindale for sure now. The one that's really spooky was Skulley. I mean the poor bastard gets out of his car and five to ten seconds later bingo, tube city!"

Mac poured out more of the strong Expresso into the perpetually used mugs. "Yeah it's almost as if the killer knew skulley's schedule or something. You know I hate to say this but I'm almost starting to think it's a cop doing cops."

Frank looked into Mac's eyes for a very long moment. Finally he replied and his voice was shaking. "We can't rule it out. We'll have to add that to our vast list of suspects. I hope to God your hunch is wrong."

Mac sipped the hot, sweet liquid before replying. "I hope to God I'm wrong to, Frank. This entire case is frustrating and frightening."

The overworked lieutenant leaned back in the chair. His voice intoned somber resignation. "Maybe it's a former cop who got drummed off the force."

"All right Frank why don't you check out former cops and I'll check out current ones and we'll compare notes tomorrow."

"Right and I'll have my boys check with local construction companies to see if they have anyone on staff that could do this shit or if they're missing any c 4."

Mac suddenly had a bright idea. "You know Frank maybe we should check to see if any of our evidence from past cases is missing. Like let's say we had a case a few years ago and some plastic explosive was being held in storage for evidence? Let's make sure we leave no stone unturned."

"Good idea. I sure hope we're wrong about this but we better cover all the bases."

Mac grinned without a trace of humor. "You got that right. By the way how's little league going?"

Frank visibly relaxed. "His team is off to a two and one start. The little monster is hitting four fifty and playing a solid second base."

Mac snickered, "You should have given him Hornsby as a middle name. He's a future fucking super star. You never know Frank he might end up on the dead sox."

Tanner got out of the seat, laughing at his boss's exaggeration. "Oh fuck off Mac. The kid's only twelve for Christ's sake!"

"Have faith Frank. He might buy you a Royce some day. Can you imagine Frank Tanner being brought to work by a butler driving a fucking Roles? Of course by then you'll be at least a Captain."

Frank left the office, still laughing at the remarks.

Mac immediately got down to some serious research. He got his computer into gear and went through personnel files for hours. Many of the names he knew, others he didn't. He wasn't sure what he was looking for. He made notes on anyone who had military training or construction work in their background. To his surprise there weren't all that many. Then he started doing cross checking of these individuals and their work schedules. He checked to see who was off duty during the times of all the murders. All the murders had been committed in the morning with the time of murder ranging from about five A:M to eleven A:M. When he finally collated the men with military training or construction background and those who had been off duty during the times of the murders he was surprised to find only four names. He made copies of the files on the four men and stored it in a new created file called 'cop leads internal'. He made a note to get photos of each. Mac knew that this was most likely bull shit but…..

The process took several hours and it was well after lunch when the call came in from Ann.

Her pleasant voice seemed to bring the dreary office back to life. "Just wondered if you could come over tonight. We can have some roast beef if you'd like."

He replied with true regret, "I'm sorry Ann. I can't tonight. I've just got a ton of stuff to go through and I'll have to meet again with the chief. It's a real zoo down here. I'll try to stop over tomorrow night if that's all right."

Only a trace of disappointment showed as Ann answered, "I understand John. Is it all right if I call you later?"

Mac chuckled, "Yeah, anytime after seven. Things quiet down a little after that. You better call me. Sometimes I can get a bit absent minded when I'm doing reams of paper work."

"Okay big guy! I'll see you later, alligator."

She broke the connection and he was back to filing reports and reviewing new evidence from the lab. It didn't tell him anything all that helpful. It only verified what Bender had already told him. All Mac could do was grasp at straws and it wasn't getting him anywhere. He kept asking himself the million dollar question. Why?

Chapter

10

MORNING SHOTS

He was quite tired, having been up all night on shift. Now he was waiting in his car outside Marco's diner just down the street from the station. Many of the police staff ate here because it was very convenient to the station, even though it was barely good enough to be classified a greasy spoon. He expected Lieutenant Barnhart soon. Apparently Barnhart was having a late breakfast because it was after nine A: M. He knew that when Barnhart came out of the popular restaurant, he was to drive him to an important destination. It was strange though, because he couldn't quite place where this important destination was located. He just couldn't think of it. Well perhaps Barnhart would tell him where to go and how fast to get there.

He began to sweat and his eyes ached from lack of sleep while he continued to watch for the lieutenant. About ten minutes later, Barnhart emerged from the diner. In moments he was at Barnhart's side.

"Lieutenant, I've been instructed to bring you to a new crime scene. We need your help on this one. It's apparently a very complex, illegal drug sale situation."

Barnhart nodded. A speck of food still clung to his thin mustache and his breath testified to the recent intake of coffee. . "All right let's get to work. Do you have a car?"

He led the way. "Yes sir, right over here. I'll drive you right over."

Soon they were driving towards the Kelley square section of the city. It was strange but the previously allusive destination suddenly had become obvious to him as if by magic. Barnhart remarked, "This intersection is the most fucked up one in the entire state of Massachusetts. I swear six streets just accidentally met here back in 1750 and they never modernized it. There must be forty or more accidents here every year."

He laughed in response to Barnhart's observation, "I know. When I was in college, my room mate got a fender bender here."

Barnhart grunted in agreement." Well that's Worcester for you, but Boston's even worse. Christ sometimes you can wander for hours trying to get out of the fucking place just to get to Cambridge. They have more one-way streets than I've ever seen. Anyway, what's the dope on the dope?"

He guided the vehicle towards some old warehouses long deserted. "It appears to be a large cache of the stuff. I ran across this last night. I've been staking the place out for some time and nobody showed up. I thought we could pick up the stuff and get it finger printed and off the streets."

Barnhart got out of the car as soon as it stopped. "All right why don't you show me and we'll take it from there."

He led the way. "Certainly sir. It's right in here."

They opened a door with a broken lock and entered the unlit building. The floor was covered with dust and various kinds of debris from decades of abandonment. The place smelled of age, decay and dampness.

Barnhart commented, "I wonder who owns these places. Christ I wouldn't want to pay the back taxes on a junk heap like this."

He kicked aside some rusted cans as they approached what appeared to be an empty office at the other end. "In here Lieutenant. The stash is in the far corner, near the window."

Herbert gave his silent order, "Now worm you vill take out your weapon and aim it at Lieutenant Barnhart. Do it now!"

Barnhart walked over to a large bag lying in the corner and upon opening it was surprised to find just some empty cans and plastic bottles. When Barnhart looked around there were two reasons for the look of bewilderment on his face. First he was confused because there were no drugs in the bag. He had quickly checked the cans and perceived they were empty. The second reason for his complete shock was because he was looking into the grinning face of the police officer who was leveling the business end of a revolver directly at him.

Barnhart growled, "What's the meaning of this?"

The patrolman smirked, "Why Lieutenant, you are being sacrificed for the good of zee master race. I'm Major Herbert Koehler of zee SS and you are about to die."

Barnhart saw the glazed look in Herbert's eyes and knew his time had come. He dove for the floor and reached for his gun at the same moment. The first surprisingly quiet shot hit him in the leg. The second hit him in the stomach. The lieutenant was one tough cookie. Even after the second impact, Barnhart was still able to raise his weapon even though he was shuddering from shock. Then his head exploded into blood and gray brains as Herbert's third shot found pay dirt.

Herbert spoke quietly. His voice held a trace of reluctant admiration. "At least you showed some spirit Lieutenant. It's a shame to have to kill a fellow German but someday the new Reich will count you as a martyr for zee cause. Now worm you vill bring the car back to the station like nothing has happened. Do it now."

He calmly left the warehouse and returned to his car and drove it back to the station. He felt utterly drained as he finally got back to his apartment and collapsed into a troubled sleep.

He dreamed of his father who was drilling him with important lessons to be learned. How he feared the thick leather belt that was used on him to reinforce his learning process. Then he would dream of the Fuehrer screaming his speeches to the adoring crowds. He was watching

"The power of Will." The Nazi propaganda film perfectly blended with his father's stern injunctions. Why wouldn't they leave him alone? Why wouldn't they just leave him alone and let him do his job? The dream took twists and turns through the present and past. He was killing Skulley near an old wharf in Boston and then Tindale was shot in his old third grade school room. He couldn't figure out why he'd kill him there. It didn't make any sense to him. Then the maniac with the mustache was telling him it was all right and he'd done a good job again…again…again…

Mac's face became white as a sheet when the call came in. He heard the words and gasped, "Are you sure? Not again!"

He stared at the light in the ceiling for a few moments after he put the phone back in the holder. Apparently some kid had been playing and stumbled across the body. In moments Frank was standing at the doorway to his office.

Mac snarled, "I just got the fucking word Frank. Barnhart's dead."

The lieutenant shuddered and quickly sat down. "I know. Bender wants to see us like yesterday."

A few minutes later Frank and Mac were in front of Bender's desk again.

Bender's eyes were flashing and his face was grim, "Our boy is back in action again. Three fucking bullets shot from the good old reliable forty five. Any bets on what ballistics will match?"

His question was met with stony silence. "I didn't think so~! The murder was committed sometime early this morning or late last evening. The coroner hasn't received the body yet. The hit was done in a deserted warehouse on Lafayette Street. There are no witnesses of course. I've already had a few of our guys down there asking questions and nobody saw a fucking thing. You two might as well go down to the crime scene. There still working on things there. Barnhart is survived by a wife and three kids." Al's voice grew low and soft in tone. He was clearly affected by this most recent tragedy. "It's a God damned fucking shame. I can't believe this shit. It's like a God damned nightmare that won't go away. We've got to get this bastard, no matter what!"

When they got to the crime scene Mac recognized a couple of guys from forensics as well as inspector Flynn. Photographs were being taken. Flynn gave them the high sign as they approached. "Hey Mac, over here! It's a fucking mess this time!"

Mac saw the sprawled body of Barnhart laying in a pool of now dried blood his hand still clutching his weapon. Mac could clearly see that Barnhart had tried to fight back but he'd been a second too late. Flynn remarked, "Your man never got a shot away. The shell casings from the murder weapon are over there by the doorway. Apparently Barnhart was checking this bag of empty cans. They look freshly disturbed."

Mac said tonelessly, "Yeah, I notice that. Frank, have the bag and all its contents fingerprinted along with the casings and front door. We might get lucky with a print."

Mac walked around the place getting a feel for the scene. He went to the front door and walked toward the room. Then he made a call to the station. When he came back he spoke with Flynn. "I just called the station and Bender tells me there was no call instructing Barnhart to come here or investigate anything like this. I take it there's nothing of value in those cans he was looking at?"

Flynn shook his head. Mac continued, "Whoever did this either ambushed him or came in with him. I think someone led him here and blew him away when he looked at the empty cans. So it either means that some informer convinced him that something significant was found or he was with another cop."

Flynn raised his eyebrows, "That's quite a long leap of deductive reasoning. I'd like to here a little more."

"Police officers rarely go to a possible crime scene alone, especially after what has happened around here in the last few weeks. I know if some thug came to me with a big find, I'd bring at least one other guy with me. If I was suspicious I'd bring Frank here so he'd get his ass shot off instead of me."

The three men laughed without much humor. Mac continued, "I'm not sure why Barnhart got into a drawing showdown. Maybe the killer made a strange noise. Maybe Barnhart got suspicious with the empty cans. Whoever this guy is, he's a damned good shot. It looks like Barnhart was on the move. It looks like he was diving for cover except there isn't any cover. The poor fucking bastard." These last words were spoken in a choked voice. Tears came unbidden to Mac's blood shot eyes.

Flynn stared down at the body and back to Frank and Mac. "I think he was definitely set up. I have to agree with you that there is a chance it was done by a cop. I'm sorry Mac. I'll give you all the help I can. I'll do anything! We've got to stop this mother!" Anger flowed from his voice like lava from Mount Helens.

Mac looked at the inspector in his gray suit and smart looking glasses. "Do you have access to more detailed military background records?"

Flynn tilted his head slightly to one side to emphasize his curiosity, "Possibly, why do you ask?"

Mac shrugged, "Just a hunch. This guy is a damned good marksman. As far as we can tell he hasn't missed a shot yet. There's also a possibility that the same guy was behind the car bombing. It's starting to look like we're dealing with a cop or someone impersonating a cop with possibly a strong military background to boot. How long will it take you to get full military records if I give you the general info you need?"

"About a week, maybe less. I think you should give me all the names of current officers and men who have left your force in the last ten years. If we're going to cover this we might as well do it right."

Frank interjected with only a hint of sarcasm. "Yeah by the book right Mac?"

The captain's face was flint as his voice rasped his response. "You bet your ass. I'll also give you our current roster. I want every option covered and chiseled in granite."

⋆ ——— • ——— ⋆

The coffee Maker was going strong as usual, while the three men went through personnel records ad-nauseum. Flynn insisted on getting all names and identification numbers of policemen current and up to ten years gone. At the top of the list were the four men that Mac had centered on recently.

"Bill I want you to get me the info on these four guys as quick as you can. These four were off duty during all the murders. Also get me the info on the guys who retired or left the force because they obviously might have been around for the murders. They'll have to establish there whereabouts for at least one of those murders."

When Flynn was gone Frank casually asked, "Do you really think one of our boys is doing this?"

Mac gave Frank a bleak look. "I certainly hope not. But this guy has the knack of being at the right place at the right time too many fucking times. A lot can happen in a week."

Frank sipped some more coffee, "If I'm not careful I'll get as addicted to this stuff as you. Actually I'm getting a bit nervous. This bastard is picking on Lieutenants now. You or I might be next on this creep's hit list."

"That's not funny Frank."

Frank growled, "It wasn't meant to be. For the last three days I Make absolutely sure nobody follows me when I'm heading home. I watch out for persons in cars who might be parked on my street. I'm getting fucking paranoid Mac! This guy seems to be working up the ladder."

Mac sighed, "All the cops killed so far have been in uniform, even Barnhart. At least we are plains clothes men most of the time. I'm hoping that gives us the edge. I don't have a clue but I'm just as scared as you, Frank. Nobody likes to get snuffed out. Christ, it's like this son of a bitch keeps getting closer and closer and we can't stop him. That's why I moved a bed in here. He's going to have to really work hard to get me. "

Tanner finally finished his cup of liquid caffeine. "Amen to that. I might do the same thing. If I were a Catholic, I'd be seeing a priest. No shit, Mac. I'm starting to get the shakes. I'll be checking on some of my boy's reports. See you in the morning if I don't go blind first."

Mac gave his friend the thumb's up and got back to work looking for that haystack needle. He frowned in concentration as he flicked through the info. Could it be a cop? How the hell could it be? Yet, the timing of these attacks was too precise, too perfect. The pattern had changed a little. This last ambush had been committed in late morning according to the coroner's report. Why was it that with the exception of the bombing, all these cops had been alone at the time of the attack? Two of the guys had been killed as they had been going off duty. It was like the bastard was a fucking mind reader. But of course, that was impossible. What was it that Sherlock had once said? Something about the improbable must be the truth when all other possibilities have been ruled out. It must be a cop. After all, if it was then at least in two of the incidents, the victim wouldn't have been alone. But why? It always came back to that troubling question.

Chapter

11

LOVE FEST

Mac was a total wreck by the time he got to Ann's apartment the next evening. He'd been at a distressing funeral service for Barnhart. Meeting the surviving family was difficult to say the least, especially when he had no answers. It hadn't been pretty. For over an hour he watched as friends and relatives bowed and wept beside the closed casket. Mac knew the morbid reason for why the coffin was closed. Arthur Barnhart's face had been half blown off. He felt hollow and sick as his stomach wrestled with anger that could not be satisfied. It felt like a serpent was wriggling around inside of him and he couldn't put a stop to it.

Ann saw the hopelessness in his face as he staggered into her living room. He just shook his head. She was almost afraid to ask. "What happened?"

He slumped onto the sofa." Just watch the news."

She sat beside him and using the remote, WBZ news soon appeared on the flat 32 inch screen. It didn't take very long for the grim story to be presented. She whispered, "Oh my God!" When she saw the story about Barnhart on world wide news.

"Tonight, the Worcester police department is under siege as the sixth patrolman has been killed in only a month. The Federal Bureau of Investigation has been brought in as terrorism is being considered as a possibility. Like the Maryland snipers, there seems to be no suspect or major leads at this point in the case. In other words, the authorities are stumped."

Mac finally croaked, "Please Ann shut it off."

She flicked off the picture with the remote and looked into his haggard face. Her hand rubbed his cheek as she shook her head slightly. "I think it's time for supper. I've made you some lovely pot roast. I think we both need a break from all this."

He smiled, pressing his hand against hers. "Is it ready for us to devour?"

She laughed. "I think so. I just have to put it on the table."

Mac got up as if he were sixty. "Well let me help you."

They went out to the kitchen and he pitched in by placing the dishes and glasses on the table. Soon they were eating the delicious meal in relative silence. The tasty supper was mildly therapeutic as they tried to forget the frightening events with little success.

He finally asked, "So how are things going at your work?"

Ann's rye smile pursed her lips for a brief moment. "A little better. The boss has been quite understanding about everything. I'm starting to get back to normal though it's lonely as hell. I keep expecting Ted to walk through that door and I haven't been able to give away any of his things yet. Sometimes I want to call the Salvation Army and then I just fall apart when I see those empty shirts and pants."

Mac finished his potato and looked at Ann with a concerned expression.

His voice was calm and reassuring when he spoke. "I hope I've been helpful for you Ann. I grieve to but losing friends and co-workers isn't the same as losing a loved one. I know it's hard, so very, very difficult. It's a bloody, God damned shame."

Ann's eyes became misty, "I know you understand. You've helped a great deal and I'm not talking about Shepard or any of the other things. I feel safe with you around somehow."

He looked into her deep green eyes for a long moment and replied, "I'm sorry I haven't been able to spend more time with you Ann but I've been up to my ass in alligators. Between the media and reports and the F.B.I. it's been a zoo. I think you know I want to know you better and well I hope you feel the same way."

Her smile was sheer radiance. "Do you think I'd be cooking you these mammoth feasts just for some small talk? HMMMMM?"

John smirked. "You're a temptress. Here, let me help you clean up."

They continued the small talk as the dishes got washed and dried and then they retired to the living room to sip some wine. Ann noticed that he didn't look so fatigued now. He was more relaxed and his tension seemed to have left him.

"So Ann, is there anything we the people of Worcester County can do for you?"

She leaned against him, "I'm not sure but I'll think of something."

Her voice became husky as she moved her face closer to his. He smelled of Old Spice and she saw his desire in his eyes. Their lips met in a long torrid kiss. In moments, his hands were massaging her back and flanks as she stroked his hair with her gentle hands. Their drinks were left only half consumed on the coffee table as they continued to discover each other. Her leg crept over his, while Mac's eager hands finally found enough courage to caress her breasts. He felt her breathing, along with the bra snugly arranged under the turquoise dress. There was something about Ann that was always green and gold.

When they finally came up for oxygen she quipped, "Are you trying to give me your best shot Captain?" Her radiant smile was shamelessly seductive.

He was holding her so close. She was so soft, so warm, so inviting.

He whispered in her ear, "The thought had flitted across my mind. Shall I continue with sweet nothings or soft everything's?"

She giggled. "That's quite a nifty line. Please John, make love to me. Make me feel alive again. Make me believe there's hope. I'm so tired of despair."

He looked into her glowing eyes again, "Are you sure Ann?"

She whispered, "I'm sure John. I want you."

His kiss sent her mind reeling and she guided his fingers under her skirt right to her damp panties. Her moans of desire and pleasure urged him to more and more exploration as he began to slowly undress her with trembling, expectant hands.

Somehow they REACHED her bed. A trail of clothes testified to the progress towards nakedness that both so eagerly sought. His pants were crumpled beside her bra. Her dress lay near his shirt. She didn't bother to remove her nylons. Ted had always told her that they made a chick look sexier. With surprising strength, Ann pulled him onto the bed atop her. She'd only had time to say two words before their mouths locked together. "Fuck me!"

They clung together in a fierce embrace at the instant they coupled. At first they were frantic with their extreme need for each other. Her kiss sent fiery signals to him and he responded by entering her lush wetness with deep, urgent thrusts. She felt so wonderful, so right to him. In moments he was driving himself deep and fast inside her willing, responding sheath.

Ann responded by squeezing tightly on him with obvious hunger. She was eager, even desperate for him. She met his penetrations with jerking clutches that left no doubt that she needed what her brand new lover was giving her. Their mutual cravings drove both of them until their love making became a totally animalistic merge.

Ann soon felt waves of passion build inside her as she locked him against her with her legs wrapped about his back. The attractive blonde widow desperately held him with greedy arms, legs and pussy as if she were clinging to a solitary life raft in the midst of a hostile sea. . There was no need for talking. Their bodies communicated everything they needed to know about each other. Each invasive penetration was met with an urgent clutch. Each lunge was met with an equally vigorous response. They were completely one.

He was fully alive at last after three long years of work and tedium. He wanted Ann more than anything right now. He had to have her! HE had to enjoy every sultry inch of her. He rammed her even harder and her moans told him she loved it. She cried out, "Yes John! Yes! Oh my God! Deeper! Faster! Faster! Yes! Yes! Just fuck!"

She felt her body tingle and then she burst and convulsed with the fiery mystical pleasure of orgasm. Her screams of joy spurred him on to a frenzy. His vicious thrusts kept Ann on cloud 29 for several glorious minutes, until he also erupted in the joy of his own answering release.

He groaned loud at the moment of ecstasy, before slumping down beside her. They both breathed fast, unaware of the perspiration that coated their skin with a thin sheen. John held her to him as if he was afraid she might evaporate. He thrilled to the heaving of her chest, the beating of her heart, the soft, sensual sounds of her tempting voice. Ann was his, all his and he was hers even while he felt himself drain inside her for those precious, glorious seconds.

She asked, "Do you think I'm terrible John having been widowed for such a short time? Please be honest with me."

John looked into those lustrous, sad eyes, "Anne, we're two very lonely people and I think we love each other. I know I do. I don't know how it happened so quickly. I'm willing to accept this miracle if you are."

She fell against him and started crying, "What a beautiful thing to say. I can't help it John. I love you. Just hold me darling. Forgive me for being weak."

They held each other, feeling the warmth of naked skin and the closeness that each yearned for. It wasn't long before their natural urges took over again and this time she climbed on him and rode his rejuvenated manhood. His mouth searched her lush mounds. Between his licking tongue and tickling mustaches, he had no difficulty keeping her nipples rigid. She laughed with joy as her body was penetrated again and again with his hardness. They resumed kissing with tongue twisting open mouthed joy. Minute after thrilling minute went by and then Ann climaxed once more. Her scream was pitched with something beyond mere ecstasy as her body shuddered from the mind numbing consummation. Although she was close to spent she kept squeezing him and moving up and down tantalizing and teasing his erect and itching member to eventually cause him to erupt inside of her lush softness for a second time.

Ann had been hungering for carnal union since Ted had been killed. It was if her body had betrayed her grief. It was as if her lust for life had become her new religion. Well, she'd think about it in the morning. It just felt too wonderful to have this handsome man thrusting inside her, driving her from one ecstasy to another. Right now, she was greedy for passion, ravenous for the excitement of carnal union.

She looked into his moist eyes unable to stop grinning. "Oh baby, you've got it bad. Would you like another rematch? Hmmmm?"

He was still trying to catch his breath from the amorous ordeal. He gasped, "You wore me out you naughty vixen. My God love! Let me rest a bit. You are so amazing! You are incredible."

Ann was still hungry but she let him relax for a few minutes before she mischievously tickled him in the most vulnerable places. They were soon laughing and wriggling over the bed. They were hitting each other with pillows and playing like lovers and children at the same time.

When they finally stopped to catch their breath he said, "I don't deserve such happiness Ann. You are like a Goddess to me."

She snuggled against him, "I bet you're trying to seduce me again, aren't you my naughty Apollo?""

He looked into her laughing eyes, "You're not just beautiful my love but you're a mind reader to. Maybe you should go into the fortune telling business."

She traced some circles on his chest with her index finger, "Well I suppose, especially seeing how I'm a goddess and a sex glutton to boot."

John chuckled even as his own fingers continued to explore in some very sensitive areas. "All right you bewitching siren, what will next Saturday's winning lottery numbers be?"

She gave him a wicked grin. "6, 9, 17, 29, 37 and 44! "

They both laughed and he started exploring her smooth, alluring skin yet again. She was a new wonder to him. He loved how she responded when he moved his fingers on her dripping, sensitive groin. Her hot kisses inspired and encouraged him again. To his amazement he was stiff and eager to resume love's pleasant labors. He couldn't recall his first wife being this horny, at least not since their honeymoon had ended, two weeks after the wedding. He wondered if Ann's desire might also fade. Was that the price humans paid for constant familiarity? Now was not the time for questions. John wanted answers which could only be found inside his new bedmate.

He moved on top of her this time. Her hands pulled him inside of her. She was frantic for him and she gasped and cried out in joy as he slammed himself inside her velvety, squeezing softness. She gasped, "Oh do me, darling! Give me that big, cop rod right there! Oh yeah, just like that! Put it to me! Oh Jesus fucking Christ! Yes! Oh yes! Johnny yyyeeeessssss!"

He answered her plea with a husky whisper. "I can't seem to get enough of you. You feel so damned good. Just hold me tight!"

In moments her legs and arms were around him holding him and drawing him deeper into her as she squeezed him even tighter and tighter with each penetration. She moaned, "Oh John just love me! Oooooo! John! John! Fucking fill me! You naughty stud! Ooooo! You're so deep in my pussy! Don't leave me Johnny! Stay with me! Yes! Like that! Just like ttthhhaaattt!"

He kissed her again and again. Soon he saw tears of joy in her deep green eyes. They blended together in love's overwhelming glory. They wanted the moments to last forever as they met each other's motions. His hands were cupped on her breasts while he moved inside her faster and deeper. He ached for her. He tingled and itched and longed to fill her with his love yet again.

This time they came together in a shuddering, violent climax that left them both totally spent and completely satisfied. He whispered, "You are marvelous, sweet Ann. I didn't know how lonely I really was until now."

She gently gripped his flagging member with two fingers. "I love you, John. I can't believe this is happening. I feel so happy and ashamed. Poor Ted must be rolling in his grave. Forgive me, baby. I just can't help it. I need you like food and drink."

John snuggled against her, enfolding her with his left arm. "You are my treasure, precious. I'll respect you in the morning, I promise."

She snickered at the remark. "You are such a bad boy. It'll take me a lifetime to straighten you out." She yawned and there was silence.

In moments they fell asleep from sheer exhaustion.

<hr>

Mac awoke to smell coffee and bacon. He didn't want to move as he lay naked beneath alien sheets. He shut his eyes, remembering a random morning when his first wife had done the same things. It had been during their honeymoon. How could he have predicted that their marriage would have lasted only a few years? She'd been so wild in bed those first months. Then there'd been the inevitable decline in the relationship. She'd complained about his long hours and there was that unspoken fear. At last she just could not take the tension anymore. All she could think of was Mac getting blown away by some drug running thug.

Ann had gone through what John's first wife had not had the courage to face, Ted's sudden death at the hands of some mug. Not only that, but the marvelous blonde was now serious about another cop. It was the last thing he'd expected or could have predicted. Yet, the past few hours had been a revelation for both of them.

He could still smell Ann. The scent of perfume and sweat and pure female was all around him. He felt relaxed as if he were floating above all the troubles of the world. For these precious moments, he'd forgotten the six dead policemen and the mysterious butcher and the fucking moron of a mayor. He sighed with contentment, recalling the startling festival which had consumed them both the night before.

With some effort he struggled out of bed and got his underwear and trousers on. Mac awkwardly stumbled out to the kitchen and she was there with just a revealing negligee on her hour glass figure. He stared at her as if at a supernatural vision.

Her smile was radiance as she asked, "Cat got your tongue?"

John replied with tenderness he didn't know he possessed. "Did I dream last night? Was it real?"

She moved into his arms, "Yes and so did I. It was a beautiful dream that's come true."

Her kiss awakened him with an electric shock that made mere coffee seem tame. He reluctantly let her go. "I know this sounds unfeeling but after breakfast I've got to get back down town after a quick change. We're still looking for Mister X. "

She pouted ever so little, "I know John. You've got a job to do. I didn't think you'd love me and leave me so quick though. I thought we could have a little rematch this morning."

He held her fast again, "Don't you believe that. I never want to leave you but I'm already late, sweetie. I'm sorry, sugar. I didn't know how lonely I was until last night. You see, I told you I would respect you in the morning." She laughed in response.

She felt better and she kissed him with more passion as his hands crept up her willing body. Ann chuckled, "You better behave, Sir John or you won't even get to work this morning. I feel like a new woman, so don't you dare be a stranger. You better be here tonight and on time."

They laughed and got down to breakfast. As he was wolfing down bacon and coffee he remarked, "Believe me Ann I want to avenge Ted as much as you do. I know you still are angry about what happened and so am I. You're a woman of strong feelings. I care about you a great deal."

She looked at him with a searching glance and saw gratitude in his handsome face. "I know John, but take care of yourself please. I don't think I could stand losing you after last night."

John finished his coffee and got up to leave, "Anne, I'm a careful man and you're my new treasure but I'm also a man of honor. I won't let my men be killed like rats in a cage. I think we're meant for each other but we have a lot more talking to do. Don't worry Anne, we'll work everything out. I've never known love like you gave me last night. It was beyond words. All I can say right now is I love you Ann and please trust me."

She embraced him at the door, "I love and trust you John. We'll see this through, somehow."

His kiss was quick and powerful and then he was gone. Ann returned to the kitchen to clean up. They wouldn't mind if she were an hour late. After all, she was the grieving widow. If they only knew what kind of a shameless hussie she actually was. Ann thought about it for a moment between washing a cup and saucer. On the other hand, perhaps it was best they didn't know. She was sure they would all think her a lecherous she cat and perhaps they would be right. Needless to say, she required a lengthy shower before embarking on her daily tasks at the office.

Chapter 12

UGLY POLITICS

Bender, Mackelroy and Tanner were sitting in the mayor's plush office inside that Victorian, granite monstrosity known as city hall. Mac was staring out the window looking at the Worcester Galleria towers, the now pathetic tribute to the great mercantile experiment of the early seventies. At that moment he remembered what one old timer had once caustically said, "They just took Front Street and put a roof over it."

The mayor snapped, "Hey Mackelroy! What the hell are you looking at? Can we have your undivided attention for a few fucking seconds? If you please?"

Captain Jack gave the gray suited politician a contemptuous smile as his gaze locked with the flashing eyes that glinted through those wire rimmed spectacles.

His retort was borderline sneer. "You were saying?"

The mayor's face visibly reddened, "I was saying that if things don't get solved in a fucking hurry we'll have to bring in the National Guard one of these days just to protect the cops for Christ's sake. So bright boy what are you doing about the situation?"

The captain of homicide was already fed up with mister mayor even before he'd entered the plush office. He decided to act like a wise ass. He just couldn't help himself. He knew it wasn't cool, but there it was. The mayor's tirades were becoming very tiresome. "Look boss, the police department is doing all it can. I've even seen Genovezzi to make sure he understands that his best interests lie in keeping us informed if any new disturbing elements show up in town. I've order that all patrolmen go in pairs now and check their cars for booby traps. I've got several officers assisting me going through scads of research into every possible lead, no matter how fucking remote it is. I have to drink more coffee in one day then you do in a fucking month. I'm getting tired of you lambasting the chief and the rest of us. It's our lives on the firing line and everybody thinks it should be easy to pick up mister nasty in like, ten minutes. You know I'm even getting fed up with the media to. I'm actually beginning to hate Piers and the rest of his turkeys. I'm even beginning to hate you, your royal amplitude."

The mayor exploded, "How dare you speak to me like that! Who the fuck do you think you are? I otta have you fired right now on the spot!"

Mac's wolfish grin spoke volumes. "Why don't you do that ass hole? I'm tired of your bull shit anyway. Just remember one thing though, I have a better handle on this case than anyone else and you never know when the sniper or the assassin or whatever you want to call the thug decides to go mayor hunting. Just keep in mind out of twelve shots fired, we found twelve casings and twelve bullets in four bodies. He's a damned good shot. He's twelve for fucking twelve so if he decided to pick you off you wouldn't have a snowball's chance in hell."

To Mac's great satisfaction he saw the mayor's face turn white with rage and fear. The mayor stammered, "Do you think he'll come after me?"

Mac actually laughed, "That's what I despise about you overpaid crooks. You talk big but when your balls are on the table you take them off real quick. How the hell should I know what the murdering prick is going to do? He's either a terrorist or an insane son of a bitch. He could be anything from a mystic rag head to a white, right wing radical with delusions of Timothy fucking Mcvay. How the hell should I know? If you fire me I'll get an easy job in Detroit or fucking Manhattan. Hell, maybe I'll relocate in Hawaii and chill out on the beach between assigning traffic tickets. I can watch those fancy broads wiggle around doing the hoola dance while I sip some brandy laced pineapple juice. It'll even be better if I can take a photo of your fucking gravestone before I relocate."

The mayor was now totally livid. "Mackelroy get the flying fuck otta here now! You're fucking history!"

Mackelroy got up and his voice hissed like a suddenly disturbed serpent. "I'm not fired until the union says so. So go fuck yourself!" The slight inclination of his head was mere mockery.

When the irate captain had gone, Bender spoke quietly, attempting to cool things down. "Please sir, try to understand. He's been under an awful lot of pressure lately. Trust me on this one. He wants this thug even more than we do. He's putting in sixteen hour days most of the time. He practically lives in his office. He's even slept there a few nights."

The mayor gave Bender a wintry smile, "He doesn't seem to like politicians does he?"

Tanner had been as quiet as a mouse up to this point. He finally interjected, "I heard him say once that he could count the number of honest politicians on the fingers of his hands. I think the most recent one was Harry S. Truman according to Mac I mean."

The mayor sat down again and sighed, "Yeah well he's got the loudest mouth in the force bar none. Bender you better keep the media away from him. I swear if he doesn't solve this crime spree real soon I will fire his ass even if I have to twist arms in the union to do it."

There was a long period of awkward silence then the mayor continued, "So Bender what are you going to do from here? Please enlighten me."

Bender shook his head slightly, "I don't know sir. We're stumped. All we have is some theories. Quite frankly we need a break. This thug has got to fuck up or we're all in big trouble I'm afraid."

The mayor gave him a sharp look, "What do you mean?"

The chief stared at the mayor as if his face was made of stone. "I mean that this guy has a thing for cops. He's definitely killed four and probably all six. He's a crack shot and might have had military training. We've got Flynn checking into military records. I mean we give the F.B.I. perhaps a thousand names and try to eliminate most of them through research. We figure it's got to be somebody living in Worcester County. Every time we can eliminate a few names it sharpens the focus a little. But there are still so many names we have to sift through."

The mayor looked surprised, "You mean you're actually looking at everybody in the county?"

Bender shrugged his shoulders in a deprecating manner. "Well not everybody. We threw out women, persons under the age of 13, persons over the age of seventy and persons with serious disabilities. Since we started we've eliminated several hundred persons with criminal records because they were in jail during the murders. We've been able to eliminate a few hundred gun owners because they were at places of employment during at least one of the murders. We've already spent thousands of man hours on this but we still have thousands of potential names to go through. We've been promised a reward fund by big corporations in Massachusetts for information leading to the arrests of person or persons behind these killings. The ante is going up to $500,000 and we've only gotten a handful of calls that have led to nothing."

The mayor looked grim as he instinctively slid his fingers through his well groomed hair. . "Gentlemen, Mackelroy's comments to the contrary, we've got to find this monster soon. The governor gave me a call last night. He's not amused. Even one of the fucking Kennedys gave me a call. He's claiming that some members of congress are implying that we don't know how to run our own state. I've got media up my ass. I can't even walk out of my office without some of those bastards asking me what the latest is, or what am I going to do about it? I have to smile at these vultures and show them confidence and excellent manners. It's a royal pain in the ass!

Look chief, if you need even more access to public records I'll have a few secretaries help. We've got complete street directories and tax records. Any information you want I'll make sure you have access to. Even if it can cut down the number of suspects to a few thousand, it might be worth it. I've already talked with some of the judges and they've assured me that you guys can have all the wire taps you want as long as you give them some faint ray of cause. Just give them something, anything at all and they'll play ball."

Bender looked at his fingers as they gently drummed on the arm rest of his chair. "I hear you. When do you want us to show up next?"

The mayor's response was an ill concealed sneer. "I want a fucking update in two days at four in the afternoon. I don't want Mackelroy here either. Let the bastard do some pavement pounding instead. I don't need his attitude in this office. He might be a good detective but he's got no tact and he certainly lacks any shred of decorum."

Bender chuckled, trying to ease the tension a little. "Well he never had that. He even told me to fuck off a few times. With Mac what you see is what you get."

Tanner and Bender got up to leave. The mayor as usual opened the door for them. "Well boys keep your shoulders to the wheel and keep me informed. I'll let my staff know they're to be at your disposal. And gentlemen, putting my own comments aside, I really do appreciate your efforts. I know it's a tough job."

Bender murmured as he walked through the doorway. "Thanks, I'll take you up on that."

• • •

Tanner and Bender soon returned to the station and found Mac drinking the usual. The chief exploded. "Mac! What the fuck is the matter with you? You don't talk to the mayor like that! I otta suspend you for a month!"

Mac had known he was in the wrong at least with regards to Bender's position. "I'm sorry chief but I just can't stomach the prick. He's an overpaid crook with hands in every kind of graft you can imagine. Just let me do my job."

Bender snarled opening and closing his fists in the process. "Well you won't be going back to the mayor's office any more and he wants results or he'll probably have you sent to fucking Siberia."

Mac gave his boss the saddest look Bender had ever seen. "I'm sorry chief. I really am. I don't mean to make things hard for you I just can't stand the bastard that's all. Actually Siberia doesn't look all that bad right now to be honest with you. At least the Ruskies give you fair warning before they shoot you. I got a real bad thought about this case. You won't like it, boss."

The chief reached the doorway about to leave. He turned and asked, "What do you mean?"

The captain looked forlorn as he met the chief's stare. "I mean I've got a theory and I don't like where it might lead. What little faith I had in human nature is likely to be totally shattered if my hunch is correct."

Bender gave Mac a piercing glance. "What the hell are you trying to tell me?"

"I mean I hope that the thug turns out to be impersonating a policeman. I hope to hell the killer isn't a current or past cop."

The chief was astonished, "You actually think it might be one of us? You gotta be fucking kidding me!"

Mac shook his head and the weariness in his voice spoke louder than his actual words. "I wish I were chief. This guy is far too knowledgeable too be so damned lucky. He seems to know the police schedules. He seems to know when or how to hit these people when they're the most vulnerable. He knows where we live. He knows how to get our attention with a phone call. He's a crack shot probably with military training. Our men are well trained at police academy and yet, they're getting picked off left and right."

Bender was clearly horrified. "But Mac it could be a terrorist to, couldn't it?"

Mac's reply lacked conviction. "It could chief. I'm certainly not ruling anything out. I just want you to know I'm getting very nervous about where the clues seem to be heading. Me and Frank are doing a lot of home work on this and we'll let you know if we find anything concrete at all. Chief you just have to trust me on this."

Bender nodded slowly. "I do, Mac. I do. I've got to get back to spinning the media now. Good luck to both of you. We're going to need it."

Mac held up his hand. "Watch your back, chief. You're a cop to."

Bender gave him a long stare, nodding slightly. "I will, you can count on it."

Once the chief was gone, Mac poured Frank and himself another cup and the two detectives got down to business. Frank decided to lighten things up a bit. "Well Mac I hear you've been spending quite a bit of time with Ann Tindale you sly devil."

The captain's retort was sharp and brusque. "Fuck off Frank! It's my ball game and I'm playing it. How the hell did you hear about it anyway?"

Tanner drank a little more before replying. "Everywhere you go Mac, I've got two guys in an unmarked car following you. If anybody makes a foul play for you, they won't get far."

Mac was genuinely surprised. "You don't say? You're boys are good. I didn't even notice. Thanks a ton, Frank. You're solid gold."

The lieutenant nodded and took another sip. "Forget it Mac. You've obviously got a lot on your mind. By the way I hope that things work out for you and Ann. I wish you the best if that's what both of you want."

Mac grinned at last. "It's a little early to be sure but things seem to be perking up if you know what I mean. But let it go for now Frank. If it happens, it happens."

Tanner raised his cup in mock salute. "Absolutely Mac. If you hit the grand slam do I get to be best man?"

"Yeah! Lieutenant Tanner will be best fucking man, all right?"

They laughed and soon both men were in their respective offices working on the tedium of lengthy lists and scanty evidence.

Herbert was entranced by the vision of the Fuehrer once again. It was clear to him that this great leader was the only true reality in an otherwise sordid and corrupt planet. The Fuehrer spoke with his loud, insistent shout. It was if he were speaking to thousands rather than to a solitary S S officer. "You did very vell disposing of Barnhart. It's good that you purchased the ammunition for your gun years ago in Philadelphia. I think it was brilliant of me to have you steal zee plastic explosive from zee armory while you were in their excuse for a military service. Now we have them on zee run. They vill crumple soon when you eliminate their top leaders. I vant you to do some research on their police chief Al Bender. Ve must eliminate him and real panic will occur."

Herbert spoke out at last, "That vill be difficult mine fuehrer. He vill be careful and Vell guarded."

The fuehrer laughed in derision. "Kill him at home you fool! All these creeps think zey are safe ven zey are at home. Just make sure he doesn't have guards there. Be careful and meticulous. If you do this, those fools vill be confused. Then you vill plant zee bombs in zee station and kill many of them. You can even send zee nasty little letter bombs to throw them off the path. Herbert, have some fun at this! It's quite amusing to kill zee enemies of zee fatherland. Maybe you get to kill some Jews in zee synagogue as reward. Americanners vill pay for ruining my plans. Their streets vill run with blood. I vill have revenge! "

The voice was screaming like it had during the Nierenberg meetings. The shadowy fist was upraised in defiance and triumph. It seemed to Herbert that the misty eyes flashed with an erie, inner flame. Herbert thought to himself that he could do all this if he could control that ever present, spineless worm. Sometimes it was so difficult to keep him under his command. It was a constant struggle to keep the slithering coward from committing such disgusting acts as being friendly with the enemy or trying to prevent him from killing more of the American swine. It would be so nice to be able to sleep for a long time and forget all this. But duty was duty and the salvation of the Fuehrer's honor was in his capable hands.

He saluted the lofty apparition as it faded into that other world that Herbert could never reach. Where did the fuehrer go anyway? Was this all for real or was it just a dream? Was Herbert Koehler just a dream? Was the world just one big fantasy after all? Herbert finally shrugged such profound questions aside and began to plan. Bender must perish. The Fuehrer had spoken.

Chapter 13

GUN GONE

Tony Visconti had been born and raised in Worcester. He was a fast rising soldier in the ranks of the local La Cosa Nostra and he certainly was ambitious. When the boss's right hand man had given him the new assignment, even if it was guarding some important cop's backside, he decided to go the second mile. Most Days he watched the home of police chief Bender. To be sure he would go there in different cars and use different disguises; however he kept a very bored eye open for hour after fruitless hour, continuously observing the residence from a safe distance. The home was located in an elegant neighborhood off Lincoln Street. It was an older home although it was spacious and well kept. A tree lined driveway led to a more modern garage. The well kept, front yard had a statue of Mother Mary circled by a variety of flowers. Tony approved of that being a staunch Catholic himself. At least the cop was a true believer.

Tony performed his confessing anonymously at a cathedral down in Providence. After all if you had to hit somebody that was part of the business. There's absolutely no reason to lose one's soul over some piece of shit that the boss wanted put out of commission. However, he had to make sure that he was unrecognized. Discretion was not just desirable, it was a necessity in this business. Besides Mister Genovezzi wasn't blood thirsty. Tony had only needed to waste two low life thugs in over eight years for the boss. Most of the time he was conducting what passed for the local extortion business and of course setting up graft contracts with the unspoken approval of the current mayor. All in all Tony figured he had it pretty good, considering the profession he had chosen.

As the tedious hours went by, he mused on some of the girl friends he had enjoyed over the years and he always had a contest in his mind to determine who the top three were. Actually he'd eventually selected Alice Mizzo for his wife. Boy was she a hot piece! Even after five years of marriage and two children later that cunt could still fuck like a two bit whore. She certainly performed her wifely duties to a tee and then some. However, a red blooded man needed some variety, regardless of a wife's voluptuous techniques.

He'd also amassed a six figure bank account and owned a six bedroom home free of mortgage. His car was paid for and he still had a dripping piece on the side over in Sutton by the name of Cathy. All and all he had a good thing going and he certainly didn't want to let the boss down. No sir. There were far worse things than staking out a house for el patrone. He didn't know why he had to stake out the chief's home but orders were orders. As long as the money rolled in, he'd piss in coke bottles if he had to.

His friend Bruno had the night shift though occasionally Tony would give him a night off and do the time himself. On those nights he would pick up Cathy, a hot little red head to provide her oral skills to keep him hard, alert and awake. For some reason, Tony had a soft spot for hot, willing teeny boppers. So he'd make his quick trip to Sutton and get some entertainment while he watched the police chief's elegant home from a discrete distance.

Cathy was an unusual novelty in that, she lived by herself for one so young. Cathy was a welfare slut and she welcomed the extra income Tony provided her from time to time. He had found her about six months ago plying her wares in a local bar. There must have been some mutual chemistry because they ended up balling on the first night in the back of his car. No question about it, Cathy was a superb, cock craving whore with the morals of a hedonistic tramp.

Tony had the routine down pretty good. As soon as the chief would leave for the office in the morning he'd get Cathy back to Sutton and bang her thoroughly before returning home for a brief nap and tussle with Alice. Then he'd be back on duty until well after suppertime when Bruno usually spelled him.

The young hood listened by the hour to his CD player. Sinatra or some of his favorite Verdi arias were usually selected. Once and awhile he'd call in to report everything was quiet or check on news updates. He only stooped to garbage rock or chucker rap when Cathy was servicing him with her very talented mouth.

He'd been watching and waiting for over two weeks and still everything was quiet. Oh well the money was good and no news was good news. His associates made sure that the old mazoolah kept filling his bank account and he only had to interrupt his routine a few times to give a couple of idiots some attitude adjustment. Yes Tony could honestly say that life was good just like in the old spaghetti commercial.

⸰⸰━━━━━◆━━━━⸰⸰

Frank Tanner parked his car near an old home located on 319 Hamilton Street. The white paint was chipped in many places and the storm windows looked like rejects from the thirties. They were the old fashioned kind that had to be physically screwed or unscrewed to replace or remove them, depending on what time of year it was. Apparently whoever lived in this house didn't really care because the storms were still screwed in with only a few exceptions. He trudged up to the front porch. Sergeant Goldstein was waiting for him in the front seat of the car to keep tabs of any calls that might come in and to protect his backside.

He knocked on the door soundly. Of course there was no response. He tried the door bell and heard nothing. He tried the knob and found the door locked. He muttered to himself, "Christ the place is like fort Knox and the stupid cunt just called a half hour ago."

He banged more loudly and finally he heard a tentative, tremulous, "Who's there?"

"It's detective Frank Tanner Ma'am! You called the department a little while ago."

Reluctantly the door opened about six inches and a furtive face peeked out. An old woman croaked, "Let's see your I.D."

Frank sighed and removed his credentials from his pocket and showed them to the woman. You'd think he was with the NKGB or something. She gave a nod and opened the door. "All right Lieutenant come on in."

When Frank entered her kitchen he thought he had been sent back to an earlier age. The sink looked like something out of a Victorian horror movie and the fridge? Was it a refrigerator or an old ice box? The stove looked like a throw back to the roaring twenties. Reluctantly he sat down at a really messy table. Frank thought to himself that the house hadn't been refurbished in decades. A tabby cat ate from a food dish on the floor and he could hear a TV blaring away in another room. Frank got down to the point, "How can I help you ma'am?"

She snapped, "It's Misses Vincent to you and it's about my husband's gun!"

Frank rolled his eyes and took a quick glance up at the ceiling. "All right Misses Vincent tell me about the gun please."

She snorted in her contrived, imperious manner. "That's better Lieutenant. Some days ago I was looking in the attic rummaging around and I discovered the gun was missing. It was one of my first husband's favorite possessions. "

He looked at her with apparent confusion. "I understand a gun is missing but what are you trying to tell me?"

Misses Vincent shook her head as if she were dealing with a helpless child. Her hair was gray with a hint of being a former brunette. Although her face was wrinkled, her visage hinted at her former beauty and her blue eyes spoke of intelligence and a high strung manner. Frank thought for a brief moment he was looking at one of those old fashioned Yankee grandmothers that literally ruled households during a previous century.

Misses Vincent took a deep breath, obviously attempting to control her temper. "I'm talking about my first husband. I was a lot younger than he was, which is why I survived and he didn't. He's been dead several years and he had some stuff he kept from the Second World War. There was a gun in the trunk and now it's gone."

He tried to move things along a bit. "Did anyone break in?"

The older lady shook her head. "No I would have noticed if someone had broken a window or something. Maybe someone picked a lock. I always go on vacation in February to escape the abominable weather around here. What's odd is nothing else is missing."

"What kind of a gun was it?"

She gave him a thoroughly acidic smirk. "A revolver of course silly! You don't think I'd have a Kentucky long rifle around here do you?"

Frank subdued a smile, presenting a dead pan expression." Believe it or not ma'am we found one in Worcester a few years ago. I don't assume anything anymore."

She continued, "Well my first husband Wilhelm, kept the gun in a holster along with his uniform in the trunk and I'm sure the gun was there last year and now it's gone."

He clenched his fist tight under the table to keep his intestinal fortitude. "Does anyone else live here besides you and your husband?"

She looked almost indignant. "I should say not! You can't trust anybody today. By the way my husband is a professor over at Clarke University and he's scared of weapons. I don't believe he even knew about the gun. I'm sure he didn't take it. I've already asked him and he was genuinely appalled to hear it was even in the house in the first place."

He opened his note pad. "What's his name?

"Myron Vincent the third. He comes from a very distinguished family in Paxton. He really is a sweet thing. He wouldn't hurt a fly. "

Frank made another attempt to make sense of the situation. "So what you're saying is that the gun could have disappeared any time in the last twelve months?"

She gave him another deprecating look, "Actually it could have been up to almost sixteen months ago. I just discovered its disappearance recently. I searched the house from the cellar to the dome and it's definitely not here."

, "Can I see the trunk where the weapon was located?"

She raised her eyebrows. "What for? The gun is gone."

He glanced upward once more, silently praying for more patience. "Perhaps if I see the holster it might give me a clue as to the make of the revolver. Also do you have any documentation on the weapon?"

Misses Vincent gave him a long look, "I don't think there was any paperwork on the gun. He apparently found it during the war. You see he was 18 years older than I when we got married. I'll show you where it was. The only thing that was odd about it all was I couldn't find the key to the trunk and I had to pry it open. "

They were climbing up the stairs as she kept talking, "I could have sworn I kept the key in my husband's desk or was it in my dresser? Anyway, I couldn't find it. Well it might have gotten thrown away. Myron is always trying to throw things out around here."

He thought to himself that he didn't blame the poor bastard. The house was a myriad of clutter. Apparently Myron Vincent was losing the battle. They finally reached the attic and she pointed to the trunk.

Frank opened the trunk and looked through the stuff as she had called it. He gave a low whistle as he pawed through the SS uniform, the Nazi medals and other memorabilia. He looked up at the old lady. Frank raised an eyebrow as he asked, "I know this may sound like a stupid question but what side did he fight on if I might ask?"

She smiled sweetly at him for the first time. "Why detective he fought on the German side. The poor dear had to escape his own country because of all the persecution over there after the war. He often told me how he was never the same after the Hitler youth camps and that demonic indoctrination. Anyway that's where the gun was, in that holster you're holding."

Frank carefully put everything back in the trunk. "Well Misses Vincent if you ever want to sell any of this stuff, you can get a good buck for it. People actually collect this, don't ask me why. I'll write up a report for you in case you have insurance and we'll keep a copy in our records just in case."

Lieutenant Tanner drove over to Clarke University later on to look up Professor Vincent and sure enough the wispy older gentleman confirmed everything that his wife had talked about. "You must understand Lieutenant I was absolutely shocked when I learned such a thing was in our home. I know the evils of such weapons. I teach history and comparative religion. If you locate that weapon kindly destroy it."

Later Frank filed the report and mentioned the entire incident to Mac. The captain sat behind his desk nursing a hot cup of his favorite Columbian brand. "So Frank you say the guy was a fucking Nazi?"

"Yeah! He's been dead over ten years. She said he had to leave his beloved Germany to get away from the post war persecution."

Mac gave a mirthless laugh, "Yeah the guy was probably a fucking war criminal. Persecuted indeed! She should have shot the son of a bitch instead of marrying him. Oh well either the stupid broad lost the thing or the burglar was an above average kind. From what you tell me the current Mister Vincent is a complete wimp and the other guy is dead. Give me the report and I'll keep it on file. By the way did you get the name of the former husband?"

"She said his name was Wilhelm. I checked up the old record and apparently he went by the name of Wilhelm Wagner but of course who knows what his real name actually was."

Mac put down his mug. "Yeah, sometimes Frank I wonder what it must have been like in those days when good was good and evil was evil. When I was growing up I talked with some of the world war two veterans. I tell you they were a great outfit. They cleaned house on the two greatest war machines since Napoleon and the British Empire combined. They would have loved to have gotten their mitts on people like Herr Hitler or this Herr Wagner." He pronounced the name the German way with the w spoken like a v. So some old lady discovers a stolen gun from a dead husband's old war chest. Just another dead lead in a dead end case. You know Frank this case is really starting to depress me. I feel like I'm a valued prize being stalked by some big game hunter. We're dying like flies and we're no closer to solving this thing then we were weeks ago. I wish I had a fucking crystal ball and could find out this thug's address. "

Frank poured them both another cup. "Well Mac I don't have any short answers. I just have a feeling that this case is going to break soon. I don't know why but I just have a hunch we're closer than we think. This killer has been a little too careless, just a little too arrogant. He'll slip up, Mac and when he does I'm going to nail him to the wall with six inch spikes."

"Yeah! I'll supply the hammer at no charge. Just to prove my heart is in the right place, I'll even give him tetanus shots and intravenous feeding to keep the son of a bitch alive for at least thirty days. I'll personally put him at the fifty yard line of Holy Cross field so that the crowd can have some lively half time entertainment. We probably won't be permitted to do those interesting things to his person but that's what I'd love to be able to do."

"Yeah, tell me about it. Torquemada would have had fun with the creep. Well I better get back to work. By the way this coffee sucks!"

Mac laughed, "Yeah I know! It's been steeping too long. Keep on trucking."

Chapter 14

HOT TROT

Mac wasn't the only one who was depressed at the horrific decimation of the Worcester Police Department. Night after night Ann kept watching the news as the political and law enforcement branches continued to flounder in evasive explanations as to why the killer hadn't been apprehended yet. CNN was now ensconced at city hall and other important places around the county as the authorities fruitlessly dug for information that was obviously not forth coming or non-existent.

Ann would curl her legs under her and watch all this as her eyes would moisten. She thought of the dead including her beloved Ted. She ached to have John hold her, comfort her and love her. However she knew he was burning the midnight oil to track down leads and she understood their new relationship needed time and patience to grow. How she wanted it to grow. She couldn't believe she could fall in love so quickly after Ted. She shuddered to think how Ted must be rolling in his grave or would he? He had once told her that if anything ever happened to him that she should marry again. Ann thought of poor , noble Ted and caring, loving John and she clenched her fists with rage as she thought of the nameless murderer walking free to kill again and again.

When she was in bed it was even worse as the phantom of Ted seemed to lie beside her. She remembered his tender love making. Ted had been so strong and insatiable and yet so gentle and considerate. He often said he couldn't get enough of her. Ted kept telling her that he was always hungry for her when they whispered together in the delicious closeness of the night. They'd planned on starting a family, once he'd been promoted and they'd saved a decent nest egg. They were still on birth control when Ted was suddenly snuffed out and now, Ann had nothing left behind except bglowing memories of her sweet darling.

Now she was haunted by John as well. He was a little less tender and a lot more unrestrained than Ted. She always felt that Ted held back A BIT, making sure he wasn't hurting her. Ann then would succumb to the ache inside her from the loneliness and think of John. Wonderful newly discovered John. Then she would hug herself and frantically rub her clit to climax. She tried to keep control over her wild emotions. But it was to no use as her fingers pushed her to another sharp release. All Ann knew was that she now wanted John as much as Ted. She knew she was wicked and wanton for letting another man into her bed just a few weeks after Ted's death but she couldn't help it. Her body was telling her, clamoring to her that John was right for her. When she played with herself it was John's name that would escape her moaning throat as she gasped with passion. How she longed for his touch, his presence, his adoration.

Ring ring! Ring, ring! Ann reached out and picked up the receiver. Her voice was still a little muddled from her fantasy.

"Yes?"

"It's me love. Sorry to call so late." Mac's voice came reassuring her out of the darkness.

Gladness crept into Ann's voice. "Hi, I miss you terribly. My door is always open to you, so don't be such a stranger."

John laughed, "I'll be so glad when this case is wrapped up. I'm normally not this busy and there's so much I want to talk to you about."

"I know honey. Can you see me soon?"

"I'll try. I'll call first so you can throw on one of your patented steaks."

Ann giggled, "Sounds like you're a glutton with many interesting appetites. I'm free this weekend. You can sneak in on me any time you like."

John became serious, "Yes Anne, I'll really try to be with you for awhile. As I said I've got a lot to tell you. I care for you a lot Ann. I hope everything else is going all right?"

She spoke in her most seductive voice, "I'm fine love. You don't think I could entice you into making a brief appearance here tonight? I could sure use some positive reinforcement."

He sounded amused. "Is that what they call it these days? Seriously Ann it's so nuts here I'm going to have to crash on my office sofa here. It really is a bitch Ann. I miss you a lot. I love you."

Her eyes suddenly moistened. "I love you to, John. It's been so sudden but a girl knows when it's for real."

His voice lowered a bit, becoming confidential in tone. "Ann you're a pearl of great price. I'd never do anything to hurt you and I know these times apart are painful for both of us. What we now have is worth fighting for in spite of everything that's happening around us. Good night Ann. Think of me as I think of you."

She couldn't help sniffling. "Good night love and take care. I couldn't bear to lose you. It would be too much."

"Don't worry love. I'm not so easy to knock off you know. By for now."

He hung up the phone and went back to checking more paperwork. As it turned out he only got four hours of sleep that night as he plowed through more dead leads and meaningless paper trails.

<hr>

Tony Visconti was ushered into Mister Genovezzi's plush office. The door was closed behind him and only the two of them were in the expensively appointed room. The highly polished cherry wood desk was definitely the center piece of the library. The book cases were made of the same wood and were filled with rich looking, leather bound volumes. To

Tony's surprise many of them were law books. Tony bowed respectfully, "You sent for me boss?"

The mob leader waved him to a chair, "Good morning Tony. There's two things I want to tell you. You've been very loyal to the family since you got out of high school. I look upon you like a cousin. As you know, Alice is related to me. I'll come right to the point. I know about that slut from Sutton you've been plowing on the side and it ends now. The next time you see her you'll pay her off and tell her to take a hike, or find her a job way out of town. I don't particularly care about the slut but I do care about your wife's situation. After all she is the grand daughter of my brother in law as you well know. Now to the other point. I want an update on the police chief."

Tony looked in shock at the white haired old man whose eyes bore through him like pointed daggers. This much he knew, he'd better give up the teeny bopper and pronto. His voice shook a little, "The chief comes and goes on a pretty normal schedule unless he's got evening meetings. We haven't seen anybody suspicious lurking around. The only people to approach the house are the mailman and the teen age neighbor who cuts the grass for them once a week. That's all we've seen. As for Cathy , I'll do what you say. I only ask that you don't tell my wife. She might not be as understanding as you."

The God father chuckled without a trace of humor. "Yeah Tony, I see that. I'm glad you didn't try to lie about it. That would have been a very bad thing. I can put up with a lot Tony but never lie to me. So see a priest and clean up your act and work hard. I understand your wife is quite the woman. You shouldn't need a piece on the side anyway but if you absolutely have to it shouldn't be so close to home and certainly not with the likes of the little tart you're with now. I mean Jesus Christ Tony she might not even be legal for Christ's sake. You could get arrested for statutory rape and then I lose a good man for a couple of years. That's bad for business Tony. Do you understand? You wouldn't want anything to happen to Miss Cathy Stone would you?"

Tony shuddered a little involuntarily. "No boss! You have my word, I'll clean up my act."

"Good, I'm glad to hear it. Keep a good eye on Al Bender. Let me know if there are any developments. So make damned sure your cell phone bill is paid up." The mafia boss waved his hand in dismissal.

When Tony was back in his car his face became red with rage. Who was that old man to tell him who he could be with anyway? Genovezzi didn't have real blood in his veins anymore. He knew he'd have to get rid of the hot little red head ASAP. You didn't even think about trying to screw the boss around. That could be extremely unhealthy. However, he wasn't going to pay the bitch off either. He'd tell her some cock and bull story about some disease he'd contracted or maybe he could find a good job in a strip club for her in the combat zone down in Boston. She'd be far enough away so he'd have excuses not to see her anymore. Now that he thought of it the strip club seemed to make more sense. She was a slut already and she'd make good money table dancing or picking up guys. The young fox had all the proper endowments to perform a variety of exciting services in the sex trade so why not? He made a strategic call to The Silver Slipper. It was a strip club in the dead center of Boston's notorious combat zone. He got things arranged and decided to go out to Sutton to speed Cathy on her new career.

When Tony got to Cathy's small apartment it was two hours before any talking took place. Tony was thinking to himself while the bedroom gymnastics were going on that Cathy was going to be hard to give up and very difficult to replace. He'd probably have to wait for the old tyrant to die before he could dip his wick in strange female pussy again. He still couldn't figure out how the boss had found out. Tony had been very secretive about his little side dish. So how the hell had his trysts been discovered? Was he being tailed? Did the boss have his cell phone bugged? It was kind of scary when you actually analyzed the various possibilities.

He was thrilled with the amazing red hot teen slut's wiggles and jiggles. He released inside her eagerly lunging body for the second time. The petite tramp was still hungry for even more. He cried out in rapture. "Jesus Christ you are good! God! Fuck!"

Cathy flashed her pearly whites at her virile lover. "I know! I'm not getting older, I'm getting better, baby. Just for you."

Tony laughed between gasps for oxygen. "I hear you. You really shouldn't put such talent to waste. I bet you could make a shit load of money down in Boston. I've got contacts you know."

Cathy looked at him speculatively, "What do you have in mind, sweety?"

She was still gently stroking him with her warm, soft hand as she gazed into his slightly troubled eyes. It seemed to Tony that she could sense something was wrong. He pulled her to him to reassure her. God she was so hot! Her nipples were still hard and when he moved his hand between her velvet like thighs he swore she sounded like she was purring. He continued, "Look Cathy, I found a hell of an opportunity for you. Wouldn't you like to make a couple of grand a week? Hell, you might even make more."

She murmured, with her lips still kissing against his hairy chest. "Hmmm! And what would cute little me have to do for that kind of serious coin? "

She raised her head slightly and gazed right into his eyes. "Some dancing and maybe a little more of what you're doing right now. There's a job available at the Silver Slipper in Boston. I know a guy by the name of Don Scarza and he told me you'd be perfect. They can show you how to dance and if you want you can get into some of the other sidelines. If you save your money for ten years you can retire."

She arched her eyebrows slightly. "And what about us?"

Tony shrugged his shoulders letting his fingers slip around her right breast once again. She felt so damned good inside and out. "Well I can come down and visit you in Boston from time to time. But you have to admit you're not making much money right now and I thought you'd jump at the opportunity. I asked Don to give you the red carpet treatment."

Cathy became pensive. "It sounds like I'd be dancing and hooking for that kind of money. Well you told me you'd try to find something for me.

I just didn't expect it so soon. It's all a little confusing. When should I call Mister Garza anyway?"

Tony did a little probing before he finally answered. "Why don't you call him tomorrow. I'll give you the number and I'll call later on to make sure everything is all right. Will you call him?"

He pulled her on top of him. The frisky vixen enveloped his re-hardened manhood with her satin like sheath, applying a vigorous rhythm. She gasped, "Yes Tony, I'll call him! But you be sure to visit me down there if I get the job. Oh Tony I just love it! I'm getting laid and I'm going to make a lot of money. Ooooo, stay with me baby! You're the best!"

She leaned down and gave him a ravishing kiss as their bodies blended and intertwined in further passion. Tony knew he probably wouldn't visit Cathy in Boston so he decided to prolong the sizzling sport with the horny slut for as long as he possibly could.

— • —

When he finally got home shortly after midnight, Alice was not amused.

His wife was a very attractive brunette with flashing black eyes and a very shapely figure. Her sexy, long legs were great for wrapping around him when they were rutting. "So Tony where the hell were you?"

Tony gave her a long kiss and answered, "Alice honey I can definitely tell you that I was on the boss's business. I can't tell you about it but I followed his orders to the letter. "

Alice gave him an appraising look but Tony had removed any traces of lipstick and had carefully showered before leaving Cathy's. He smiled at his wife, "Alice I love it when you're jealous. You know I'd never do anything to hurt you. I'm glad you're jealous because it means you love me as I love you. Now why don't we go to bed and I'll try to make up for my absence tonight okay?"

She replied only half joking. "All right Tony but if I ever find you with another woman I'll cut her cunt out with my Ginsu knife and make her eat it raw. You know I'm a very hot blooded woman and I can hate as fiercely as I love."

He whispered in her ear as they entered the bedroom, "Don't I know it."

In moments they were naked in the bed and Tony slowly slipped his hands and tongue over the intimate areas of Alice's warm, velvet skin. He was trying to buy himself a little more time to get sufficiently aroused to perform his expected marital duty. Cathy had thoroughly drained him and the ride back from Sutton had only taken a half an hour.

Soon, Alice was moaning and crying out very loudly while Tony gently licked her juice oozing cunt with quick up and down movements with his lips and slurping tongue. He stimulated her exposed clit until it swelled and moistened. He gently licked or nibbled it, teasing that tingling little knob until Alice couldn't deny him anything. Instinctively she moved her legs around his head forcing him even closer to the target area. Alice hadn't had him in almost two days and she was hungry for him. "Oh Tony, I need you inside me ssssooooo bad! God you feel good! Fuck another kid into my cunt you fucking stud! Hmmmm that's nice! Just a little quicker! Yeah! Right there! Oooh yes, yes! Fuck!"

At last, Tony was ready to rock. Nothing quite like plowing two chicks in the same day to turn a guy on to the max. He spread her legs wide apart and then pushed them back as he entered her and began to slam her just like she liked it. Waves of joy flashed through Alice as her body was pounded by the thrilling penetrations of Tony's pulsing cock. She met his thrusts and then she climaxed. She was pleasantly surprised at his longevity. Her language became absolutely florid, the harder and faster he slammed his manhood into her. Tony eagerly drilled her clenching snatch until his hot wife convulsed with two more cataclysmic orgasms. Her cries and swearing grew louder and louder the more he drilled her ravenous slit.

Sometime later, they had a mutual release with Tony pouring what felt like a river of spunk into her vaginal paradise. When it was over Alice purred, "that was nice my darling. I wish you could perform like that every night my Italian stallion. I know you've been busy lately but when you get back to a normal schedule I expect you to service me just like that for several months in a row."

Tony held her close, breathing against her neck. "You know, baby, you're the best. I adore you, every inch of you."

She still gripped his member with her damp hand, reluctant to let him escape her libidinous clutches. She was a little disappointed that it had shrunk however, he'd given her a pretty wicked ride. Her semen soaked hole still tingled, aching for more. Seductively, she pushed her tits against his chest to no avail. He was done for the evening. Sometimes she wondered if he had been stepping around. So she cuddled up and said nothing. However, she would try to keep an eye on him in future.

Tony thought to himself as he drifted towards sleep, maybe he didn't need a piece on the side after all. Alice was pretty darned hot and a damned great lay. Maybe he could walk the straight and narrow at least for awhile."

◆━━━━◆━━━━◆

Major Koehler was preparing for his next assignment. He had it all planned out. He new precisely where the house was. More importantly, he knew just how to approach and enter it. It was a shame to eliminate the wife to, however that's the price of conflict. He was meticulous. This time he'd make sure that it would be carried out when he was on duty just to throw the bastards off in case they were checking on things. He knew he had to be careful, ever so careful. All he'd have to do would be to slip out for awhile during desk duty. Well he'd be an honorable asset to the fatherland by God. He'd show the world that the fuehrer had been right after all. It was time to destroy this Democracy of utter stupidity and Bender would be the beginning of the end of America's social stability. The first six cops had just been the warm up tosses. It was time to get serious.

Chapter 15

DOUBLE DOWN

It was a lovely sunny Thursday afternoon. Tony was comfortably ensconced in his dark blue, Grand Marquis as usual, keeping Bender's home in view while munching on some chips. He was parked on a nearby side street, somewhat hidden by mature shady maple trees. The tranquil scene was accented by a brilliant, blue summer sky. No clouds, no noise and the smell of fresh cut grass tempted him to complete relaxation. He was listening to an aria from Tosca when he saw the policeman approach, alone and on foot.

At first, he wondered if the cop was tracking him down. However, as he watched, the cop headed straight for the police chief's home. Tony thought to himself it was a little odd that the guy was alone and hadn't driven up in a car. There hadn't even been a motorcycle or he would have heard it even in the distance. In due course the door opened and after a brief pause, the lone policeman entered. He reasoned that if the chief's wife permitted the cop to enter, it must have been an expected visit. So he sat back into content relaxation while Verdi filled his soul.

Misses Bender was a very down to earth woman who eschewed vanity. Even though her lovely, long hair was graying rapidly, she refused to die it. She was in her mid fifties as the chief was. She was wearing a long blue dress with white cuffs and collar. Her shrewd dark brown eyes appraised the police officer in front of her. She asked, "I don't understand this. Why are you here? Did Al send you?"

The officer answered, "The lives of you and your husband are at risk. I've been sent to guard you until further arrangements can be made."

She closed the door behind him, "My God! Is it that bad! What happened?"

The policeman bowed a little to show his respect, "A very explicit threat came to the department today and it was decided to play it safe. I'm here to see that no harm comes to you from that or any other threat."

Misses Bender gave a sigh of relief, "All right, can I offer you a cup of coffee or tea while you hang around?"

The officer smiled, "Tea would be splendid. Thank you very much."

They went to the kitchen and she rapidly prepared some water and got two cups out of the cupboard. She asked, "Have you been on the force very long?

The patrolman laughed good naturedly, "Not very long. Your husband does a very fine job. I was fortunate to be assigned to him. I've learned a great deal since I've been on the force."

She returned the smile as she retrieved two tea bags. She turned then to check on the water which had started to boil. When she turned back she was staring at the business end of a revolver. She looked into the eyes of the policeman and they had become glassy and distant. His smile had turned into a face of stone. Of course she screamed. She heard a strange sound as the bullet tore through her leg and she crumpled to the floor. She cried out, "Stop! Please don't kill me!"

The gun was aimed directly at her head now and his voice changed to a harsh clipped tone. "Misses Bender you must die for zee glory of zee fatherland! Ven your husband returns home he Vill Die also. I vill take zee leadership away from zee police and they vill become a useless chaotic body. I vill cause anarchy and vill revive zee Reich."

From her innermost depths, she found courage she never knew existed. She understood all too well, her time had come. "They'll get you, you insane maniac. I only wish I could be there to see you blasted to oblivion. Into God's hands I commend my spirit."

Her eyes blazed with defiance until the moment the second bullet ripped through her valiant brain.

The patrolman calmly emptied the tea cups and placed them back in their place. It was obligatory that his hands were protected with plastic gloves. One didn't want to leave any prints around. Carefully, he stepped around the body to make sure no footprints were left either. Stoically, Herbert Koehler sat down around a corner from the kitchen. He knew sooner or later, Chief Allan Bender would return home. And then....

For once, there were no special meetings that Thursday evening. A brief inquiry with Maxine, the chief's secretary had inadvertently set the planned execution in motion. The sound suppressor on Herbert's revolver was certainly useful. It kept noise down to a minimum. It definitely made life, or in this case death a lot easier.

• • •

Predictably, about six o'clock, Police Chief Al Bender parked his car in his stone tiled driveway and calmly entered the house. Even after several days, the chief hadn't noticed anyone watching his home. Tony was thinking to himself, the chief's wife must be having a thing on the side because that other policeman hadn't come out yet and he'd been there way over an hour. Well the shit would hit the fan now.

When Al Bender entered his home he called out for his wife but there was no answer. He muttered, "Christ where are you, doll?"

When he entered the kitchen he saw her, lying in a pool of blood. He just stood there in disbelief. His mind couldn't accept what his eyes were apparently seeing. Still in shock he leaned down and saw the goo that had been his beloved wife's face.

"Good evening Herr Bender. I am Major Herbert Koehler at your service."

Bender looked up in stunned surprise at the revolver aimed at his head. "But you're…"

The patrolman interrupted, "You vill die for zee fatherland. Zee fuehrer has ordered your execution along with many others. If it means anything to you, your vife died well. She vas a brave woman, better than you I think."

Bender jumped from his kneeling position with a growl of rage and raw hatred. Unfortunately all the patrolman had to do was pull the trigger. The first bullet caught Bender in the stomach and the second blew his brains out. However the blood spattered onto the killer's uniform. He shook his face in disgust and he quickly went into the bathroom to clean himself up. He was careful to use a face cloth to remove any possible fingerprints or blood stains from the floor or counter before fastidiously wiping off the splattered blood from his uniform and his face. It was most distressing because he'd have to get to a laundry mat real quick. Oh well, it was one of the hazards of the enterprise.

He searched the kitchen and finally located a plastic bag, carefully folding the wet face cloth before placing the bag in his pocket. He checked to make sure he hadn't left any blood stained footprints around and to his relief he hadn't. The killer went to the front door, took out a handkerchief and opened it. After all, there might be the odd blood stain on his gloves. He'd have to destroy his gloves and perhaps his trousers. Yet, it was a small price to pay to literally get away with this double murder. He was still amazed that the police chief hadn't taken any security precautions regarding his residence. The idiot must have thought that nobody would be audatious enough to attack him in his sacred lair. Well, he and the Feuhrer had proved the dead chief wrong. He chuckled while shutting the door behind him.

Tony watched as the patrolman closed the door and put what looked like a white cloth into his pocket. The cop proceeded to retrace his steps the way he had come. Then all returned to serene normal. Little did he realize that the sound of silence was becoming ominous.

A few hours went by and Tony was enjoying an aria from La Force Del Destino when he noticed something odd. The lights didn't come on in the Bender household. They always came on shortly after sundown. He waited and everything remained dark. He knew that the chief had entered the house and the car was still in the drive way. Why wasn't the light on? For that matter, why wasn't the car in the garage? Bender almost always did that.

Tony called information and to his surprise he actually got a listing for Al Bender. He muttered to himself, "The guy isn't a paranoid bastard after all."

He decided to call and ask for Roger Erickson and pretend he'd gotten a wrong number. It would be pretty safe from the cell phone so he dialed after putting in the privacy code. The phone rang and rang and rang but there was no answer until the voice mail clicked on. He grumbled, "What the fuck! I know the bastard's there."

He tried again with the same result. Tony listened in vain and at last he hung up. HE was starting to get a bad feeling about this. Did the guy have his ringer off? Curiosity was building up like a bull rally inside his mind as he tried the call yet again to no avail. Finally he said, "Fuck it!"

He got out of the car and approached the chief's home. Tony looked like a prosperous businessman in his elegant dark blue suit. He took out his handkerchief and used it to cover his finger just before he pressed the door bell. The English chimes rang eight familiar Big Ben notes that could easily be heard from outside. Tony put the handkerchief away and waited. The sound of the bell faded away and there was absolute silence. He waited but nobody answered the door. There was no yell, "Who's there?" There was nothing but the sounds of crickets and muffled sounds of televisions coming from the neighbor's homes. Tony thought to himself, "I know the fucker is there. He covered his finger again and rang the bell three more times and nothing occurred. He muttered, "If that didn't piss him off, nothing would." He was thinking that maybe the guy was getting laid. That's the only reason why this could be happening. No lights were on and the door bell and phone hadn't accomplished anything. Curiosity kept gnawing at him like a hungry lioness stalking a wildebeest herd. Keeping the handkerchief in hand he tried the doorknob and to his shocked surprise the door opened easily. He listened carefully but the darkness was equaled by complete silence. All he could hear was the refrigerator running from the kitchen. He was drawn into the home like iron filings to a magnet. Tony was trembling with apprehension and then his nose caught the faint smell of gun powder. He knew that smell from the necessary activities of his dubious occupation. A frown of concentration creased his forehead as he quietly shut the door behind him. He snuck quietly around the living room and found nothing. He went through the dining room and moved as quietly as a ghost. He couldn't see much but the moon light streaming through the windows just made it possible. He entered the kitchen and saw two dark forms on the floor. His hand was still covered by the handkerchief and after a few fumbling moments he turned on the light.

"Jesus fucking Christ!"

◆——◆——◆

Captain John Mackelroy found himself being carefully guided into the inner sanctum of Genovezzi's compound. He had responded to a phone call at about ten o'clock that evening. To his own surprise he'd only come with patrolman Winkler as his driver. His car was waiting for him about a hundred yards up the road.

Mac was briskly ushered into the plush office of the crime boss. He noted that Mister Genovezzi didn't look happy and there was another well dressed man sitting near the ornate desk.

The mafia lord stood up and moved to shake Mac's hand. Reluctantly he grasped the warm, firm grip for a moment. Mac asked, "All right what is this important information you have for me?"

Genovezzi gave him a mirthless smile. "Forgive me for being the one to tell you what I must tell you. Please permit me to introduce you to one of my more reliable associates. His name is Tony Visconti. I've known him for over ten years and he's married to one of my relatives."

The captain's brusque tone indicated that he wasn't in the least bit interested in Tony's social connections. "That's nice! So what's the big deal?"

There was genuine sadness in the crime bosses face. "I've just found out that your friend and associate, Al Bender was shot dead this evening. I'm sorry."

Mac just stood there stunned. His face grew pale with sheer shock. "What the fuck?"

Then the boss barked, "Tell him Tony!"

Mac sat down, feeling as if he'd aged fifty years in seconds. Tony explained what had happened. "I'm telling you the cop must have been the one who did it! He was let in by somebody and he left by himself. The only other person to enter that house was the chief himself. On my mother's soul I swear it!"

Mac sat in stunned silence as he tried to assimilate what he'd just heard. Bender and his lovely wife had been blown away as easily as gunning down a couple of cows for slaughter. Mac glanced furtively from man to man. He finally asked, "Do you have someone guarding me as well? "

Genovezzi smiled, "You bet your ass. I told you the last time you were kind enough to visit me that killing cops is bad business. It gets everybody upset. That's a very bad thing. If some suspicious jamoco had showed up at Bender's home, maybe Tony would have interfered, but he figured a cop wouldn't be a problem."

Mac asked, "I've got to use your phone for a minute, all right?"

The boss extended his hand, "Be my guest."

When Mac finally got through to Tanner he said, "Frank, you better get an ambulance and a few squad cars over to Bender's place right now….Yeah that's right…..I'm not kidding Frank, I think they've been murdered…… No shit Frank! (Further pause) I'll be there in a few minutes myself."

He hung up and sighed, "If the bullets match the others than it will clinch the fact that it's a cop or someone impersonating a cop. I would advise you, Mister Visconti to stay in town. At the very least you'll be needed as a witness."

The crime boss saw the distress in Mac's eyes. "I'm sorry, captain. I really am. I admired Bender. He was an honest man and like you, he played by the book. I'll keep Tony in town as well."

Mac spoke quietly as he stood up to leave. "Thanks for the thought. If everything checks out, it would appear I'm in your debt and for some reason that scares me."

Genovezzi laughed, "Oh it's not as bad as all that. If I ever need a favor from you I'll try to make sure you remain on the straight and narrow."

Mac shook his head in disbelief and left. The God father remarked after a minute of silence, "Tony there goes a good man. Don't ever cross him. Men like that can be very dangerous because they can't be bought. They are men of honor and integrity. You never want to get a man like that to start playing outside the book because he'd stop at nothing to get revenge. He actually came in here a few weeks ago and threatened me in my own house. He's got balls, I'll give him that. So Tony you make sure to be a good witness if it comes to that and don't mess around with him, you understand?"

Tony stared into those cool, appraising eyes, "Yes boss, I can see he'd be dangerous."

Then Genovezzi exploded, "Than why the fuck did you go into the fucking house? Jesus Christ Tony, if they don't find the right bullets or they don't make the right connections they might accuse you, us! I ordered you to guard the place not go inside! Why the fuck didn't you just make an anonymous phone call tipping them off and high tail it. If he suspects you at all, my ass will be in the fucking frying pan. You're so smart why don't you use your fucking head for more than a damned hat rack?"

Tony was inwardly in a panic. He'd never seen the boss this angry in a long time. "I'm sorry boss. It's just everything was so strange and I did tell you as soon as I found out."

Genovezzi sighed, "Yeah, at least you did that. By the way I understand that mister Scarza is going to interview a certain young red head soon. That was well done. You got the bitch out of town and set her up in a good paying job. Now you're going to stay in town like I agreed and you keep out of the way of any more cops or cunts. You're going to be a good family man for a few months and just help out on some bookie business for awhile, Kapeesh?"

Tony nodded, "Yes boss and again I'm sorry."

The boss waived his hand, "All right but next time, don't be so curious. Just do what I tell you and you'll stay out of trouble. Christ Tony if he needs you as a witness, you'll show up in all the fucking newspapers. If you gave a phony name to Cathy slut she'll know you're real name now. She might even try to black mail you. You see why I'm so upset?"

Tony became thoughtful, "Somehow I don't think Cathy will be a problem. If she tries anything like that, well she might find it might be bad for her health. I'm not going to let some little bimbo cause me problems. As far as the papers I can lay low for awhile or maybe me and my family can move to another city to help keep tabs on some other competitor's turf. Even if my name gets into the papers most will forget in a couple of months."

Genovezzi gave him a frosty grin, "Well we'll cross that bridge when we get to it. For now keep a real fucking low profile, okay?"

Tony stood up, "Absolutely boss! Can I go now?"

Genovezzi nodded and for quite awhile after Tony had left, he gave a lot of thought to the current situation. He wasn't happy with Tony entering the police chief's home but at least he'd been honest with him about everything. If Tony wouldn't lie about the cheep cunt or discovering a dead policeman than at least perhaps the man could be trusted and that was important. If only the stupid son of a bitch would think intelligently. Well, high school education wasn't as good as it used to be. He sighed and turned out the lamp, deciding to retire for that evening. It had been a very long day and he wasn't young anymore.

Chapter
16

HEART'S TRUTH

The captain was out of it. Between the unusually pale face and the dark rings around his bloodshot eyes, it was pretty clear that Mac had not had a very good night. He nursed the inevitable cup of strong half and half. The lieutenant stated the obvious. , "John you look like shit."

Mac just nodded and stared at him. He raised an eyebrow ever so slightly as if to ask, what's up?

Frank answered the unanswered question. "All right, I've got the low down from forensics. No prints, no clues, no nothing except the four bullets were fired from the same gun that killed Tindale and all the rest. It's the same blasted weapon and it's the same fucking bastard pulling the trigger."

Mac glared down at the empty cup. "It's a fucking cop Frank. The city is in a volcanic uproar. I've just had to listen to fuck head Flarity foaming at the mouth for ten minutes. The cock sucker is threatening marshal law for Christ's sake! Why the hell didn't mister gun man do Flarity instead of Bender. Poor fucking Bender. You and the chief were the best men I've ever known and some psycho kills him for nothing! Christ, Frank! Bender was almost like a second father to me. Do you understand? For absolutely fucking nothing!"

Mac suddenly stood up and flung the empty cup against the file cabinet and it splintered as it crashed to the vinyl tile floor. "Mother fucking cop killing son of a bitch! It's too much!"

Frank watched in total despair as his friend and mentor sat back down and started sobbing into his hands. He knew it had been building up for a long time. He quietly got up and went down the hall for a moment to retrieve a new cup and give his boss some privacy. Returning to Mac's office he filled it with more coffee. Then Frank placed a gentle hand on Mac's back and said in his gentlest voice, "Here drink this, it'll help you feel a little better. That's it Mac let it out. I don't have any more tears to shed myself. It's a great big mother fucking shame."

It took Mac a few minutes to get with it. Finally he drank his beloved half and half, while he wiped his eyes with his handkerchief. Finally, he smiled at his friend, "Sorry Frank, I'm just a basket case today. Thanks!"

"No problem man. Just wait till we get our hands on the son of a bitch."

Mac's face became flint. "We're going to check everyone in this fucking police department. We're going to go over all the records again. If I have to I'll get a search warrant for everybody including myself if I have to. We'll get him Frank. By the nails in Christ's cross we'll get him."

Tanner saw the grim determination in Mac's face, "I'll get all the personal records accessed on our computers. I'll go A to M you take the rest. We'll even check out anyone who's left the force. There aren't many but they might have kept a uniform. I just want one favor."

"What's that?"

"I want to be in on the kill."

Mac gave his friend the high sign. "You got it buddy."

Over the next few hours both officers reviewed the records and Mac called Frank back into his office. There was yet another fresh batch of coffee perking away in the dependable maker. Mac motioned for Frank to sit and he spoke excitedly. "You know Frank something just clicked. You recall that I told you the first call didn't make much sense?"

"Yeah!"

Mac continued, "Well I thought it was strange that a killer would try to put himself at the scene instead of saying nothing. It was as if he wanted us to know he was there instead of somewhere else. Well that would make perfect sense if he were a police officer on duty or off. The main point is that he wanted to establish his whereabouts as other than where he normally would be. So let's say he was supposed to be patrolling Gleason dale at the time. He calls from the phone booth and slips away while the regulars show up. The old lady I questioned didn't notice any cars leaving the area, you know the one with the dog?"

Frank nodded, "Yeah I read your report on her."

Mac's most evil grin widened. "Yeah well remember there was only a short distance involved and a short time like ten minutes max between the time of the call and when our boys showed up. So let's say for the sake of argument that the killer lived within walking distance and he's actually off duty? How many of our finest live around that neighborhood?"

Frank stared at the captain, "As I recall, Al Wagner lives around there some place, but he might not be the only one."

Mac shifted his attention back to the computer. "Let's find out."

Frank went around the desk to watch as Mac went from record to record. They knew the streets quite well from years of investigating the city. In ten minutes they had only three men who lived within a mile of the first killing and of course Wagner was one of them.

For the first time in weeks, Mac's face was intense with excitement. He was onto something. He looked up at his friend. "Let's go for a walk."

Fifteen minutes later they were walking from the warehouse to 27 King Street. Sure enough if they walked fast they could make it in a little less than ten minutes. Then they did the same thing with the other two, the residences of patrolman Mason and Sergeant Summers. They both took close to fifteen minutes each. When they returned to the car Frank commented, "I checked the recent retiree list or persons we have fired and they all live out of town except for Bronson and he lives way down on Pleasant Street beyond Chamberlain Parkway. That's over three miles from here so I think we can write him off for now."

Mac stared at his friend for a long moment, "I think it's time we had a long talk with our friend from the F.B.I. mister Bill Flynn."

A few hours later Frank Tanner and John Mackelroy were sitting in front of Bill Flynn's desk in the small field office in the old Denholmes building. Bill was sitting back with a non committal look on his face as Mac told him what they had discovered from the circumstances that had led to the dead chief to their recent little hike. "I tell you Bill that Mason, summers and Wagner should be put under surveillance and further in-depth checks done beyond our own. Right now these three are tops on our list but I don't want to start any bad feelings if they prove to be innocent. I'd like you to play it close to the vest."

Bill thought over what he had heard for a long time. When he finally answered his voice was trembling with rage. "To think a cop is probably doing this. I pretty much agree with your gut feeling Mac. I also understand why you want us to bring in some fresh faces that the three suspects aren't familiar with. It will make surveillance easier. I can have my boys in position by tomorrow evening and if you e mail me what you have on file, I'll see if I can find out more. We're normally not quite this accommodating but hell, my old man was a cop and we're all in this together. I'll keep in touch. If we see anything suspicious at all, be ready to get a search warrant and proper arrest warrants. Now let me get to work."

⚬━━━━◆━━━━⚬

Ann was riveted to the news that evening with shocked silence as she nibbled on some short bread. She was perched on her normal position on the couch as the electrifying and horrible news report about the double murder of Chief Bender and his wife was reported on every channel including CNN. The mayor looked like he was about to have a stroke as he struggled to keep his composure. Fear could be seen in his eyes as he stammered out his statement of outrage and condolence. Her stomach was knotted in cold fear as she thought of the peril John was in. After all, if Ted was killed by this nameless thug then why not John? She was gripped by the hopelessness of her complete inability to help him. John had done so much for her. His love had saved her from the depths of despair and his concern had helped her find a trust worthy manager for her money. He'd even talked briefly with her boss to let him know what kind of stress she had been enduring as if Tom needed to have been told anyway. John had been little less than a miracle and now this. Why couldn't they get the cop killing bastard?

Ann couldn't stand the loneliness any more and she called him. Mac was working on a search warrant when the phone rang. He could hear the desperate loneliness in her voice. "Please John I need to see you now. I'm falling apart over hear."

John heard the tears in her voice. He couldn't do all that much tonight anyway. The damned warrants could wait until the morning. It wasn't like the three suspects were going to blow town overnight. Besides this was the woman he supposedly loved wasn't it? He hadn't been with her in days. Was he a man or a mouse? He replied in his gentlest voice, "All right love I'll be over soon. I've got to get away from all this shit anyway. My heart is breaking to."

Ann sniffled with happiness and regret. "I'm sorry dearest, I know Al Bender was your friend. I'll try to help you get over it. I love you."

About an hour later when Mac entered her apartment she flew into his arms before he could say a word. Her lips devoured his with such hunger that it literally took his breath away. Her arms were around him as if she were clinging to a life preserver. When she finally came up for air he whispered, "Love, love what's the matter?"

She whimpered, "I saw the news! Oh John he's going to try to kill you to! Don't say anything just love me!"

Her passions were like a volcano as she practically dragged him into her bed. In moments most of their clothes were tossed on the floor. There were no preliminaries as she pushed him down with his socks and undershirt still on while Ann hadn't bothered to remove her nylons or bra. She was like a tigress as she launched her body onto his, ramming him from on top and impaling her desperate aching flesh with his trembling manhood. His gasp of surprise was smothered by her ravenous kisses. They rocked and lunged together as their torrid bodies became one.

Their arms and legs were quickly entwined together while their inner lust grew exponentially. Ann's moans and cries of pleasure urged him to greater acts of powerful love making and they soon climaxed in a delirious rapture of ecstasy as they both released within moments of each other. It took a few minutes for their breathing to come back to normal and their blood to stop racing as they still kissed with inexpressible joy. They both knew they were smitten with the most glorious of human passions. For those brilliant blinding seconds they were immortal, they were as God to each other. At the supreme moment they saw stars in each other's eyes or at least they thought they did. Somehow, in all the confusion and discord that swirled around Ann and John, Cupid had found them and smitten the new couple with his amorous arrows.

John finally caught his breath and spoke to his new bed partner in a low, husky voice. "Anne, I see in your beautiful eyes that you love me even if the rest of you didn't scream it to the heavens. I've never been loved by anyone as you have. No I'm not kidding. What I'm trying to say is I want you to marry me. You are so precious to me. I wasn't sure until now. If you feel we should wait for a few months for appearances sake I'm more than willing to wait. If you believe in my love than I must be considerate of your feelings."

Ann stared directly into his eyes. She spoke with fierce determination. "Fuck appearances John! I'll marry you tonight if you can find a JP!"

Mac laughed, "Wow! What a woman! Let's set it up for the first Saturday next month all right? Is that soon enough my darling?"

Ann moved him inside of her again and she smiled wickedly at him. "That will be fine love but I want to enjoy some coming attractions right now. After all, I should find out exactly what I'm getting, don't you think?"

Mac lay back and his smile was pure happiness. "Why am I so lucky? You feel so grand, so soft, so hot! Ohhhhh Ann please keep going!"

She leaned down and before she kissed him she whispered, "Your wish is my command. You feel so good inside me, I want it all. Don't hold back, baby. Just do me!"

Ann artistically moved and twisted in jerky squeezing movements as he grew larger and larger to fill her emptiness. He'd recovered quite quickly. The nearly naked blonde shamelessly reveled in the pleasure of his hot, throbbing hardness with each movement as it jolted to the inner core of her being. Their love making was slow and appreciative for quite awhile and then he rolled on top of her and banged her silly. She screamed with the thrill of multiple orgasms. There wasn't any need to speak. She wrapped her arms and legs around him so he couldn't possibly escape. She wanted him deep and dirty. Waves of jolting passion ripped through her as her body told her that this was THE man for her. He was tender and savage. He could gently arouse her or plunge inside her like a wild animal. She met his thrusts with eager willingness as again she burst with another mind numbing climax. At these sublime moments, Ann only cared about the here and now. She wouldn't think about tomorrow she just wanted him inside her and to be fucked as hard and fast as possible. Her body and soul demanded his powerful, penetrating thrusts with desperate insatiable longing. "Oh John fuck me! Please John harder! That's it baby! Don't stop! Do every inch! Oh yes, yes, I love you!"

The lust craving woman that was Ann Tindale thrilled with the unleashed passions of a wild beast as she felt his rising tension and his breathless anticipation. She continued to service him with some exceptionally expressive fleshy caresses. She knew he was close, close closest! Then his tingling cock finally drove him to a tremendous explosion of ecstasy. He actually screamed as his seed was wrenched out of him. His creamy essence gushed like an uncontrollable jet stream into her vaginal vortex. Ann continued to vigorously perform, extending his pleasure for many precious seconds. He gasped, "Oh my fucking god Anne! Oh my sweet Jesus! You're so fucking good!"

When he finally lay exhausted on top of her she still held him with her arms and legs. He whispered to her, "Sorry about the bad lingo. I couldn't help it."

Ann giggled, "Oh baby, I loved the way you love me. I just love to hear your words, after all I'm a very naughty girl. I hope you don't think I'm terrible loving you so soon after Ted?"

He just lay on her and enjoyed the feel of her chest moving up and down as she breathed. He felt the beating of her heart and the sticky fluid inside her. His member had become limp, but it remained lodged in her tender, passion sheath. He finally got his voice back to normal. "Ann I love you just as you are. In spite of my recent conduct I actually do respect you as a person a lot. I wouldn't change you for the world."

Ann felt content for the first time in days. Her radiant smile was on her face and in her voice. "Oh darling, I don't want to change you either. I'm just so afraid of losing you. When this terrible investigation is over I beg you to give some consideration to an idea I have."

John looked into her green gaze. "What's that Anne?"

She stroked his hair tenderly with her fingers while her pelvis began to clutch him ever so gently. She couldn't help being greedy for him. "I know you are a policeman and I don't want to change that but would you be willing to move to a small town somewhere? Someplace nice and quiet where it's less likely to be so dangerous? I'll do anything for you. I'll love you even better and more than tonight. I'll cook your food and work at raising our children. I'll work part time if you want. I'll care for you when you're sick or when you're sad. But love can you meet me part way and get a safer police job?"

Mac stared straight into her moist eyes as desire crept back into his penis with her gentle seductive movements. "There's no such thing as a perfectly safe police job Ann but you're right about NowhereVille being less likely to be so violent. Such a town would be safer for our kids to. All right Ann if that will make us happy, it's a small enough price to pay."

Her kiss was passion and gratitude and then she laughed. "Oh John you dear wicked boy! You still have your t shirt on! I need a little more of your complete attention, so why don't you take it off and get more comfortable?" Her coquettish smile encouraged him to continue the joy ride of mutual blending and soon they both forgot the outside world and its cares and dangers.

Next morning John and Ann were finishing breakfast when he said, "You know Ann it will take a little time to do what you want."

She looked at him a bit sharply. "What do you mean?"

John grinned at his soon to be wife. "Well first we have to figure out where we want to go. Like what state and then I have to find out if they have a job available for an old detective like me. Some of those small towns are quite tribal if you know what I mean."

Ann sighed with relief. "I know what you mean." She'd had a brief preminission that Mac might have changed his mind.

He went on. "But I promise you it can and will be done. As soon as we're married I'll start looking. It would be nice to go someplace like the Deep South where we wouldn't have to endure nasty winters. We have the whole country to choose from, although I don't think I want places like Montana or Minnesota. If you think winters are bad around here just go out there and see."

She hugged him, "Well darling you would have a better excuse to warm me up at night."

Her kiss was a solid gold thrill. He remarked, "I absolutely draw the line at Alaska though."

She couldn't keep her hands off him as they went to her door. "All right Mac, Alaska's out."

When he had gone she sat back down on her sofa and for the first time in weeks she was completely happy. She knew deep down in her heart of hearts that John had let himself go completely with her during their incredible love feast the night before. She felt fulfilled inside like she'd just won the lottery or gotten a free trip around the world. Her emotions and her physical being proclaimed to her mind that John was the boy for her. She didn't put on the news now but watched a game show rerun before she got fully dressed and went to work. Life would definitely go on.

Chapter

17

DEAD FAST

McBride's funeral home was an elegant tribute to the late Victorian period with its classy bay windows, occasional stained glass and exquisite woodwork that would have been virtually impossible to replace in the modern world. Rich, oriental carpeting adorned the visiting area which added tasteful coloring to the somber setting. Friends and relatives were gathered to talk or pray beside the pair of closed coffins. Recorded Bach organ music flowed in its eloquent softness, giving the room the perfect ambiance of solemnity required for such an occasion.

Frank and Mac spoke in hushed tones to Bender's son and daughter in law. As it turned out, Brian Bender was a new and rising star in the law profession. He was a fair haired slim man of an imposing six foot three and his eyes flashed with suppressed anger. His voice had the cultured clipped accent of Harvard University. His manners were impeccable as he greeted the guests and accepted the vast array of condolences. Everyone from the police department to the mayor to the news media to men and women in his profession came by. Even some of his most competitive opponents in the legal world gave him sincere condolences. In fact the biggest surprise that Brian received was when Judge Barker stopped in with tears in his eyes. The crusty old sarcastic judge had often embarrassed Brian in the courtroom. Barker expected and demanded no nonsense, professional and competent behavior from all lawyers, policemen and forensic experts, bar none.

The judge never suffered fools gladly. In other words, he took no prisoners. Not to say that Brian was a fool. He was far from it with his exceptional academic background and an IQ in excess of 150. But like all new lawyers he was learning his craft. Now, however, the judge was grasping his hand as Mac and Frank watched with disguised amusement. They'd never seen the judge act this human before.

Barker said in a voice surprisingly quiet and tender, "I'm so sorry Brian. Your loss is insupportable. I knew your father well. If there's anything I can do for you outside of the courtroom just let me know. If you need to talk with me, I'll listen. Your father was a credit to the force and an outstanding citizen. "

After Brian closed his slacked jaw that had been caused by the surprise of the judge's humane words he replied in a shaking voice. "Thank you, your honor. My father always referred to you as tough and fair. He respected you a great deal as I do. It's like someone has ripped out my heart and trampled it. Thank you so much for coming here. I must admit it's a pleasant surprise."

The judge grinned with a twinkle in his eye. "I bet you thought I was just a nasty old buzzard always waiting to pounce didn't you?"

He could see from Brian's face that he'd hit the mark. Barker laughed, "I have to keep you young cubs in line and make sure the older ones don't get complacent. Really Brian I'd do anything to bring your parents back for you. We can only hope now for justice."

With those last words the judge's face had become hard and grim.

Brian nodded and his eyes flashed with inner fire. "I hope when they catch the bastard he ends up in your court. Please excuse me but I've got to see to some more guests. I'd appreciate it if you could be so kind as to speak with Marion. She'll be quite grateful to talk with you. Thank you so much for dropping by."

The judge squeezed Brian's shoulder for a moment and then spoke to Brian's wife. The grieving lawyer went over to Frank and Mac and shook their hands. "Thanks for coming Frank, Mac. I understand you're still attempting to hunt the SOB down. It's too bad we still have laws against cruel and unusual punishments. I can think of a few from the medieval period that could be quite appropriate."

Frank's grin lacked the faintest trace of humor. "I know what you mean. You'd have to stand in line I suspect."

"Well I'd just get an injunction preventing anyone else from yanking a slow rope, but I guess we're too civilized these days."

Mac grasped Brian's hand. "I'm sorry for all of it. The chief was a great guy. It was an honor to work for him and I'm not just saying that. It's the God honest truth."

The lawyer recognized the sincerity and sadness in both men's eyes. "If I've lost a father and mother you've lost a close friend. I won't forget your kindness even if I have to cross examine you some time. I can assure you it won't be personal."

The three men chuckled a little and in moments Brian moved away to greet even more guests. It was incredible. The visiting hours had to be extended as more and more people came to wish Brian and Marion well. The two coffins were covered in flowers of every kind and description. The bereaved son was amazed at the frank admiration and grief by so many for so few. To be sure he knew some officials came just because it was there duty or to make brownie points. But for the most part the guests were honestly touched by the sadness of the occasion.

When the two detectives got through at the funeral home they stopped by Bill Flynn's office, just to check on things. They were soon ushered in to get an update. Flynn had his jacket off and was carefully perusing some papers when Mac and Frank entered the small room where the G-man did so much of his work.

Flynn looked up and smiled, "Hi guys, we've got our eyes on the big three, at least while they're off duty. Nothing exciting to report."

The two police officers sat down. Both men's faces were pale and drawn. Mac said, "I just saw Brian Bender at the funeral home. It's a fucking shame. Any big tidbits on the background checks?"

Mason and Summers are pretty straight forward but your boy Wagner has quite the military record. Apparently he was in the commandos and was a crack shot as well as sure handed with explosives. According to some conversations I had with a certain Sergeant Major who will remain unnamed, Wagner was a top marksman. I mean this guy could pick off a dime at a hundred yards and those are the sergeant's own words. Apparently Wagner was promoted to gunnery sergeant but unexpectedly after ten years of service he left when his re-enlistment came up. Everyone was surprised as he seemed very dedicated. Wagner was a bit of a loner. He didn't make any friends, just acquaintances if you know what I mean. Apparently he had no steady girl friends either. His relations with women such as they were apparently were limited to those brief encounters that can be purchased. My operatives did some checking at a massage parlor near his former base and he was an occasional visitor there. Wagner might not be our boy but I think we should focus on him first."

The two policemen nodded before Frank commented. "Perhaps we can get the search warrants set up and you guys could serve them. That way if the guy turns out to be innocent he won't be too upset with us. We always have to consider politics with all this bull shit."

Bill gave him a speculative look, "Yeah Frank, I know what you mean. You never know when your life might depend on whether or not a certain cop that you put through the ringer might have to save your ass."

Mac countered, "Precisely!"

Bill shrugged his shoulders, "All right gentlemen. I'll serve them but we'll have to get a federal judge to okay them because it's the only way I can legally serve the warrant. However it would be nice if you get a little more to put on the plate. If this guy is our guy I wouldn't want him getting off on a technicality like there wasn't sufficient cause to issue the warrant in the first place. I think we're close. If we could get one more connection I think it will fly. I'll be upgrading the three suspects to full twenty four hour surveillance on the morrow, so I don't think he'll be able to pull any more hits assuming he's the one. Maybe one of the other two is the one but I'm beginning to think our Mister Wagner is the most likely. "

The two homicide detectives got up to leave. "All right, we'll keep digging. I've got the warrant pretty well set up pending a little more homework. I'll put those comments of yours on the Wagner warrant when I get back. It shows he has the capability of committing those crimes, considering his marksmanship and demolition skills.

Mac finished yet another cup of incessant coffee while he reviewed the Wagner warrant. He thought gloomily what could possibly make an apparently fine soldier and cop go so far wrong? He slammed down the paper work and stared at the ceiling. His mind drifted to the contemplation of his new found world. His mind dreamily saw Ann naked and panting in front of him as he vividly recalled her demands and caresses. To him it was a miracle a gift from the Gods whoever they were. She was fire and angelic spirit. She was glorious and animalistic. She had opened her heart to him in every possible way. It frightened him to know how much he wanted her close to him, moving on him and with him through love's fantasy land. Perhaps her astonishing sensuality was the result of a rebound, perhaps not. He wasn't about to question his good fortune. Only a complete fool would walk away from love's arousing abundance.

"Captain? Hello Captain!"

Mac looked up with a blank expression on his face. A young patrolman stood in front of him. He was a well built dark haired, brown eyed tough looking guy who wore just the faintest trace of a smile on his ruddy face.

"I'm Mark Mason, Captain. Could I speak with you for a few minutes, Please?"

Mac motioned him to sit down. "I'm sorry Mark I have a lot on my mind."

Mark looked Mac straight in the eye and said, "Captain, I've heard through the proverbial grape vine that I'm actually suspected as being the cop killer? Is that the case?"

Mac raised his eyebrows. "The grape vine eh? Well to be frank with you I guess you are."

Mark exploded. "You've got to be fucking kidding me! I've only been on the force a year. I wouldn't have a chance to make those many enemies. Christ captain my old man's an ex marine. I love this country and the laws that made it great. I could never do such horrible crimes."

Mac saw the hurt, pain and anger in the younger man's eyes. "If it means anything to you your not our primary suspect. You happen to live within easy walking distance of a significant location in this investigation. I had hoped to spare you this if our more likely candidate had turned out to be the one. I'm sorry Mark but you know as a cop I have to check out everything, especially in a cluster fuck like this."

Mark tightened his jaws muscles and spoke with grim determination. "All right captain. Let me have an opportunity to get my name of this shit list. I want you and anyone else you wish to bring to search my home, garage and yard. I've already talked to my old man about this and he wants you to search his home also. In fact I'm even willing to be placed in solitary until the thug is caught or kills another cop just to prove I'm not the one!"

Mac stared in disbelief and not a little admiration at patrolman Mason. He finally said, "All right Mark if it will make you feel a little better we'll make the search. I don't think you need to go to the slammer. "

Mason got up and leaned towards Mac with a menacing gleam in his eyes. "Well captain it isn't about how I feel so much as I don't want any black marks on my record. I want to be a career cop and you don't get very far being suspected of being a mass cop killer do you?"

"I can't argue with that. You've got a point. I'll get Frank Tanner over here and we'll take you up on your offer. Again I'm sorry about all this. "

So they went to Mark's home and searched it from the cellar to the roof. They checked the garage and the yard with metal detectors and found nothing except some spare ammunition Mark had in his bedroom for his service revolver. They went to his father's home and found nothing there either. Both Mark and his old man even went to the trouble of helping them search a suspended ceiling in their respective basements. When it was all over and back at Mac's office Mac quietly said, "All right Mark you're off the list. There's really no need for you to place yourself in custody but if you want to stuff all this down my throat you've got a three week vacation coming up. Why don't you go to some place exotic like Hawaii or Rome? Just to show our hearts are in the right place we'll chip in part of your plane fair from our slush fund. I'm really very sorry about all this."

Mark had finally cooled down. "All right captain, apology accepted. I guess I'll need a vacation after this jolt. At least I have the satisfaction of knowing that I have a thorough commanding officer. I hope you get him by the time I get back. I think I'll opt for England. I've got some distant relatives over there and there's a ton to see." He grinned, "I'll send you my bill in the morning."

•———•———•

The Silver Slipper was a strip club and then some. Cathy entered the dark smoke filled den of iniquity to keep her appointment with Don Scarza. She watched for a few moments as she saw two women prancing and swirling naked in front of several gawking customers. The bar tender was serving drinks to one couple at one end of the long strand. One of the customers moved his hands over the scantily clad girl who was smiling and giggling at him. The loud disco music rocked the place as it drowned out almost every other sound. Finally she approached the bar keep and shouted in his ear, "I've got an appointment with Scarza! How do I find him?"

The bartender looked down at the flashy red head and smiled, "Come this way."

Cathy was led to a well concealed door, before passing through into an antisepticly clean, white hall that was brightly lit, complete with spotless, white walls and clean light green floor tiles. The contrast was quite an impact. She went from a dark, noisy choking place to this hall of opposites. Tony's former girl friend walked down the hall, her high heels clicking until she reached a polished oak door at the end of it. She knocked. "Come in!" rewarded her efforts.

Scarza looked up to see the sassy, shapely red head enter and close the door behind her. He asked "What can I do for you Doll?"

"Tony sent me. I'm looking for work as a table dancer. At least that's what he calls it. It looks more like a naked belly dance to me."

Scarza laughed with a raspy voice. "You're not far from the truth. Have a seat. What

Is your name kid?"

She sat down and gave him a sultry look, "I'm not a kid. I'm what Tony calls excellent material. He tells me I can make a shit load of money down here and he said that you could show me how. My name is Cathy Stone and I'm almost 18. So when do I start?"

Don leaned back in his chair and chuckled, "Well, well, well, you're quite the one. I love your brass chick. All right you're hired. You don't seem to have many illusions for someone your age and Tony told me a lot about you already."

A faint blush came to her cheeks. She asked, "Did he tell you everything?"

Don gave her a leering grin, "Everything tootsie. He told me your extracurricular activities were of the highest quality. However we don't have to be concerned about that for the moment."

Cathy gave him a piercing look. "What do WE have to be concerned about Mister Scarza?"

Don became serious, deciding to get right down to business. "All right Cathy let me draw you a map. You're walking right into what we euphemistically call the sex trade. There's a lot of lonely guys out there. There's also a lot of guys who just like to get a good look at a hot little number so they can jack off when they get home. There's all kinds as you'll soon learn. You can make a lot of money in this business if you're smart. If you're a little lucky and really good at your job skills you can easily dredge in a couple of grand a week. The trick is to save your money and don't burn yourself out. It's far better to do ten tricks a week rather than thirty because even though you make more money in the short run, you might pick up a nasty disease or get into the drug scene. Drugs can eat up money faster than the fucking IRS. As a matter of fact if you work for me you just do table dancing until you're eighteen. Don't worry babe you'll make about seven hundred dollars a week. I'll get Glenda to show you how to move on the floor and hustle drinks. You'll get felt up a lot but that's all. Are you really serious about becoming a rich lady?"

"You bet I am. I'm tired of welfare bull shit. Those ass holes couldn't find me a job if there lives depended on it. I'm going to try to avoid paying taxes as much as possible as well. I know eventually I'm going to have to fuck for my money and I don't want to be screwed by the government to."

Don chuckled and nodded at her pluck. "Right on, Cathy. Once you've worked here a few months, get a good lawyer and get incorporated. You can write off everything including your room rent. When you get established you can write off your bed, your clothes, your make up and transportation costs if any. If you do it right you can even write off a lot of your food expenses and travel trips. You can save some taxes by having your corporation pay you a modest, personal salary. Some of the money you get will be in cash and you can buy some gold coins and salt it away in a bank vault box and cash it in on a later date and claim it was handed down by a relative if there are any questions. I'll show you the ropes babe, every one. When you reach the tender age of eighteen I'll introduce you to some friends of mine that will get you started in some interesting sidelines to go along with your work here. I know this is going to sound corny but I do care about the girls who work for me. That's why I've got two tough bouncers on staff at all times. Even when you start sleeping around, we've got safe guards and high quality referrals. You can be a success as a party girl for some of our rich clients. All you have to do is keep your mouth shut in public and wide open in bed. I really do hate to see any of my girls get into drugs though. You're best approach is to avoid drugs even if they're offered free. Just say you are not into that. Tell you're client you're into sucking and fucking and you're damned good at both. I'm being straight with you. "

Cathy carefully appraised this handsome fair haired middle aged man, who seemed to be giving her excellent advice. "Well Mister Scarza when I'm eighteen I assume I will be at liberty to choose what I want or don't want to do?"

Don nodded, "Absolutely. I'm a happily married man so you don't have to worry about me. I've seen it all and believe me I've done it all before I met Loretta. Let's just say she leaves nothing to be desired so don't be afraid to ask me anything at any time. By the way you need an exotic name. How about Cathy Diamond or Ruby Redbreast?

Cathy laughed, "I think Cathy Diamond has a little more class so that will be fine. How about I dance wearing only a belt with big glittering fake diamonds on it?"

Don smiled, "that's the idea, give them a good look and a good show. I'm sure Glenda can fill you in. By the way I've got a message for you from Tony. In a way it should be your first lesson. I know you like Tony a lot. As you probably know or at least suspected he's married and certain pressure was brought to bear for him to permanently give you up. He's not a bad guy he just likes breathing even more than fucking to quote him. You can draw your own conclusions. You shouldn't forget that he did try to help your career such as it is. I guess that makes him better than most scoundrels. Believe me in this trade Cathy you'll run into far, far worse than Tony, trust me on that. If you play your cards right, you can be a millionaire well before you're thirty. Don't play the stock market because you know nothing about it. When you make some money put it into treasury bills or something else that pays a good return and is safe. Mortgage funds aren't bad. If you follow my advice you'll become a rich woman. Just remember in this life there's always a price to be paid. You have to decide what you want and how much you're willing to pay for it, do you understand?"

Cathy gave him an appraising glance before she replied. "I know I totally don't understand what you're telling me but I know I have to approach this as a business and not as a lark. It hurts that Tony has dumped me. I thought I was someone special. I literally did everything I could for him and just like that he tosses me aside. As you say at least he recommended me. So do you have a real cheep room I can rent while I get rich?"

"I think that can be arranged. Just speak to Glenda and she'll get you the keys and help you get set up." Cathy got up to leave. "Oh, and by the way, I'll be paying you under the table until your birthday. Just playing it safe. You're a bit young but good girls can be difficult to find. Let me know when you're ready to rock."

Scarza was right about one thing. Glenda sure knew her way around. In just a few hours, Cathy was set up and ready to work in the historic combat zone.

Chapter

18

TERROR'S EDGE

Herbert's gaze was riveted on the dominating presence of the Fuehrer. It seemed that each time he encountered the "great man", the power of that image became more glorious and intimidating. The shimmering, ghost like glow lit the darkest corners of Herbert's mind. He so wanted the great leader's approval and guidance. Vell Herbert, I see you've disposed of the police chief. They are frantic vith concern and fear. Fear is zee mightiest weapon you have at your disposal. Soon you vill have them at their knees. It vill become easier and easier to eliminate zem vith ambush and exploding vehicles. Vhen they bring in zee national guard you vill be able to kill them vith poisonous gas in their barracks. You vill be able to mine their offices. Because you are in their excuse for a police force you vill have zee access to do all this easily and efficiently. I think it is time that you killed off those busy bodies, Lloitenan Tanner and Hoffman Mackelroy. It should be easy to set up a trap for them. You can use one to bait zee other or you can kill zem both at zee same time. It was a stroke of genius when I told you to bug McElroy's office. Yu vill know everything that fool vill do."

Maniacal laughter filled Koehler's brain from the frightening phantom. The laughter grew and grew until Herbert was screaming to drown out the horrible sound. He fell to the floor but the cackling and hysterical laughter continued until he collapsed into senselessness.

⚬⚬⚬⚬ • ⚬⚬⚬⚬

Al was aware of the clock ticking. He noticed he was already five minutes late. He put on his police cap and hurried out his apartment to his motorcycle. He didn't like the noise it made so it was used as sparingly as possible. He had to get downtown quick. His colleagues didn't like to be kept waiting when night shift came around. Well, it was all part of the job, protecting the tax payers from crooks, drug lords and worse.

When Mac entered Ann's apartment that night they had hungered for something other than supper. It was left to simmer on the stove while they lay together, letting their own stimulated blood reach the boiling point. They were becoming more creative and experimental in their love play now as they switched positions with each other and explored the new sensations of unbridled passion. Ann's sex cries drove John absolutely wild. He kept penetrating inside her grasping, eager vaginal orifice or hungrily sucking mouth. They finished up in the exotic sixty nine position with Ann on top giving him the works. When he eventually released into her moist throat she swallowed and gagged at the same time at the still unfamiliar taste and texture of his love juice. When she finally got her voice she giggled, "After all honey, I was thirsty. You dragged little old me from supper because you're such an animal. I'm so helpless when you take me like this."

He rolled on top of her and kissed her still sticky mouth. "You sleazy vixen. It's you who have control of me. I have no choice when you look at me with those witches eyes of yours. You're a phantom of every delight. You're a winsome wench and you've stolen my heart. I've never said so much foolishness in my life and meant every word of it."

She wiggled her hips suggestively. "Hmmmmm, I think we should have some supper before we resume festivities. I need to keep your strength up. I expect Herculean service tonight. "

John gently pinched one of her nipples, "Hang on a second I have something for you."

He got up and went to find his pants. They were lying in the corner in a crumpled heap. Mac carefully searched his pockets until he found a small box. Returning to the bed, he handed it to her.

With eager fingers, she opened the box and gasped when she saw the exquisite engagement ring. Joy came to her lovely eyes and she cried out, "Holy fuck John! What a rock! Oh thank you my darling, thank you! The answer is yes!"

She slipped it carefully on her finger before savagely pulling him down again. Her kiss was pure fire. Her hand slithered over his manhood, moments before she guided it back inside her hot, fleshy tunnel. As they started the enchanting dance of love once again she gasped, "You know how to keep me hot, you devil! A girl doesn't have a chance with you! Oh John! Keep it coming just like that! You really are a letch and I love it! Yeah, make little Annie earn that rock! Make me work it off like this for the rest of my life! Oh God Johnny it feels so good! I need you so much!"

Supper could wait.

⊷━━━◆━━━⊶

Quite awhile afterwards, they finally were sitting at her table, wolfing down the evening repast. Sex gave both of them a very healthy appetite in more ways than one. He finally said, "I should have told you sooner but I think we're close to solving the case. We have a prime suspect but I can't tell you anything more right now. The truth about the killer is shocking if it's who we think it is.

"Oh John, please be careful. Don't take any chances."

He was touched by her genuine concern. "Don't worry love I don't intend to go down to such a worthless thug. All I can tell you right now is he's someone local and the truth surprised us as I'm sure it will you. He's still a suspect and it could be someone else of course. We're playing it carefully. I have a little time for us because I don't have so damned much paperwork to deal with now. You know Anne, I feel like I'm reborn when I'm with you. I was married before as you know but I swear to God you're a world apart. It's like she was silver to your gold."

She smirked with the cat got the mouse grin on her lovely face. "Now, now, now, you naughty boy. You should know by now that flattery will get you everywhere with me. Don't look at me like that. You finish your food and we can get reacquainted. After all I'm still working on the first installment on this marvelous ring. Where did you steal it?"

John chuckled as he forked another chunk of chocolate cake. , "that's a trade secret. That's a two karat ring I'll have you know. A certain to remain unnamed jeweler owed me a big favor and I got that wholesale. Do you like it?"

"Like it? I love it! I love the giver of the gift more. Seriously John you didn't have to do this. I know you want to make an honest woman of me. It's your heart I want. A ring is just stone and metal. But you are fire to my oil. I'll always treasure this moment."

Tears rushed to her eyes as she looked at the beautiful ring and then to her new found lover. She sniffed, "Now look what you made me do. I hope you aren't jealous of Ted. I remember him to. I still love him or at least his memory. Can you accept that? Can you accept my weakness?"

He went to her and embraced her for a long moment. "Hush, love! There's nothing weak about you. Ted was a fine man. I knew him well. I consider myself lucky to be worthy of your affection. That's why I want you to be the next and last Misses Mackelroy. Are you sure about us?"

She gave him such a dazzling smile, it took his breath away. "You listen to me, Mac! I'm so sure, I'll go to the justice of the peace in ten minutes. Now finish that cake and let's resume our little get together."

When supper was over she led him back to her bed and as she positioned herself on top of him she grinned, "It's time to play rock and roll baby. I'm already working on our wedding plans. Would you like Disneyworld or just a cabin in the woods someplace for our honey moon? Hmmmmm?"

In moments, he was hard inside her and she was moving with vigor. John was licking and sucking her nipples just to get the fires burning at full temp. She gasped, "I can't get enough honey! How long do you want the honey moon to last?"

His hands became totally possessive. Soon, he groaned, "Forever!"

She practically purred her approval of his amour. "You glutton! Be serious!"

"All right Ann. I guess I'll settle for a month but I expect you to spend your time barefoot and at the end of the exercise you're to be one hundred per cent pregnant."

She giggled while she clenched his urgent thrusts. "Well if you keep doing these outrageous things to my person, I suspect our chances are good. You really are a very naughty boy you know. I just bet when you were in high school you corrupted a whole bunch of innocent girls who didn't know what you'd be getting into. Tell me the truth love."

Her pussy grips increased exponentially. It felt much tighter to him as she pretended to be seducing the truth from him. "Oh Ann just like that! It's so good! I had a few girlfriends in high school but nothing like this."

Her squeezing became very intense. "Are you sure, Captain Jack? Come on make me feel full! Oh Jesus! Oh my sweet Jesus! Oh yes, yes! Oh my God!"

Her climax was just the threshold of a romp which lasted for over an hour. They loved and talked and planned their new life, their new world. Even though they caught only about four hours of sleep that night they were refreshed in the morning. They felt like new people and in a way they were. They were completely transformed by the power and majesty of true love. Their souls had finally and completely touched.

This time they kissed at her door and he whispered, "Don't worry love. I shall return."

She looked into his gentle eyes, "I know Mac, I know. So two weeks at Disneyworld and two in the back woods of West Virginia. "She gave him a dazzler. "And when you get me there I want you to take me apart. I want to try absolutely everything with you. Now get back to work before I drag you back in bed all day."

He gave her his most enchanting smile. "I'll go honey but when we're on that honeymoon you'll see what kind of an insatiable monster I am."

At the moment he opened the door to leave she gave him a love pat on his behind and quipped, "Promises, promises! This lady has to see to believe."

Mac gave her a wicked grin. "Believe it woman!"

Ann took about a half an hour to get ready for work. For the first time in weeks she was humming to herself with her new found happiness. She kept looking at the dazzling ring as if it would disappear from her hand. She felt like Cinderella two minutes before midnight. She got dressed in one of her most favored outfits, finished washing the dishes and got her stuff ready for work.

She picked her shoulder bag and opened the door. Ann gasped in shocked surprise. A policeman was standing in front of her with a gun aimed at her face. "Gooten tuck Frau Tindale. You vill come vith me please?"

Mac was into his second cup of coffee as he was going over the evening reports. The phone rang.

"Yeah, Mackelroy here."

"Goot morgin Herr Hoffman. I have someone here that I think you'll vant to talk to. I understand she's a close friend of yours, a very close friend. I bet you two get very cozy around zee midnight fire eh?"

Mac grew cold with the chill of abject fear coupled with sudden rage. He knew the answer even before it would be given. "Who is this?"

"Ah mine Herr you sound upset. Zee young lady is here safe vith me. I believe her name is Ann. If you want to see her alive again you must do precisely what I say. Do you understand?"

Mac's voice croaked in an attempt to keep from screaming. "Yes!"

"Very goot mine Herr. You vill come alone to zee Howard-Bateman building on Vernon street. As you know it is a deserted old office building. We'll be vaiting for you on zee second floor. I'll be watching to make sure you're alone. If you're not she dies. If you try any tricks, she dies. I've blind folded her so she can't recognize me. I'll let her go, it's you I vant. You're the head now and you must go. It's your life for hers. Let's see how noble you are."

Mac voice was thick with rage. "How do I know you've got her?"

"Oh ye of zee little faith. Wait a moment."

He heard the muffled whimpering of a woman and then a familiar voice screamed into the phone. "Don't do it jack. Bring the fucking army and waste this creep!"

Then he heard the sound of a blow. Ann cried out as she was hit and dragged away. He could hear her crying in the background. The familiar voice came back. To Mac's surprise the voice was angry. "Vat is it vith you Americaner vomen. They all think their heroines or something. That stupid bitch has no fear. You still vith me Herr Hoffman?"

Mac growled, "I'm still with you. You slimy son of a bitch! I'll kil you, you mother fucker!"

"Tsk! Tsk! Tsk! Temper, temper Mackelroy. You get here alone in twenty minutes or she dies."

There was a click and the return of the dial tone. Mac slammed the phone down in utter rage.

He had to think quickly and clearly. All right where was the fucking building? He looked at the wall map showing the streets of the city. Vernon Street was near the old factory section and not too far from the old, abandoned train station. Then a plan crystallized in his mind. He ran down to Frank's office. Tanner was sitting at his desk talking with someone. Mac cried out with all the frantic desperation in his voice that he'd ever have. "Frank get down to your fucking car and follow me right now. It's life and death! I'll explain over the radio! Come on Frank! Do it now!"

<hr>

Herbert was looking at Ann with a crooked smile on his face. So Frau Tindale do you think your new fancy lad vill show up? Hmmmm?"

She retorted with utter scorn in her voice. "He vill!" , mocking his accent. "And when he does buster he'll blow your fucking brains out!"

He actually laughed at her bravado. "I don't think so. You see as soon as I see him show up I'll have him in zee site of zis gun. You can have zee pleasure of seeing him eliminated for the good of zee Reich. Zee fuehrer has ordered it you see."

His voice was calm and conversational as he watched the street in front of the building.

She snarled with an inner rage she hadn't known existed. Standing just a few feet away from her blindfolded eyes was the monster who'd killed her Teddy. . "You're as nuts as a fucking fruitcake! The fucking Fuehrer's been dead since 1945. The cowardly bastard shot himself in the mouth when the Russians were knocking at his bunker door!"

"Tsk, tsk, tsk! Such fowl language from such a pretty lady. Vell zee Americanner vomen have no class. I bet you've never listened to

Brahms or Bach like I have. But you have no culture, no breeding, no proper civilizing influences. Zee fuehrer wanted to bring his great ideas to zee world. He tried to bring order and security to us all. But zee Jews in America and zee communist Red devils from mother Russia were his downfall. That bastard Roosevelt and zee Jews he controlled hired the industrialists to bomb holy Germany into rubble. Zee fuehrer tried to save zee world and he vas betrayed by zee degenerate scum of zee earth. Vell I have come to change all that. Ah here comes zee lover boy now. Right on time! How touching! Oh he does look handsome. I can see why you spread you're legs for him. Vell he soon vill be dead and so vill you. "

She struggled against the ropes that bound her hands. The blindfold effectively prevented her from running anywhere. She shouted, "I'll stop you, you evil son of a bitch!"

A split second later, he'd gotten over to her and slapped her hard across the face. She cried out and in that moment he stuffed a rag into her throat. He snarled, "That vill keep you quiet you miserable vixen!" Herbert was livid. This loud mouthed bitch had taken him away from the window for the precious seconds he could have used to blow away the intrepid captain, before he'd had a chance to enter the building. He hit her again for good measure.

Mac slowly opened the entrance door to the long abandoned Howard Bateman building. It would be to his advantage to approach this killer as silently as possible. Just maybe he might be able to catch him by surprise. The inside hall was quite dark except for a little light let in by the door and a half boarded window. It always amazed Mac how cold abandoned buildings were, even in the dog days of summer. He moved slowly, attempting to make sure that the floor didn't have any creaking spots. It proved to be quite solid and the remains of a ragged, worn out carpet helped smother any sound his progress might make. . He listened with deep concentration to every sound from the occasional drip of water to distant traffic noise.

Ever so softly, Captain Mackelroy approached the stairs to the right of the useless elevator shaft. He crept up each step as if he were consolidating new territory. Although the building was old and the steps wooden, he was not betrayed by any tell tale creak. Mac kept his movements slow and deliberate, allowing time for Frank to get into position about a block away. Tanner had come in from a different direction to make sure he was out of sight. Mac drew out his gun and released the safety. His heart pounded with increasing rage and apprehension with each ascending step. At least he'd gotten one major break. There was a hallway at the top of the steps which meant that unless the thug exposed himself, he could not see Mac's quiet assent. Thoughts flashed through his mind. Questions without answers fear without hope plagued his mind. How the fuck had the maniac gotten to Anne? Wasn't Wagner supposedly being followed by the Fucking Bureau of Investigation? Maybe it wasn't Wagner after all. He reached the second floor landing and snuck over to the first door. He saw Ann lying a few feet beyond the entrance to a long abandoned office. She was tied and blindfolded. Well the bastard had to be in one corner or the other. Should he jump right or left? He listened and looked at Ann. She was sticking her left leg towards the left. Was she pointing towards something or someone? Or was the gesture meaningless? He saw the gag in her mouth and understood. She couldn't know he was there. Was it an act of faith on her part? The leg stayed in the same position as if deliberately pointing. He waited a few more seconds, hoping to hear a noise from the cop killing monster. Only the distant sounds of traffic invaded the silent building. Should he wait here for Frank? Should he jump in? Should he try to reason with the bastard? It was as if his entire life came down to this most critical of moments. In those precious seconds, he made the soul wrenching decision. He mentally spoke the Gladiator's prayer to himself, straining for the courage to act! 'Hail Caesar! We who are about to die, salute you'. He gritted his teeth. Gun in hand, he leapt through the doorway.

Chapter

19

SHOWDOWN

Ann heard a loud thump followed by a quick shot and a blip along with corresponding grunts of pain. She felt so helpless and useless with her hands tied behind her back, her mouth gagged and eyes blind folded. She had a vague idea where the doorway was and she slowly wriggled toward the source of the very faint draft.

Herbert saw the blur of the captain come hurtling through the door and for a split second he was surprised because the policeman was taking quick aim. Apparently the cop had guessed right. Herbert fired with the expert training of an excellent marksman. The silencer lowered the sound of his shot to a weird sounding blip. A split second later Mac's gun roared its own defiance and Herbert's left arm felt the shock of hot metal. He was thrown back against the wall.

Herbert's bullet had penetrated Mac's right thigh. The captain's sudden, quick attack had saved his life. However, the shot felled him. In addition, the stunning impact of hitting the floor caused his gun to fly out of his hand. It landed ten feet away on the dusty hardwood floor. For a moment there was silence and then it came. It started as a chuckle and grew to a maniacal laugh as Herbert struggled to his feet and slowly crossed the short distance to the hand gun. "Very goot captain. You actually scored zee point. I think I'm lucky though. The bullet did little more than graze zee arm. I better get that gun out of harm's way."

He kicked the gun away, then calmly resumed his little chat. "You see Herr Hoffman it's all about order! Zee new order! Zee fuehrer has chosen me, Major Herbert Koehler as the first to bring in the new Reich! You silly

Americaners with your loose vomen and big cars. You lazy fools who lack culture or discipline."

He knelt down even closer so Mackelroy could more easily see the look of triumph on his face. "You see Mackelroy it vas easy to trap you. I put a bug in your room. Hahaha! I knew everything important you were going to do. I knew where to find your pretty little slut. I knew you were starting to get on my trail. But you were wrong Herr Hoffman. You thought that worthless vorm, Albert Vagner had done it all. That spineless piece of shit couldn't find his own way to the toilet! He's a veakling! He's a fool! It was I, the true savior of Germany who killed your fellow degenerates."

Mac stared into the glazed eyes that gleamed and glistened with an inner fire he could only guess at. The laugh came again. "I think I'll make you suffer first. I have plenty of zee ammo for my father's gun. You see my mother kept it for me though she didn't know what I vould do vith it, of course. She thought it vas just a memento, but it was my key to your down fall, you supercilious idiot."

The deranged cop stood up and snickered, "It's time to end this farce. I vill first put bullets in your remaining leg and arms and then you can watch your little tramp die in front of your eyes. Then you vill join her. A fitting end to a vorthy adversary! You were better than zee rest, I think."

He cackled with his over the edge laughter as he raised his weapon.

"Freeze sucker!"

Mac caught a glimpse of Frank appear in the doorway, but Herbert's back had been turned to the door for that critical moment. To his and Frank's amazement Herbert whirled around and fired and caught Frank in the stomach crumpling him to the floor. With a supreme act of will and training, Frank actually kept hold of his weapon and fired back. Herbert was thrown back as the bullet tore through the right side of his chest. The infamous forty five clattered to the wooden plank floor just inches away from Herbert's twitching hand. Mac painfully crawled over and picked the hand gun up, securing it from any further destructive mischief. To his amazement the insane patrolman was still breathing. At that moment he aimed the forty five at the head of Al Wagner also known as Herbert Koehler. Mac knew that he could easily make it look like a suicide. It was time to end it.

Frank moaned with a trembling voice. "Don't do it Mac! The scumbag isn't worth it!"

Mac stared at the limp form of patrolman Wagner who apparently thought he was some Nazi avenger. It was the most difficult decision of Mackelroy's life. His finger itched to pull the trigger and eliminate this creature from the face of the earth. He thought of all the cops this slug had killed. Just a tiny pressure from his trembling finger pressed against the metal trigger and he could terminate this struggle for all eternity. It would be so easy. Just a little twitch and this maniac could be done away with. Yet something deep inside him kept his finger tense and motionless. Perhaps it was his training. Perhaps it was his religious background. It was as if two magnetic poles were pulling on him, at the same prolonged moment. To kill or not to kill, that was the ultimate question.

Frank's voice broke through his steaming brain. "Don't Mac! He's a piece of worthless shit! Don't fuck up your career because of him. Trust me!"

At last, Mac lowered the weapon. In that moment, he wished that Frank's hit had been more decisive. He'd done the right thing but every fiber of his being was rebelling against his choice with a plethora of torturing regrets. With sheer agony shooting through his thigh, he crawled over to retrieve his own gun and somehow holstered it. Then he crawled over to Frank and gave him Al's forty five. "Hang on Frank! I'm going to free Ann and she'll call the cavalry. You still got your gun?"

Frank's nod was all that was required before Mac painfully moved over to Ann. "it's all right, love. You're safe now."

First he removed her blind fold and then pulled out the rag from her moaning mouth. "Don't say anything Ann. I love you. Frank's hit bad. You can save his life."

He untied her wrists as he spoke. "When I get this damned rope untied go down to the first floor and out to my car. It's right in front of the building. On the front seat I have a cell phone. Call 911. We're at the abandoned Howard-Bateman building on Vernon Street. Tell them that captain Mackelroy demands ambulances from Saint Vincent's hospital like yesterday. That's the closest. Tell them to hurry there are three cops down! Now tell me what you should say!"

Ann saw the face of the trained professional now. He wasn't afraid. John was disciplined and calm and it rubbed off on her. She stood up and gently massaged her wrists. "I call 911 and tell them there are three policemen down and badly hurt at Vernon Street. They are on the second floor of the Howard-Bateman building and to get Saint Vincent's ambulances over here right now."

Now go! I'll hold the fort here!"

Ann ran down stairs as fast as her trembling legs could carry her. Mac crawled over to Frank who was lying on his side. His hands were bloody as he held the right side of his stomach. "They're on the way Frank. Hold on buddy. Help is on the way. Frank you're the bravest son of a bitch I've ever known. You'll get a fucking medal for this!"

Frank grimaced in pain as he tried to laugh. He rasped, "Christ Mac Plese don't make me laugh….it hurts to much. But we got the bastard at last."

Mac had tears in his eyes, "Yeah Frank we got one for Bender. Just hang on. They'll be here soon. Don't you dare die on me. I'll never forgive you if you do."

Tanner was breathing shallow but he was still awake. He grinned up at his boss. "It'll take more than one bullet from that bastard to put me out. I'm tougher than I look."

They heard the siren in the distance. "You saved my life Frank and you saved Ann."

"Stow it….You'd have done the same for me."

Mac tried to smile at his friend but the tears in his eyes were spoiling the intended effect. "I'm going to the head of the stairs, you're going out first and no back talk. That's an order."

Frank smiled back. His face was pale and shock was beginning to set in. "Yes Sir Herr Hoffman."

Mac chuckled, "I'll make sure they save your ass so I can beat the shit out of you later for that wise crack. I'll make you eat that medal."

Frank gasped a chuckle and Mac crawled to the stairs. In moments he saw two Para meds running up the stairs with a stretcher.

Mac yelled "Get the man right behind me first. He's got a nasty stomach wound. I can wait! Fucking do it!"

To his relief Frank was carried down to the Ambulance in less than a minute. Ann was back at his side, "I was out in the road waving them hear. I wanted to make sure the idiots found us quick. "

Mac was sitting up against the door frame grinning up at his intended. "I think the bastard is still alive. So keep your distance. I've got his gun. "

She knelt beside him. Tears streaked her cheeks. Her hand instinctively clutched his, but for the moment, she couldn't say anything. All she could do was look into his troubled eyes.

"Anne, please forgive me. I didn't know the prick had bugged my office. You almost died because of my carelessness and that evil man. Please can you find it in your heart to still love me after all this?"

Her answer was a long breathtaking kiss. "Oh you valiant fool! My sweet, sweet boy. Everything will be all right. I hear another siren right outside. You'll be well in no time and then we'll shack up in Disneyworld or where ever you want to take me and I mean take me."

There eyes locked. It was as if both were hit by a ton of bricks. "I love you Ann."

Two more medics got to them as they saw Ann kissing Mac again. One of them coughed.

Mac regained his voice of authority. "Hi guys, you better get the other one in that room over there. He's got a serious chest wound.

One of the medics looked down at Mac's bleeding leg and pulled out a tourniquet from a pack. " I better put this on before you loose anymore blood. It'll only take a second. I'll get you down as soon as the other one is attended to."

In moments the tourniquet was secured on Mac's leg. Thirty seconds later, Al Wagner was being carried down the stairs on a stretcher.

Ann and a medic helped Mac down to the ambulance a few minutes later. Then they took off to the nearest emergency surgery rooms at Saint Vincent's.

⸺ • ⸺

Mayor Flarity actually stopped in to see Mac a few days later. "Good morning Captain Mackelroy. I've got some great news for you. It looks like a promotion is in order. You did a hell of a job!"

Mac growled, "Get those media jackals outa here!"

The mayor turned and waved them out. "Sorry about that Mackelroy. They are persistent chaps."

Mac glared at the politician he so thoroughly despised. "Frank Tanner is the brave one. He saved both me and Ann Tindale. So give HIM the fucking medal and promotion."

The mayor was taken a little aback. He'd expected some appreciation from the hard crusted dick head. "So I heard, so I heard. I'm sure Frank's going to get quite a commendation. He'll probably get promoted to. You know he might even get to be captain."

Mac had no use for those glass rimmed gray eyes or that artificial grin. "This is off the record mister mayor but you can take your promotion and shove it up your ass sideways. I'm getting married just as soon as I get out of this place. I'm going to find a small town some place in the sticks and get away from this madness. If you really want to do something for us you can write me a glowing letter of recommendation seeing as how Bender didn't make it, the poor bastard!"

"If you want that letter Mac you can have it. I must say you don't show much gratitude."

"That's not true Mayor. I've got plenty of gratitude to Frank Tanner. He's worth ten of you. Now get out and go back to stealing from the voters."

The mayor stood up with a pronounced frown on his face. He scowled at Mac who was comfortably lying on the clean hospital bed. "You know Mac you really are a caustic son of a bitch."

"That's better Tom. Coming from you I consider that a compliment. Just make damned sure that letter is solid gold and don't let the door hit your ass on the way out."

Later that day Ann was in to see him. She was conservatively dressed, having just gotten out of work. She ran to him breathless and her kiss was very stimulating. Mac grinned in obvious appreciation. "Another kiss like that and you better shut the door."

"If I didn't think I would reopen the wound I'd take you up on that. You're worth waiting for you big lunk!"

Mac grew serious, "How's Frank?"

She smiled, "He was hurt pretty bad but he'll pull through. It was touch and go for the first forty eight hours. They've got him pumped with antibiotics and he's on intravenous feeding. It'll be awhile before Frank gets a rock solid meal. He was in surgery for over six hours. A nurse told me to tell you he'll be right as rain in a couple of months."

Mac held Ann's hand as if it would disappear. "Ann I really mean what I said. I can't take any more of this shit. We're going to Smallville U.S.A. even if I have to take a cut in pay. I never want to see you in danger again."

"You know when that creep said he was going to kill us both I was praying to god like I never prayed before."

Mac held her close and smirked, "I hope you didn't make any promises you can't keep."

She gave his face a playful pinch. "Oh you! Can't you ever be serious? I prayed that if God got us off the hook that he'd convince you to give this up. He answered my prayer big time, right across the board. "

Mac's voice became very tender and he gave his bride to be a serious look. "I see the soul of an angel in your lovely eyes. You know Anne, you must believe me I would bring back Ted if I could. I know that's easy to say and it probably doesn't mean much, but what I'm trying to tell you is that I'd never do anything to hurt you."

She gave him another very dramatic kiss. "I know love. They found the bug by the way. It was something he saved from his army days."

"Is that creature still alive?

"Afraid so! It figures the scalpel couldn't slip at the right time. Look on the bright side, you'll be able to pull the switch."

Mac smirked with little humor. "Not likely, Massachusetts has no death penalty. Maybe he can be sold to the Chinese for experimental research."

"I don't think they'd have him Mac."

"Probably right." His hand was mischievously moving up her leg and flank. When it inevitably reached her large, tempting breast she slapped him away. "Behave! You're an injured invalid and I've come to help you recover, not harm you. Oh John I could just eat you alive!"

Mac had a wicked gleam in his eye, "That's a thought."

Ann retorted with mock disgust, "Oh you! Men!"

Two days later Mac received a totally unexpected visitor. To be sure, most of his co workers had dropped in. Brian Bender had stopped by and Judge Barker had actually spent an hour with him one night a little after normal visiting hours. He'd even got a brief visit from an apologetic Bill Flynn. He was sorry that the killer had somehow eluded the F. B. I. surveillance team.

However, he was completely unprepared to see the mafia Don, standing in front of him. Of course the patrone was dressed immaculately. Mac raised his eyebrows with astonishment.

"You're the last man I expected to see mister Genovezzi. Have a seat."

The boss answered dryly, "Thanks, you look like you're coming along fine. Have the nurses been good to you?"

Mac couldn't help grinning conspiratorially at the Don. "Ann Tindale has been making sure I get the best of care and letting the nurses know that I'm spoken for. So what brings you here. We're on opposite sides of the fence you know."

"Well captain I admire a brave man. I looked in on your friend Frank Tanner and it looks like he'll recover. He's doing a lot better. They'd only let me see him for a moment. He told me to tell you he's coming back to whip your ass."

Mac laughed, "You know I'll tell you something funny that just dawned on me. When the mayor was in here a few days ago I basically told him to bugger off. I couldn't stand him being in the same room with me and yet I talk to you like you were my grand father or something. I guess it goes down to the old saying hate the sin and not the sinner."

The elderly crime boss looked contemplative for a few moments. "You know Mac we don't live in a perfect world. In one way or another we all play the cards we're dealt. If your father had been a major crime figure like mine was, you might have chosen differently. I think the main difference between myself and the right dishonorable Tom Flarity is that I'm an honest crook and he's a hypocrite of the worst sort. I do what I do for the good of the family. Believe it or not, we're attempting to become more legit. In two more generations we'll be as respectable as anyone else and they'll be new crooks to replace us. I know you won't believe this but I wish deep down inside I could have lived differently. I don't take any satisfaction in seeing an enemy destroyed or innocent persons hurt. I admire men like you and Frank and Al Bender because you have principles. You play by the book and because of that I play by the rules also. I don't kill cops Mac. I never have and I never will. If you believe nothing else, believe that."

Mac became pensive, "You know it's a strange world. When I was a kid I used to watch the cops bag the robbers. You know, Robert Stack, Clint Eastwood and all the rest. Everything was black and white. Life was crystal clear like antique glassware. Then I got older and the vision became blurred somehow. White was white most of the time but occasionally there were gray areas. I've never condemned a man if he had to steal a loaf of bread because he was hungry. Sometimes I wonder if the worst crooks aren't the guys in the jails but the ones who slink around in high places. You know what I mean?"

"I think so, captain. You know we have a code of honor believe it or not. After all, it's such an unjust world. We've learned over the years that you get as much justice as you can purchase or grab with your bare hands. Just look at the O.J. Simpson case. How many hours do you think it would have taken to convict him if he'd been a poor black janitor making twenty thousand bucks a year?"

Mac couldn't argue the point. "I know, the system sucks but it's what we got. I heard someone once say, "Democracy is a poor form of government. However, the others are worse.""

The Don nodded and stood up, relinquishing the comfortable chair. "Well I better be going. I've always got things to attend to. You know captain if you ever want to stop by for a drink just to talk, you're always welcome. Peaceful co-existence, eh?"

As the Don stood up Mac extended his hand. "Thanks for the sentiment mister Genovezzi It was nice of you to stop by. By the way I don't think we'll need Tony Visconti to testify. Actually I'm glad he did what he did. His information was the vital link. Indirectly it saved my life. Could you thank him for me?"

The boss smiled, "He'll be happy to here that. He's really a good boy at heart. He just has to grow up a little more and figure out how to avoid being stupid."

Mac glanced up at the ceiling. "Don't we all."

Genovezzi waved and was gone.

Mac turned on the television awhile only to watch the red Sox blow another three run lead in the ninth inning. He shut it off with disgust and shook his head. "Some things never fucking change."

Chapter 20

HOLLOW JUSTICE

Two weeks later, Mac moved all his furniture and personal effects to Ann's apartment. What they couldn't fit they stored or sold off. When she was at work he would lie back on her bed and watch TV or walk a little to keep up his muscle tone. She really enjoyed taking care of him in every way. The food was infinitely better than the hospital fare and Mac found strength creeping back more and more every day. At first their lovemaking was confined to gentle, tender sessions of mutual oral love but as his leg improved and his strength returned she would ride him from the top, exhibiting all her deepest feelings for her intended.

Needless to say Mac felt great most of the time. She made sure his dressing was properly changed and the nurse who would come in once per day, mentioned that he was progressing nicely. Ann smirked when she thought of the interesting activities which verified that Mac was gaining in strength and endurance.

Mac riley commented, "That's more accurate than you can imagine."

Of course they were making plans for the honeymoon and decided not to put too much strain on his leg by standing in lines for eons at Disney world. Ann gave him a wicked smile, "You'll have to expend your stamina for more important activities than waiting for Mickey Mouse rides, my sweet lad. I think we should keep you relaxed and totally corrupted by your new strange woman don't you?"

Mac was shamelessly staring at her completely undressed condition as she sprawled on top of him and winked at him. His hands automatically roamed all over her tempting curves and moist, tender places, including her lush portal of love.

She was practically purring. "Hmmmm that's nice Mac. I see you're warming me up again. You really are an insatiable letch you know. My mother warned me about guys like you. But of course, I wouldn't listen and now look at me. It's far too late to reform."

His hand noticed her wetness increasing, "Was it a warning or advanced publicity do you think?"

She gave him a very appraising look, encountering those mischievous eyes of his. "I'm not sure but I think it's time to give you some more exercise. I've got to keep your blood flowing and your muscles kept in perfect condition. I certainly wouldn't want you to get flabby on me."

She gently maneuvered him into her while she talked, "Oh that's so nice Mac. You really aim to please. I expect much more of the same. I think we'll go camping in that little lake resort in Virginia. We can do a little sight seeing on those rare occasions when I can get away from your wicked clutches."

He was meeting her lunges now and enjoying the thrilling sensations of their joining. "Well Ann I don't think that will be very often. After all I've got to produce an heir and I predict it will take many long hours of hard work to make sure that occurs."

She moaned, "I bet! At the rate you're going you'll have the job done before we ever get hitched! Oh God it's so good!"

Her kiss sent a fiery jolt through his very soul, while her movements increased to a torrid frenzy. When they reached fever pitch, she climaxed for him. She was beyond excited when they were together like this. She sighed, "I bet you want me to continue you glutton. You've really ruined me you know. You just love to keep me nice and spoiled."

He gasped, "I'm the one who's spoiled! Nice and quick! Just like that!"

She gave him a demonic smile when he finally erupted inside her clenching flesh. "Naughty, naughty, naughty! Look what you just did to your helpless little girl!"

He was still trying to catch his breath. "Christ woman, you're anything but helpless. You're a temptress and I can resist you nothing."

She laughed, "A month beside the lake and we'll be all alone with nothing to do except what we're doing right now. Do you think you'll survive? After all you're doing a nympho and you otta know all nymphos never get enough. Am I your little nympho darling?"

He grinned, "If you're not you're damned close. The lake sounds lovely. Do you think we'll get a chance to swim in it?"

⋯⊷━━━━━━━⊶⋯

The day of the wedding was the following Saturday afternoon. Late summer had generously graced New England with its fairest gifts, a cloudless sky and a dry 80 degrees Fahrenheit. The effect was perfected by that telltale hint of crisp coolness which insured chilly evenings even during Indian summer. Frank still looked a bit pale and shaky. However, he gallantly fulfilled his role as the best man. Ann's father gave her away shortly before the marriage vows were exchanged. The First Congregational Church was a lovely, turn of the previous century building with massive stained, glass windows depicting Christ, glorious with angels and representations of the Holy Spirit flanking the ornate walls.

Ann was stunning in her flowing wedding gown. To adhere to custom, the gloves, waste band and veil were in a light shade of yellow, signifying that this was her second marriage. However, she'd had the Taylor refine the lines of the dress to imitate a historic, Georgian style that had caught her fancy. She was the living picture of arcaic elegance as she posed for the cameras. The new bride held a dozen roses in one hand while shaking the hands of each departing guest as they stood at the entrance to the church. . Mac had a chance to talk with many of his old friends and cronies. Without exception they all wished him well along with compliments about Ann's exquisite taste in gowns.

Later they enjoyed some excellent food and drink at the reception hall. The establishment was rented by the police department for such events. A D J was systematically flipping out one song after another, filling the large room with loud music that sometimes made it hard to hear what was said. For this reason, many were forced to shout at times when a particularly wild number hit the skids.

Frank caustically mentioned, "When you get back from lala land they're going to be dealing with the Nazi nutcase. I figured you'd like to be in at the kill."

Mac sipped some more Champaign, "Wouldn't miss it for the world. You look good Frank. Thanks for attending. You're my best man in more ways then one. It'll take more than one slimy bastard to take you out thank God."

Frank gave him a lop sided smile, "Yeah, well I'm starting to think the old timers were right, shoot first and ask questions later. If I hadn't warned the bastard, I wouldn't have missed so much ice time."

"Yeah, they sure had a lot of common sense in those days. It's a different world now and I don't know if it's better or worse. Let's just say it's different."

Frank chuckled as he changed the subject. "You know Mac, the mayor is pretty pissed off at you. I guess you didn't say the right words to the old boy."

Mac's grin was almost demonic. "Yeah, I know he's actually considering you for police chief. Good for you Frank! As far as mayor tom Flarity goes, he can piss up a rope."

They both laughed as Ann looked on with a wicked smirk on her face. "Seriously Frank both of us wish you the best. Just remember one thing Frank."

"What's that?"

Mackelroy became conspiratorial as if sharing a great trade secret. "Make sure you have an unlisted number."

Frank chuckled between sips of wine. "You got that right. I'm tempted to confiscate all forty fives also but they probably have a law against it."

Frank got up to rescue his wife from a particularly aggressive dancer. . "See you later you love birds. Don't do anything I wouldn't do."

Ann giggled, "Christ Frank! That's like a blank check.

When they finally had a free moment, she whispered like the tempting devil in his ear. "You really are a beast you know and I expect you to act like one the very second we reach the cabin."

His eyes met hers with the wickedest gleam she'd ever seen. "Your wish is my command great lady. What do you say?"

"Let's blow this joint."

⋅•◦•⋅ — • — ⋅•◦•⋅

Mac and Ann were back in town after a 3 week honeymoon that both of them considered to be the equivalent of any ancient orgy of Rome or anywhere else. Ann was definitely pregnant from the incessant interplay which had occurred even before the honeymooning had taken place. They actually fit in some time, sight seeing. They saw Mount Vernon, Arlington cemetery and Robert E. Lee's home. They walked arm and arm through the battlefields of Gettysburg, Sharpsburg, Bull Run, Fredericksburg and Yorktown. They explored the lovely colonial homes at Williamsburg and even looked at Jefferson's home at Monticello. But most of the time was spent in very serious baby making efforts which obviously were successful.

When Ann told Mac she noticed a surprised look on his face. She spoke in mock disgust. "Well, don't look so shocked love. Just think of all the wicked things you did to me for over two months. A girl just doesn't have a chance with you around. You made me miss my period, you randy beast!" Then she gave him one of her most demonic smiles, "Besides I loved every second of it!"

"If it's a boy I want him to be called Percival."

Ann put her hand over her mouth in mock shock. "Oh my God John! What a horrible name. Percival Mackelroy. It sounds like an upper crust limey with a roll of dimes up his ass."

Mac chuckled, "All right how about Foster?"

Ann gasped, "Worse and worse! How about mark?"

Mac tested the name. "Mark Mackelroy, it does have a certain flair to it. Sounds quite distinctive without undo affectation. All right! Mark Mackelroy it is!"

Ann gave him her singsong teasing voice. "But honey bun what if he's a she?"

Mac came right back with, "Zelda!"

She howled with laughter. "You've got to be fucking kidding! Get real! That's a horrible name!"

Mac retorted, "It's distinctive, nobodies likely to forget a name like that."

Ann groaned, "That's the whole problem with that name. How about Julia or Margaret?"

Mac quipped, "I like the alliteration. My vote is for Margaret."

"But what if we have twins my lusty laddie?"

Mac stared at her; "If they turn out to be identical we'll have to put ID tabs on them. I knew two brothers in college who were identical and it could get quite confusing. They used to switch girlfriends all the time. They'd compare notes and give each other enough info to pull it off in more ways then one."

Ann threw up her hands in mock despair. "Men!"

The police commendation ceremony was quite the solemn affair as Frank Tanner was the heroic centerpiece at the function. The medal of valor was presented to him along with an embossed citation. The mayor praised his conduct in saving the lives of captain Mackelroy and Ann Tindale. Mac and Frank got equal recognition for the capture of the cop killer, Al Wagner. To Tanner's great surprise, he actually was promoted to chief of police.

Later when they were sitting around eating the prime rib and drinking anything and everything Mac mentioned to Frank, "Flarity did it to spite me, but I don't care. Ann and I are leaving Worcester for good anyway."

Frank raised his eyebrows, "Christ Mac I didn't know that! I don't get a chance to hear you call me boss! What a let down!"

Mac gave him a deadpan face. "All right boss, we decided to leave this den of iniquity almost two months ago. We need a safe place for the kids to grow up and Worcester County ain't it."

Frank smirked before sipping some more wine. "I see what you mean. Well this town has some pretty bad memories for us both but I'll stick it out for the time being."

"Before I leave I'm going to give you my special file I have on Tom Flarity. Perhaps you may find it useful if you need to lean on him to help him do the right thing. I've got enough on the bastard to possibly indict his ass. Get some legal council first and make sure it's a lawyer from out of town. There's a certain hard nosed judge who I'd love to see clean out Tom's clock."

Frank winked back. "Sounds like the right honorable Arthur P. Barker."

"No shit, he'd be great on two counts. He'd make sure you did your homework and he won't show mister fucking T any quarter if you get a conviction. I'll give you the files tomorrow."

The new chief became suddenly thoughtful. "So where will you go?"

Mac sipped some more wine before answering. "A small town in southern Georgia. The letters of recommendation I got from fucking Flarity did the trick, especially when they found out I helped snare the notorious cop killer. I'll get paid almost as much and living expenses down there are much lower than up here. I'm going to be a deputy sheriff with detective duties. I'm second in command again. They're really excited to have me on the force and they haven't had a murder in that town in thirty years. It's like going back to the fifties. I'll be working for Sheriff Hayes and when I get settled down there I'll contact you so we can stay in touch."

"So when are you leaving Mac?"

"Well I've got to hang around for the Wagner case but hopefully we'll be settled down there before Christmas. It'll take me a few months to wrap things up here and some time to get a house picked out down there. Just think I'll own my own home and have a fresh start. You know Frank I was afraid for you. You were lucky."

"Don't I know it. I'm finally getting back to normal. I can even eat food again. Sometimes, God is good. Well I hope you are as happy as I've been. That file should be very interesting reading."

Mac knew he would miss his old friend. "You got that right! It strengthens my faith in human nature. If you ever get T.F. behind bars send me photos all right?"

"You got it!"

Mac became almost maudlin. "Frank, I just want you to know, it was an honor working with you over the last few years. I put in a few strategic words on your behalf because I think you'll make a hell of a fine chief. Let's just say there are some individuals in this state who wield a lot more power than fuck face Flarity. I think you learned enough from Bender to hang in there. Don't let the bastards wear you down. Good luck, Frank."

Chief Tanner lifted his eyebrows in amusement. "I didn't know you were so influential, being a mere captain. Well, I'll try to live up to your expectations.

Mac laughed, "I'm sure you will, cheif."

Frank smiled and grasped Mac's extended hand. "I might be chief but you'll always be my captain. Best of luck."

The rest of that evening was caught up in talking with coworkers and a few persons from the Worcester Telegram and Gazette. Mac thought it was nice to be a hero, at least for one evening. He could see where it could get boring if it went on indefinitely though. He thought of the many people he had met and befriended in Worcester County during his lifetime. Certainly he would miss many of them but Ann was his world now, along with their future child or children. Apart from all that, he was looking forward with eager anticipation to the indictment of one bad mother, Albert Wagner.

⸻ • ⸻

It was a rainy gray day in late October in a closed room in the top floor of the old courthouse. Mac, Frank and the district attorney were sitting across from a manacled Al Wagner, a prominent psychiatrist Norman Filson and a Cracker Jack defense lawyer Robert Gould. Judge Barker was presiding over the special meeting which was only attended by a few members of the press.

The judge spoke in his no nonsense voice, "All right gentleman this private hearing will commence to determine if there will be a trial. Mister Filson I'd like to hear from you first so everyone else keep quiet until he finishes."

There was a court recorder in one corner and the bailiff swore in Doctor Filson. Filson was a distinguished man with graying hair and soft looking brown eyes. He carefully removed some notes from his coat pocket and related his findings to the group. "I have examined Albert Wagner for almost two months and I can attest to the fact that he is not competent to stand trial. Albert Wagner strangely enough is innocent of any wrongdoing. He does not

220

remember any of the crimes committed. As far as he knew, he was a good policeman, doing his job. You see to keep the discussion of his pathology in simple terms he has a triple personality. His second personality is Major Herbert Koehler. The name was his father's actual name. Herbert changed his name after the war to protect his identity. He arrived in America shortly after the Second World War. That is when he altered his name to Wilhelm Wagner and he married a woman who is currently known as Misses Vincent. Major Herbert Koehler A K A Albert Wagner stole the gun that had been saved by his father as an heirloom. He retained some ammo from his army days including some c four and detonators. It seems that Herbert Koehler was a meticulous planner and used all the information that Albert Wagner had picked up in the service. You see Herbert was aware of Albert but Albert didn't know about Herbert. It gets even more complex. There was a third personality. It was the visionary presence of the so-called Fuehrer. This mystical presence gave Herbert all the plans and commands. The crucial figure in all this is this Fuehrer figure. It's a combination of Adolph Hitler and Albert's father. When Albert was just a little boy, Herbert actually brain washed him. He was forced to listen to recordings of Hitler speeches, to memorize passages from Mien Kumpf and watch a video called "The Power of Will" which is a movie showing Hitler at the height of his power in the late thirties. I believe it takes place in Nierenberg.

At any rate, Albert rebelled against this intrusive insanity while the Herbert personality followed it like a bedazzled slave. The love-hate relationship was so extreme at its opposite points that his mind couldn't accept one or the other. I've learned a great deal from performing hypnosis on this individual. I must tell you being of Jewish descent, I found many of Herbert's conversations extremely disturbing. He believes in the master race, in the Reich as the blueprint for world order. Mind you this is not just a theory, he actually believes it. The Fuehrer figure is hard to reach. It's like his own personal deity. Only deep hypnosis can reach this mystical presence. It was quite a shocking encounter and the apparent power of this presence was formidable. It was like hearing the maniac himself except it was even more twisted and deranged than the real thing, if that's possible. It's a complex question. If you could remove these two destructive personalities and just leave Albert Wagner by himself, he'd be a safe, law-abiding citizen like you or I. My current prognosis for Albert isn't very good. Without a great deal of therapy Herbert Koehler will eventually subvert and imprison Albert's personality deep within the subconscious. It's a frightening and complicated pathology and it will take years of therapy. The damage is so deep I don't believe he'll ever be completely cured. It is his father Herbert Wagner who should have paid the debt owed to society. It was he who created this monster living inside the mind of Albert Wagner. I'm certifying that this man is clinically insane. You can bring in all the doctors you want and once we all have an opportunity to interview him and search his mind through hypnosis I'm sure they'll come to similar conclusions. I just want to add that Albert Wagner has complete remorse for what Herbert and the other have done. He has something to say to you now if he can be permitted to do so I think you will better understand."

The judge nodded, ordering the defendant to proceed. Albert spoke in a lifeless monotone. "All my life I'd tried to do my duty to God and this wonderful country. I don't remember any of the crimes that I'm accused of. They are terrible, heartless acts that demand death as the ultimate penalty. I have listened to the Doctor's recordings of my other voices under hypnosis and I was shocked. It would seem that the evil that Hitler propagated lives on. We are still not free of that terrible chapter in human history. I know all of you are afraid to ever let me see freedom again and I agree with that judgment. I am pleading guilty with the following two requests. First that even if I am supposedly cured that I will be kept as a ward of the state and never be released. Who could say if my cure was only temporary or not. I am willing to sign or have my attorney sign such an agreement. Further Doctor Filson has recommended a secure asylum that is out in the country far from the evils of the world. He has indicated that my pathology is so unique that several experts in the field will study my mental condition and see if certain medications will be effective. They and myself will try to fully understand what my father did to me. My request is that you permit me to go to such an institution that doctor Filson is recommending. If I could bring back those that were killed by sacrificing my life I would gladly do it. Your honor those are my only two requests. I can only pray that God has mercy upon me. I dare not ask for forgiveness from those families who had relatives who fell by my hand."

The room was silent for a long time and Judge Barker asked, "Are there any objections from the prosecution?"

There was another long moment of silence and suddenly Albert stood up and Herbert started screaming. "You miserable fools. You think you vill win, but zee fuehrer vill be victorious! He vill crush all his enemies. I demand to be treated as a prisoner of war! I am Major Herbert Koehler of zee SS. My serial number is 17675. I demand that this mockery of a trial be stopped. I killed enemies of zee fatherland! I vill not refute today what I've believed all my life! Hile Hitler!"

His cuffed arms shot out with an attempt at the stiff Nazi salute and then he sat down with his eyes blazing. He whispered, "Deutschland Ueberallis!"

Mac looked at Frank, "You should have let me kill him."

Barker was shocked and he order that the bailiff restrain the man and have him taken out of the room. When order had been restored the judge looked at doctor Filson, "I see what you mean. Is there any objection from the district attorney to the terms of the plea?"

The district attorney cleared his throat and looked squarely at the judge. "There are none your honor. I'm satisfied at the security arrangements of the facility. The man is obviously insane."

Barker coughed a few times before continuing. He kept staring at the empty chair where the defendant had been sitting. "Sometimes, Justice is a stern taskmaster. It is regrettable that these proceedings could not have had a more satisfying conclusion. Yet, it is also the test of a civilized society that we treat those who are incompetent with such mercy as is prudent and warranted. Therefore it is my judgment that Albert Wagner be remanded to the Park Hurst home for the permanently insane located in Amherst, Massachusetts. He is never to be released even if technically cured from this terrible condition. I wish to make the observation that it is unfortunate that Albert's father could not have stood trial for these unspeakable acts against those who protect our society from every evil. In the case of Albert Wagner it isn't that we don't want to be more merciful it is rather that we do not dare. I know the sorrows that this sick man has done to this community during his reign of terror. I know for a certainty that this decision by this court will not be popular. Scores of persons would have liked nothing better than this man be given life in solitary or worse. It is nevertheless the measure of a truly advanced culture that we hold harmless those who are not mentally competent to be responsible for their actions. Gentlemen I will accept the signatures of doctor Filson and defense counsel. I note that Albert Wagner has also signed but because of his infirmity it is superfluous. This proceeding has been the most depressing case of my entire career. I sincerely hope I never live to see another of its like."

He banged down the gavel and adjourned the court. Immediately after he said, "Just so you know I'll be reviewing the paper work on this over the next few days. Albert Wagner should be kept in a city jail cell until next Monday. I need some time to consult with doctor Filson. I thank all of you for coming today.

Barker sat back and watched in stony silence, as everyone else left the courtroom. He thought about Brian Bender and the funeral home. He thought of some of the other individuals he had known and respected. He was sixty-three years old and he now knew for a certainty that he was getting too old for all this. For many moments, he gazed at the symbolic hand carved portrayal of blind justice hanging on the wall beside the American flag. Sometimes the price of justice came very high. The blind goddess held her scales as if mocking the very people who struggled with right and wrong, truth or error. It wasn't as simple as checking some weights. How could one really evaluate the complicated human soul? Perhaps it would have been more merciful to end the insane man's life. And what about the victims? How could Justice compensate those unfortunate people for all those years lost at the hands of a maniac? The judge shook his head. In the sullen silence of that empty courtroom, voicelessly making a heart felt prayer for the dead. When he finally stood to leave, there were tears in his eyes. Just before he left the chamber he turned to face the image of Justice once more. His whisper was little more than a croak. "Blessed are the merciful. Yet, even mercy has a price."

Chapter

21

BLACK DAWN

Southern Georgia turned out to be a different world. The people were so hospitable and helpful. It had been a pleasure to do the house hunting and his new wife had been treated almost like royalty. It was a bright, sunny day in early January, much warmer than New England would have been to say the least. Mac was thinking to himself that one could sure get used to this. It was the first official meeting with Sheriff Hayes since he'd been placed on the force. Some time had elapsed in order to move down and get properly settled in preparation for the new phase of Mac's career.

The sheriff was a middle aged man with graying hair and a sizable paunch. He possessed a friendly, open, quick to smile face, further highlighted by a very relaxing and pronounced southern drawl. He had a laid back attitude that quickly put Mac at his ease in the no frills office.

The desk was definitely world war two vintage and the file cabinets were of similar age. A manual typewriter on a small cadenza in the corner could have been classified as an antique and amazingly was still being used by the part time secretary. The only thing that looked relatively modern was an IBM Pentium computer on the sheriff's desk.

Mac sat in front of the sheriff with the all too predictable cup of coffee in his hand. Of course, his new acquaintances weren't aware of Mac's Columbian vagary…yet, although he was certain they soon would be. He'd heard many synical comments about his coffee drinking over the years, so he was used to it.

Hayes called out to his secretary. "Hold the calls, please!"

It was a long time since Mac felt relaxed in a police office. He gratefully leaned back in the comfortably padded chair and spoke directly to his new boss. "Thank you sheriff Hayes for all the assistance you and your friends gave us to get settled here. Our new home is lovely and so pleasantly quiet. It's like a different world down here."

The sheriff was sitting back in his swivel chair with a freshly lit cigar sticking out the side of his mouth. "Well son if you want to get along with me you call me by my nick name. Everyone I consider a friend calls me Bucky. Hell, even my enemies call me that. You only need to call me Sheriff Hayes on exceptionally formal occasions and they are far and few between."

Mac grinned warmly as he sipped the coffee, "Well thank you sir, I go by Mac."

The sheriff continued, "I was talking to Chief Tanner a few days ago and he told me about the trials and tribulations you went through. I'm honored to have a man like you as my deputy sheriff. I'm just surprised you chose such an out of the way place as Bonaire, Georgia. I mean, we're on the edge of nowhere. "

Mac sagged back in his chair and looked somewhere beyond the grinning, pleasantly plump man who was the law in this part of the county. "I guess it was time to slow down the pace a bit. I mean I don't think the job will be a cake walk but at least I won't have to worry about my wife getting mugged or our children being exposed to drugs or worse in the local school here. I've talked with the principal already and I've been assured of the strict standards around here. In that regard you have my whole hearted support. I'll finally get a chance to breathe for a change."

The sheriff nodded his head and shoved the stub of his cigar into the ash tray. "Just sounds real fine Mac. You see we're quite old fashioned down here. You probably already know we're part of the Bible belt down here and we don't cotton to strangers very often, current company excluded of course. Everyone in Bonaire has heard of your exploits already. All it takes is for somebody's wife to pick up a phone and in twenty four hours the entire town knows whatever the important news is. Reputations have been made or lost in this town literally over night."

Mac took another sip and asked, "So Bucky how long have you been sheriff here?"

"Well I took over from Sheriff Al Tolliver about twenty years ago. He was the best man I ever knew. He was a decorated veteran at the battle of Anzio. Have you ever heard of that?"

"Yeah, I heard it was tough."

"You bet it was. However, this here little get together isn't about Tolliver, it's about you." Bucky chuckled a little before going on. "I've been on the police force in one capacity or another for almost thirty five years. I know this area like the back of my hand. I grew up here and I know every hiding place, every cave, every sparking place and every back road or hunting trail. I know all the families here going back three generations in most cases and I can tell you for the most part they are fine citizens who love this country and believe in law and order."

"If you don't mind me asking, are there any racial issues I need to be aware of? I mean I don't want to offend anyone or mess up the status quo."

Hayes lifted his eyebrows slightly, "Well son it's like this. I know that segregation is no longer legal or even desirable. However down here, like seems to stick to like. Many of the old neighborhoods are still either black or white depending on how they were occupied for the last hundred years or more. The blacks still tend to be less affluent then the whites and I'm afraid prejudice is something that laws can't easily remove. That being said blacks down here will tell you they prefer the more open prejudice down here than the carefully covered up type up north. Do you understand what I'm saying?"

"I think so. Some years ago I saw a show on sixty minutes where a blonde bombshell and a black girl went to a head hunter in New York City to get a secretarial job. The black girl had far superior credentials and did much better on the typing tests. The personnel consultant firm didn't know the two ladies worked for sixty minutes. They later discovered that the workers at this firm had a special little code on the applications so that undesirable candidates could be weeded out on a very subtle basis. Needless to say, the blonde bombshell got hired in hours while the black lady got the run around. Then these idiots in politics can't understand why blacks are so bitter and so many of them resort to crime. Hey if you want to make a good living you sure as hell aren't going to make it on welfare. When it comes to employment rights, they've got to equalize things in this country or the next civil war will be the Hispanic and black community against the white."

Bucky gave Mac a level glance, "So you perceive the racial problem in this country as primarily one of opportunity and economics?"

"Precisely! I mean I'm not going to care if somebody calls me a nigger if I'm making a hundred thousand a year and I'm living in an upscale neighborhood. When I was up in Worcester doing my job as a detective and somebody called me a pig or the fuzz or whatever I just let it slide because I knew that in many cases it was jealousy for the excellent job I had. Sometimes it was pure hatred to but every time I put my paycheck in the bank I have a knack of forgetting the insults. Names will certainly never hurt me."

The sheriff had a good natured laugh before replying. "Well, you'll probably find us a bit better mannered down here. We haven't had a murder in this town in over thirty years and that's because we believe in high profile. We actually have a few cops walking the beat down the main drag and we've always got some of the guys cruising around looking for anything suspicious and I mean ANYTHING. You might say my brand of police work is proactive. We take small complaints like family arguments very serious here so we can help keep the little problems little. We've got a Cracker Jack family counselor here by the name of Edna Adams. She put out more than one fire in her day. Mac I think you'll like it here. We're a caring community. Treat others the way you would want to be treated, I always say."

Mac reflected for a moment before speaking in an emotionally subdued voice. "I just want to personally thank you for the help you gave us getting settled here. You've made us feel like we've finally come home and that means a lot to us. Ann's still getting over a personal tragedy and well chief Bender was a good friend of mine. When he was killed it was like part of me died along with him. Hell, he was like a second father to me."

Hayes looked back at Mac with misty eyes, "I understand and I'm so sorry. Are you satisfied with how everything came out?"

Mac shook his head, "Not hardly! This SOB kills an innocent woman and several cops and gets to live it up on some lovely funny farm so he can be pampered and tested by experts in the field of psychiatry. I should have blown his ass away. I had the chance and I didn't pull the fucking trigger!"

The sheriff grew serious. "But you had to do the right and honorable thing. Sending him to his maker wouldn't have brought back the others. Sometimes Justice can be a hard wench. I just want you to know I understand your frustration. I lost my daddy in Nam. He was a recon officer in the marines. We never even got the body back. Sure that was war but it's still an empty feeling, even after all these years. You know Mac you can talk about anything that bothers you anytime. I've seen it all and heard it all. I'm on your side."

Mac grinned at his new boss, nodding in agreement. "Gee thanks a lot Bucky. The same goes for you. If something's bugging you let me know. Just because you're top dog around here doesn't mean you can't have a bad day."

As Mac got up to meet some of the other staff, Bucky shook his hand. It was the warmest shake since Frank. The sheriff spoke with sincerity, "Glad to have you aboard. Now let's get you introduced to the others."

⊶⟶•⟵⊷

A few weeks later, Mac came home to a great steak dinner with all the fixings. Ann was in top form and met him at the door with a hug and a kiss. "Welcome home stranger. Everything go okay with training and all?"

Mac held her close. He imagined he could feel the beginnings of the little one, lodging in her stomach. He replied, "Couldn't be better. How's mother feeling?"

She smiled as happiness glowed from her face. "Oh I'm fine darling. I just found out from the hospital that we're having a little boy soon. I take it you're happy with Mark?"

He laughed, "Mark it is doll. Now we better have that steak before it gets cold. I'm ravenous!"

He was true to his word as he sat at the kitchen table and wolfed down the mouth watering supper. Ann noticed that his appetite had dramatically improved since he'd gotten away from the stress of the big city. The home they had purchased was about twenty five years old with four bedrooms, a study, dining room, eat in kitchen and a very large living room. There was a spacious two car garage with cement driveway. The home rested on a mature, well kept half acre. Beside the property was a huge vacant lot, half field and half woodland. The nearest neighbor was some 300 yards down the road. It was a lovely lot among the quiet back roads of Bonaire Georgia.

Ann asked, "So are you getting to know your way around yet?"

"Yeah but it's like a new world down here. The people talk different and act so friendly. When you knock on a door they actually answer it. It's amazing really."

"I know, when I was at the hospital they didn't act like I was a number. The doctor was so kind and actually talked to me for 15 minutes. I'm so glad we came here. I know it's not utopia, but I think we'll be very happy here. We've been able to get away from the horrible memories to some extent and this is a place we can raise a family with some sense of security."

"Yes and Bucky Hayes is solid gold. He gave me a map and even filled in the private roads that weren't listed. He introduced me to everyone. He said it'll take about a month to get totally oriented but I felt like I'd known these people for years the way they treated me. When I asked Bucky about it he said, "Well Mac they think you're a hero after all. You got the worst cop killer to come along in decades.""

She did justice to another piece of her own portion of steak. "They just are glad they've got someone on the staff they can count on in a tough spot. They wouldn't think you were a hero if they saw what you do in the privacy of our bedroom." She followed that comment by swallowing a liberal quantity of tea.

Her smile was enchanting as usual. He smirked after chomping some more meat to digestible shreds. "Yeah, they don't give medals for what we do behind closed doors. I better cool it down a bit with big, bad mark starting to push his weight around."

She stuffed another piece of steak into her mouth and after devouring it she responded. "Well I guess I'll just have to get on top to keep your massive weight off little Mark. That way I can still get off with fun and games without possibly injury to the little one and I'll keep my hunk of a husband under wraps. After all a big girl like me still has these little urges and appetites that have to be taken care of properly, you know. And…I'm not talking about this steak either."

He swallowed some tea and asked, "Is that a not so subtle invitation? Is that a promise of adventures yet to cum?"

She forked up some mashed potato and smirked back at him. "Well honey, I think you'll have to wait until bed time to find out, won't you?"

The phone rang the three irregular rings that indicated a long distance phone call was being received. They both looked at the phone at the same moment. Ann answered it, being closer to the side table where the device had been placed.

"Yes!....Why hello Frank!....It's nice to hear from you......Oh we're doing very fine down here thank you!.........Well I'm pleased to hear that, would you like to speak to Mac?"

In moments Mac was handed the phone and Ann said, "It's Frank Tanner darling, he's officially the chief now and things are going fine, he wants to speak with you."

"Hello Frank, how the hell are you?"

Grave concern dominated Frank's voice as he answered, "I hope you're sitting down Mac. I've got grim news."

Ann could see Mac's face tense and hear his voice become serious. "What happened?"

"That son of a bitch psycho got away from fruit land. Fucking Al Wagner escaped from the place they sent him and we can't find the son of a bitch. It's an absolute cluster fuck."

"You're kidding!"

"Nope, I wish I was. Happened yesterday evening."

To say that Mac was astonished would have been an understatement of the highest magnitude.

"How the hell did he get out?"

"The bastard knew martial arts well enough to kill a guard and incapacitate a receptionist. He grabbed some clothes, took about a hundred dollars in cash, the guard's weapon and stole the guard's car. He could be anywhere and the biggest problem is that he's a smart, nasty psycho."

Mac groaned, "It looks like the race isn't over frank. It's like a bad version of the Ben Hur movie with Hitchcock's Psycho thrown in for good measure. Overnight me some photos of the bastard so I can have the guys down here keep an eye open for him. You never know he might be looking for me to. Whatever you do Frank watch your ass big time. He doesn't like us one bit."

Frank chuckled with forced mirth, "You got that right! The entire force is going to have to wear flack jackets if we don't find him pronto. I just wanted to give you the good fucking news."

When Mac put down the phone he sat and stared at the remains of his supper. Ann asked, "What is it love! You look like someone got killed."

He stared up at the ceiling. His voice trembled with sudden rage. "You aren't going to believe this. I don't believe it myself. It's like a bad dream. It's like the Gods have mandated that that damned psycho is going to be my tragic flaw or something. That useless creep, Al Wagner escaped from the fucking funny farm and they don't know where he is. Do you understand? That God damned fucking killer is on the loose! Frank's sending me some photos so everyone down here can keep an eye open for him. It's absolutely unreal! "

Ann was suddenly crying. "It isn't fair! Won't we ever be free of that cursed animal?"

Mac sighed and stared down at the remainder of his supper. He didn't feel hungry now. "It's all right honey dear. I'm sure he'll get nabbed. He probably doesn't even know where to find us. It's Frank I'm afraid for. But don't you worry I'll tell Bucky about it in the morning and we'll keep in close touch with Frank's department every day. I'm not going to let that maniac hurt you any more."

Ann jumped when his fist hit the table. "Fuck! I should have shot the mother fucking bastard! I was holding the gun just a few inches from that fucking cretin's head! I had the chance handed to me on a silver, sodding platter, and I didn't take it! Now the little fucker is on the loose! Please forgive me Ann."

Ann got up and embraced him. "There's nothing to forgive. You did the right thing because you're a man of honor. You don't go around shooting people who are critically wounded or helpless. We'll get through this baby. Fuck supper! Take me to bed!"

—————•—————

Herbert was catching forty winks at a rest stop in New Jersey. He'd stolen about three hundred dollars from a variety store in Connecticut and had sped south. Thanks to learning a few important facts from listening to the news he'd found out that Mac had left town. He'd called Frank tanner's home pretending to be a friend of Mac's and actually gotten the teen aged moron to tell him where Mac had gone. The kid hadn't known much except that Mac had gone to Georgia. Next day, He'd strolled into a college library located near Princeton and used a computer to access the latest telephone directories for Georgia. He just loved libraries. One could find out almost anything by looking through a few books or using their public service computer.

After a few hours the tenacious maniac found a number listed for J. Mackelroy in Bonaire Georgia. It was a new number listing. This almost had to be the one. One of these evenings he'd give it a call from a phone booth and check the voice just to make sure. After all, it wouldn't do to rub out some worthless civilian who didn't have a clue anyway. He figured he'd get a road map in Georgia when he got there and find the damned place. Leave it to Mackelroy to try to hide amid the stupid red necks. Well, what could one expect? He had no breeding or culture. He was an overpaid pawn who served law and order on a gilded plate for the benefit of Jews and other worthless liberal elements.

—————•—————

It was after dark. Herbert was sitting on a bed, staring at his inner God. He gloated as he spoke to the Fuehrer. "So I took your advice and left zee area of Worcester for now until things cool down. You'll get zee useless svine hunt, Mackelroy, vhen he doesn't expect it. Zen we go back for Tanner and those other morons."

The ghostly vision strutted back and forth in the murky darkness of Al's subconscious. "You vill kill Mackelroy and zee other worthless policemen down in his new haven. He thinks he vill be safe but it shall be his grave! Then you vill disappear for a time. You can get some odd jobs in places like Looser Ville, Georgia or some other worthless state. It vill be very easy. Grow zee beard and wear zee sunglasses and act scared of people. You must hide after your little rampage in Bonaire Georgia. Act like Eric Rudolph. In four of five years you can go back to your old home area and kill that dumb, dog Tanner and zee rest. Don't vorry, Herbert. I'll guide you every step of zee way. I reward your bravery and sagacity by promoting you to zee rank of colonel. You have done very well. You have proved you are worthy of the volk! You have done very vell indeed."

Herbert was ecstatic! He was serving the leader of the German people expertly and effectively. It felt so grand to be back in action after that brief stint in the nuthouse. He could have escaped sooner but he'd had to wait for his chest wound to heal. He'd stolen the dead guard's car, switched number plates at a Norwalk parking lot, bought some second hand clothing at a Good Will store and headed south. His military training was invaluable. The little worm, Al Wagner was safely subdued now deep in the recesses of his over wrought brain. Herbert felt exalted because he'd been strong enough to submerge Al Wagner at long last. The Fuehrer was right once again, as he always was. The power of will was the ultimate truth! Colonel Herbert Koehler had finally taken completely over and there would be hell to pay! His chuckle grew into a triumphant cackle, filling the third rate Georgetown motel room. "I vill crush you like zee bug you are, Mackelroy! You vill die!"

He raised his fist in both anger and salute. He still felt a twinge of pain in the right side of his chest from the wound Tanner had inflicted, but it wouldn't interfere with his gun hand. He would take his time and plan carefully. He would be meticulous and follow the Fuehrer's mandates to the letter. Then when that interfering bastard least expected it, wham! Mackelroy would be history!

The end of the beginning!

Acknowledgements

The following is a brief explanation of real locations used in the book.

Dunkin Donuts A very popular fast food chain with locations all over the United States. There actually is a Dunkin Donut shop at the corner of Park and Chandler in Worcester.

The Worcester Art Museum actually exists on Lancaster Street and there is a painting of John the Baptist by Andre Delsarto proudly displayed in that museum.

St. Vincent's Hospital an actual hospital in the city of Worcester

Merryl Lynch Prominent investment firm

Paine Webber prominent investment firm

WBZ An actual radio and Television station located in Boston Massachusetts

Worcester Telegram and Gazette. This is the name of the actual newspaper that is widely circulated in Worcester County.

The Silver Slipper is the name of an actual strip joint in Boston's combat zone, not to be confused with the Glass Slipper.

Several of the street names are actual streets in the city of Worcester. However, the scenes depicted on or near such street locations are again, purely fictitious.

Streets named: Hamilton, Lafayette, King, Oread, Franklin, Pleasant, Chandler, Park, Congress Main, Chamberlain Parkway and Old English Road.

The towns of Boston, Shrewsbury , Cambridge, Worcester, Clinton and even Bonaire Georgia actually do exist but again, are only used to support fictitious scenes or individuals.

Any similarity to persons, living or dead is completely coincidental.

Further Biographical Notes:

I had the privilege of growing up in a neighborhood where many World War II veterans spent the more productive years of their lives. Sometimes they spoke of events that occurred during the war years along with depression decade reminiscences. They were a class act, by in large. In their quiet way, they left us a warning concerning the horrors of Nazi Europe which they'd had to remove, first hand. I remember one man in particular who'd fought in the war as a British marine. He was still bitter about the fact that his military training had turned him into a killer. However, it wasn't his training that was to blame. It was the reaction to the Nazi monsters which made such training a necessity. So ultimately the blame goes back to the Fuehrer and all those misbegotten ideals that renegade stood for. In Broken Cross, we see the direct link between the modern citizen and the goose stepping morons that forever impacted the world. We can never be the same again, after the disgusting images of those death camps. Today, I can't endure to watch them. In all my life, I have never seen anything worse than those hopeless faces, heading to their collective doom. Yet, in the story, Herbert Koehler was unable to learn from it. He is not alone. Look at the horrors that were committed in Cambodia and to a lesser extent in Yugoslavia and Iraq? Even now, the Neo Nazis claim the holocaust never happened. They claim it was allied propaganda. Tell that to the British veterans who had to march into the hell known as Bergen Beltsin! How could you artificially make human bodies shrivel into such things as were buried there?

At least our anti-hero doesn't have any illusions except for the great one. He knows that death and destruction are the only way that his Fuehrer can get back into power. He knows that racial purity is the answer. At least for him there is no hypocrisy and it is his only questionable virtue.

Our hero, John Mackelroy stands for the strong arm of Justice. It is for him to drag the offenders before the blind Goddess's scales. To him, the world is white and black with only the occasional shading of gray. He is a homicide captain with years of experience and training to help him solve such frightening mysteries. Yet for weeks he is stumped because of the apparent randomness of the attacks. The only two common factors are the same hand gun is being used and only policeman are being killed until the unfortunate Chief's wife is at the wrong place and the wrong time. She turns out to be the sacrificial offering which turns Koehler's mission into a pact of blood and hatred.

As Mackelroy progresses through this journey of fear and self discovery, he learns what it is to truly hate. His men are being gunned down. The leader he looks up to is taken down in his own home. He even tells the local mafia boss that he would sell his soul to catch the thug. Yet through all this, Mackelroy is able to preserve his own sanity, his own inner strength. Somehow, he saves that which is the best in him. At the last moment, he doesn't pull the trigger when his gun is just inches away from the helpless killer's head. Perhaps in that moment, John Mackelroy achieves his greatest victory although he may live to regret it.

There are no easy answers. There are no comfortable truths. The world is a place where anything can happen. However, it is in the mind of man where so much goodness or evil can emerge. Mackelroy learns this through his search for the killer and his relationship with Ann. In mere hours he climbs to the summit of glorious human love and then he is plunged into the cesspool of heartless hatred and violence. Somehow, he survives with his soul intact. He is still a man of honor although the devil himself could not have tempted him with more power. However, deep in Mackelroy's psyche, he recognizes that he must leave the terrors of big city existence. There is only so much the mere mortal can endure and he is wise enough to recognize that. Broken Cross is more than just a murder story. It is a challenge to discover the perilous truth that may lurk within ourselves.

⚫━━━━━━⚫━━━━━━⚫

I actually did grow up in Worcester County, Massachusetts. As a result, I became very familiar with the way things are done in that neck of the woods. First hand, I personally met many WW2 vets while I attended grade school and high school. Perhaps I was more of an idealist then, but I looked up to these men as being a cut above the current herd. They cared about their community. They backed up the teachers, sometimes to my chagrin. You couldn't do anything in that town without it becoming national news. I recall one humorous event. I kicked a can into the street just because I wanted to hear the sound of metal hit the tar. By the time I got home which was perhaps fifteen minutes later, my mother met me with utter rage, demanding why I'd tossed a can into the street. Apparently someone had called her. I was so shocked; I didn't even try to deny it.

That's the way it was and I didn't realize how fortunate I was at the time. Those people cared about themselves and everyone else's kids. Perhaps they were the finest generation. So in an indirect way, Broken Cross is in tribute to them.

All that being said, I personally have been influenced, some would say warped, by Monty Python, Archie Bunker and Richard Nixon. Whatever your position on the matter, my view of the world changed dramatically between the years, 1970-1980. I learned that government is more concerned with its own perpetuation rather than the collective good of its citizens. Justice is a matter of economic strength. In today's world you generally get as much justice as you can afford. That is indeed the reason why O.J. Simpson got such a fair trial. The little man truly has become a statistic, an unimportant victim in the hurricane of modern civilization.

However, let's return to our story, Broken Cross. We see directly into the sinister lie of the super race. The hero, Mackelroy is a modern version of what those veterans went through. Can you imagine for a moment, what it must have been like to land on a French beach on D Day or at Anzio and see many of your friends mown down? On a smaller scale, this is what happens to our redoubtable Captain and naturally it leads to the great confrontation which all readers love to experience through the power of the imagination.

I conclude by pointing out that all characters in this novel are fictitious. Any similarity between these characters and people in the real world are coincidental. I refer to some locations in Worcester which actually do exist, such as the town hall and the Worcester Galleria. Yes, even the Dunkin Donut shop exists at the corner of Park and Chandler. However, the events depicted at these locations again are completely fictitious. Any mistakes that may appear in the text are completely my responsibility. In that way, the publishers and distributors of this book can sleep nights once Broken cross has been sent out into the universal realm of entertainment. So with these remarks, I sincerely wish you the limitless blessings from He who is the author of all things.